WILD LIFE

LIAM BROWN

LARGE
PRINT

First published in Great Britain 2016
by
Legend Press Ltd.

First Isis Edition
published 2017
by arrangement with
Legend Press Ltd.

A catalogue record for this book is available
from the British Library.

ISBN 978–1–78541–363–6 (hb)
ISBN 978–1–78541–369–8 (pb)

Published by
F. A. Thorpe (Publishing)
Anstey, Leicestershire

Set by Words & Graphics Ltd.
Anstey, Leicestershire
Printed and bound in Great Britain by
T. J. International Ltd., Padstow, Cornwall

This book is printed on acid-free paper

This book is for Elliot and Felix.
Grow up! Stay wild!

ZERO

Peel back the skin. Beneath the well-oiled order of the world. Behind the sterile veneer of concrete, steel and glass beats something else. Something wild and animal, crouched in the shadows, just aching to shake loose. You can catch a glimpse of it now and then, if you look in the right places. If you keep very still and stay very quiet.

It's there in the alleyways you're scared to walk down at night, where broken bottles and discarded syringe cases glisten in the flickering street lights, crackling under foot like first frost. It's there in the aerosol-propelled acronyms scrawled under bridges and along embankments, a smudged alphabet of affiliation and violence. It's in the faded bloodstains spattering the pavements outside all-night bars and in the cremated body panels of burnt-out cars. It's in the age-blackened creases of a badly photocopied missing person poster. It's in the long shadows that slink towards your dustbins at dusk and at dawn. It's a stirring in the hedgerows, a shriek in the wind.

It sleeps in shop doorways and it roams in packs.

Most people don't look. They don't want to see that world. They cross the road, avoid eye contact. They change the channel, flip the page, close the window. Hit Escape. They keep their heads down — or worse, they keep them filled up with an ever-expanding list of distractions and diversions. Politics. Football. Social media. Shopping. Things that trick them into believing they are part of something tangible. Neat. Knowable. Things that reassure them that life is a game, that it is playable and can be won. If only they follow the rules.

And so they follow the rules.

They work hard at school and attend a good university. They graduate and join a well-established firm on the ground floor, quickly catching the eye of senior management and hauling themselves up two or three rungs. Their salary doubles, triples. They enrol in a pension plan, health plan, insurance plan. They start an investment portfolio. They join a gym, play tennis at the weekends. They eat a nutritionally balanced diet and leave a column marked "grooming" on their monthly expenses spreadsheet. They go for minibreaks in Barcelona, Milan, Copenhagen. They meet someone and begin viewing apartments. They get married, and within months realise they're going to need a bigger place. Meanwhile the years roll on. Twenties slide towards thirties. Weekends at the gym make way for barbeques with friends, until suddenly they're forty. IBS, grey hairs, an unlimited line of credit. Another promotion, a waistline expanding parallel to their salary. A bigger car, a second child, a new home, the whole story pixelated and edited into a neat, nourishing narrative to preserve indefinitely in online shrines to their own success.

They do not drink heavily in the evenings. They do not open a secret bank account in order to deposit funds for gambling or develop a cocaine habit or sleep with their twenty-four-year-old secretaries. They do not fuck everything up.

They play an active part in the local community, organise charity quiz evenings, participate in politics. They take pride in their garden, imposing an artificial order on the natural world with the sweep of a petrol strimmer and the pump and spray of carcinogenic herbicides. They stay at home at night and stream HBO dramas while tracing patterns on their iPads. They check the gas, the kids and finally the burglar alarm before they go to bed each night, happy to believe that their personal hygiene routines and their bland domesticity and their positive bank balances will deliver them from evil, will somehow inoculate them from the wildness of the world. Will keep it locked outside. But they've forgotten something.

You've forgotten something.

Because for all of your shopping and shaving and talking and texting, you're still nothing but an animal. Fucking. Fighting. Taking what you want without

3

asking. You can wring a tie around your neck, anaesthetise yourself with garden furniture catalogues and Internet pornography, but you can only hold it back for so long. The wildness is in you — *is* you — and no matter how the wooden blocks of your successes stack symmetrically on top of one another, your education, your job, your car, your wife, your kids, all it would take is for a single lapse of concentration, one fumbled false move and your entire sorry life will come tumbling down around you, leaving you thrashing around in the dirt with all the other beasts.

And who knows what you'll be capable of then?

So I ask you — and I know after all I've put you through I have no right to ask such a thing — to try and remember who and what you are. Beneath the mousse and moisturiser. Under the coats of concealer and fake tan. At night, go to a dark place and look upon ancient things. Stars. Galaxies. Things that make the world seem new again. Kneel down and let your hands run through the living, beating earth. Let the filth get under your fingernails. Feel around in the cracks for the people who have already slipped between them, knowing that you could join them at any time. That the only thing separating you, one way or another, is chance. Don't be afraid. Pick the scab. Gouge the flesh and poke around. Look. Look.

I dare you to look.

WINTER

CHAPTER
ONE

It's a well-known fact that every gambler has a tell. An involuntary twitch of the eye or a scratch at the back of the neck that gives away the anguish or elation of their hand. Even the best players in the world, those hard-bitten, card-counting, bookie-sponsored, professional poker "stars". Those multi millionaires that grin and grimace for the cameras as they crow around the private tables of Vegas casinos in mirrored shades and cowboy hats. Even they can't escape the revolt of their own bodies. An incongruous clearing of the throat, a bead of sweat on a cool autumn day. Even they can't craft a truly perfect lie. Or so the story goes.

Me, I'm not so sure. See I've done a lot of gambling in my life. Not just on poker either. Blackjack, roulette, baccarat, fruit machines, football, Korean indoor women's lacrosse — I've bet on almost any uncertain event you can imagine. I once forfeited a month's salary at my four-year-old's sports day when I caught another father speculating aloud on the odds of his own son scooping gold at the egg and spoon race. Another time I walked home — a full fifteen miles — after losing my car over a game of scissors paper stone. Like I say — I've gambled a lot.

And sure some people are easy to read, their spasms and tics like braille to a blind assassin. But the truth is those people are amateurs. No, the pros — the *real* pros, the ones who aren't content with just gambling money, but with anything and everything that holds any value — those guys don't mess around when it comes to calculated deceit. There is no tug of the ear, no clench of the jaw. There isn't even a "poker face", as such. They're far too refined for anything as unreliable as that. No, the pros understand that the best way, the only way, to tell a lie is to swallow it yourself. Better still, you have to let the lie swallow you. You have to commit to it totally; to eat, breathe and shit the lie twenty-four hours a day until it becomes part of you, inscribed not only on each and every strand of your being, but on the genetic code of future generations of relatives yet to be born. It's a tough trick to pull off — one usually reserved for elite politicians and tabloid journalists — but I've managed to master it.

Which is hardly surprising when you consider I've been doing it for most of my adult life.

Fifteen seconds. That's how long I had each morning before I remembered the shuttle crash my life had become. Fifteen seconds to lie cocooned in the warm pocket of my family — my legs nestled into Lydia's back, Flynn burbling beside me, the alarm only two or three squawks into its daily tantrum — before it all came rushing back with sickening clarity.

But I'm getting ahead of myself.

Because as I luxuriated in those fifteen freeze-frame morning moments, the world was still a generous, happy place to live, and I was able to see myself as the outside world might: Adam Britman, successful account manager at an award-winning, pan-global digital marketing agency. Attentive husband and hands-on father to two TV commercial-cute children. Keen tennis player, wine enthusiast and owner of a new BMW 6 Series Coupé, finished in Alpine White. My kitchen was large enough to warrant an island midway across it in order to break up the journey from the cast-iron Aga to the limited-edition Smeg refrigerator. I was the living, breathing, Savile Row suit-wearing embodiment of a winner.

At least I was for fifteen seconds . . .

That's when my training kicked in.

Step one was to tell myself everything was normal. Swallowing down the hangover and self-loathing, I swung one leg over the edge of the bed and willed myself to get up, repeating the mantra that a solid routine was a liar's best friend. And boy did we have a routine.

It was important to be rushing. It seemed in those days that we were always late, no matter what time I set the alarm. For authenticity's sake it was vital every task was undertaken with a clenched jaw and a bark in my voice. Flynn's coos had already transformed into yells for chocolate-coated Chubby Cubs, his demands spat with the spite and natural authority of a third-world tyrant in training. Lydia meanwhile was up and out of bed, blocking the bathroom with her morning cleansing ritual, despite the fact she would spend the rest of the day ensconced in her studio, stapling bits of fabric to live pigeons or sloshing red dye over a plate of raw oats or whatever her "art" consisted of back then. I used the opportunity to go downstairs and intercept any unwanted mail, finding with a mixture of fear and hope that the postman had yet to arrive.

Peering over my shoulder to ensure I wasn't being watched, I pressed my eye to the front door, checking there were no nasty surprises lurking out there for me. It was still dark, the frosty road reflecting the street light, yet from what I could see the street was deserted. At least no one I needed to worry about. I straightened up, then leapt back in terror as I spotted Flynn, crouched in the shadows behind me.

"I want Chubby Cubs," he said. "Now."

After I followed him through to the kitchen and poured out a bowl of what looked suspiciously like diabetic dog biscuits, I opened the fridge, spotting the bottle of vodka next to the milk.

"Hurry up, Daddy," said Flynn.

Shielded by the enormous steel door, I reached for the bottle, unscrewed the lid and swallowed down a single, burning shot. Then, just to prove how perfectly normal behaviour this was, I had another.

Leaving Flynn to his ADHD-inducing breakfast cereal, I raced back up the hall, stopping only for the briefest of seconds to check the mat for letters and scan the street before sprinting up the stairs as I knock-knock-knocked on Olivia's door. I counted to three and then burst in, hitting the light switch to reveal the groaning corpse of my daughter.

"I don't feel well," she said, her voice muffled by the layers of duvet wrapped around her head.

"Of course you don't feel well, Ollie," I said, tearing back the curtains. "It's Monday morning and, spoiler alert, nobody feels good on Monday morning. That's what Monday's were invented for. But you need to get up, now. Before you make us all late."

Olivia leant forward just long enough to shoot me a look that would freeze helium before collapsing back onto the mattress and pulling the covers over her head. "What's the point?" she said, her anger escaping the layers of hypoallergenic microfibres. "We spend all day learning things we're never going to use in the real world. When am I ever going to need to calculate the third side of an isosceles triangle? Or quote from Act Three, scene one of *Hamlet*? Why can't they teach us something we'll actually need, like social media, or how to choose a mobile phone tariff. It's all so . . . futile!"

It was sad really. At just twelve years old she'd already figured out something that took most of us at least half a lifetime to realise — that school wasn't really about filling your head with practical knowledge to prepare you for a journey of success and personal growth. It was simply a production line designed to turn out a legion of obedient, identikit consumers; a method of ensuring the next generation doesn't think too hard or question the established order of things. It was all just a way of breaking you.

Of course, I didn't say any of that to Olivia. After all I had a role to play — a lie to uphold. So instead I marched forward and forcibly yanked back the covers, threatening her with all manner of irrational punishments if she didn't *rise and bloody-well-shine*, all the while staring at the shivering almost-woman and wondering what the hell happened to the plump, pink bundle of unconditional love I'd held to my chest and promised the world to a quarter of a lifetime ago . . .

But there was no time, no time, NO TIME for any of that. Not when we were so busy pretending to be late.

Fleeing Olivia's wrath, I nearly bumped into Flynn, who was standing on the landing, a Batman figurine clutched to his chest.

"Have you finished your breakfast?" I asked.

"Pew-pew-pew," he said, pretending to shoot me.

"Have you finished your breakfast?" I asked again.

"You're dead," he said. "Dead people can't talk."

"Batman doesn't have a gun," I countered, then pretended to die anyway, crumpling to the floor and attempting to stem the imaginary blood flow from the imaginary bullet wounds while Flynn stood above me, laughing, until Lydia emerged from the bathroom, smelling like a tropical storm.

"Time to get dressed," she said, scooping Flynn into her arms. "You're going to make Daddy late."

"No, I won't!" he said, kicking his legs as he tried to work his way free. "Daddy doesn't have to go to work anymore."

This time I stopped breathing for real, rigor mortis instantly setting in.

12

"What do you mean?" said Lydia.

Flynn paused, catching perhaps the fear in my eye. Had he said something bad? Was he about to be banished to the naughty step?

"Flynn?"

I felt my consciousness clambering to escape as I teetered on the brink of an out-of-body experience. This was it. Game over.

Flynn shrugged, deciding to risk it. "He's dead. Dead people don't have to go to work."

How we laughed at that.

Rising from the grave, there was just enough time for one last check of the doormat, along with — for the sake of staying in character — a final visit to the fridge, before I dived into the sanctuary of the bathroom, sliding the latch behind me. I hit the taps and paused for a moment to inspect my waning smile in the full-length mirror.

When I was starting out in the marketing game, back in my early twenties, I remember somebody bought me a self-help book, a sort of a joke present. *Make it Happen: Seventy-Seven Steps to Sterling Success.* Now, for the life of me I can't remember what seventy-six of the steps entailed. But I do remember the first page. And right there, in the author's introduction, there was an instruction I followed unwaveringly for the next two decades. It was about positive visualisation. According to the book, the key to health, wealth and eternal happiness was to stand in front of the mirror each morning and picture the trappings that success would bring — the sports car, the model home, the perfect wife — the idea being to meditate on it, to lust after it. To vow you wouldn't stop until all of it was yours.

For years I took this advice as gospel, filling my bathroom mirror with all manner of earthly treasures, until eventually there was no need any more — if I wanted to see a sports car all I had to do was go down to my garage. The reflections were real. That morning though, I felt the need to summon up a mirage in the mirror.

Stepping out of my dressing gown, I surveyed my greying temples, my crow's feet, the paunch of my gut, the flaccid droop of my penis. I took a deep breath and tried with all my might to conjure the future as it should have been. The winters in Barbados, country bolthole, the twenty-something mistress. Yet as I stood there shivering, the glass frosting with steam, I watched as the ghosts of my future life warped and ran, taking on a nightmarish quality. A skeleton with my face cowered before me, while the ghoulish figures of bailiffs, tax inspectors, magistrates and prison wardens formed an unbreachable circle, queuing up to first flay then fuck me while my family looked on, Flynn keeping time with the beat of a toy drum.

I dived for my dressing gown and fumbled in the pockets until I found a small cling film wrap. Then I chopped out a line on the cistern and inhaled deeply, the white-cold numbness that followed resembling something like peace.

After that I stood in the shower for what felt like a long time, swaying slightly while all around me the

14

world carried on as if it was just another Monday morning. Somewhere adjacent to me Lydia screamed at Olivia to get out of bed, while downstairs Flynn smashed something and pretended it wasn't him. And up and down the street and throughout the city, in houses identical to ours, the morning ritual played out in much the same way, people waking, washing, rushing; like sharks, terrified of what would happen if they stopped moving even for a second.

I stayed in the shower until the water ran cold, but even then I didn't move. Instead I stood there, wondering if maybe Flynn had been right all along.

Maybe I was dead.

CHAPTER
TWO

Eight hours. In my old life it was never enough. I would pull sixteen-hour shifts without thinking. I would work Friday night through to Monday morning on two hours' sleep. My phone was always on, constantly pulsing with calls, text messages, emails, appointments, status updates. I didn't even consider it overtime because *all of my time* was simply an extension of work. There was no separation. Picking up the kids, going to the toilet, arguing with Lydia; they were all just bullet points on an infinite to-do list. Just one more thing to be ticked off and filed under "Done". That was how I managed my life.

Then everything stopped, and eight hours seemed like an impossible stretch of time to fill.

For the first few weeks I did nothing but drive. The moment I dropped Flynn at nursery and Olivia off at school I'd hit the motorway, slipping into the outside lane, heading for nowhere as fast as possible. It was comforting to zone out behind the wheel, the grey scenery repeating endlessly like the backdrop of an old cartoon. Occasionally I'd pull off and wander aimlessly around a service station, each one a sterile clone of the one before, like a train station or an airport, everyone strangers, everyone just passing through. It was perfect. Other times I'd be driving and I'd forget where I was — who I was — and presume I was off to a meeting or a business lunch. I'd panic then, desperately trying to recall the details of my client, fumbling for my phone only to find my diary clear, my inbox empty. Then I'd remember. The only people who called any more were looking for money.

One evening I was hurtling down a dual carriageway on my way to collect Flynn when a blue light detonated behind me. I hesitated, my mouth instantly dry as I pictured myself triggering a Hollywood-style car chase, complete with helicopters, shoot-outs, and spike-strips, before I was consumed by the inevitable fiery climax. I hit my indicator and pulled over, the hard shoulder crackling under my tyres like the sound of a record that's run out of songs. As I killed the engine, I cupped my hand and blew into my palm. A hot wave of vodka echoed back into my face. I vaguely wondered how over the limit I was. Watching the policeman approach in my rear-view mirror, I desperately tried to keep calm, to fashion an excuse that would prevent me from blowing my guilty breath into his tube, before a sharp rap of knuckles at my window cut short my thoughts. This was it.

"Sorry to bother you, sir, but one of your back lights appears to be out . . . "

After that I was too paranoid to drive. I might have been a drunk but I wasn't an idiot — I knew my luck wouldn't hold out indefinitely. Instead I stayed local, parking up as near to home as I dared and then spending the day stumbling around bars and bookies until my money began to run out and I switched to wandering around supermarkets, my empty trolley squeaking down the endless aisles, time slurring to a standstill as I did my best to avoid the suspicious eye of the in-store security guard. Wherever I went I was paranoid, convinced that every woman I passed was Lydia, terrified she was about to leap out from behind a display of low-fat ready meals — though whether I was more scared about her finding out the truth or of the very public scene she'd inevitably create once she did, I'm not sure.

In the end I abandoned the city centre altogether, sticking to the least populated places I could find — patches of wasteland, canal walkways, the grounds of abandoned buildings — the hours crawling by as I shuffled along, trying my best to keep warm. Once or twice I thought about starting a fire, but decided against it in the end. It was hard enough to explain away the booze on my breath every evening without also having to account for the smell of petrol and smoke on my jacket. Instead I plunged my hands deep into my trouser pockets, bowed my head against the wind and walked. And walked. And walked.

One afternoon I found myself on a narrow dirt track alongside a fenced-off railway embankment. It was late February by this point, and though not yet spring, the first strangle of nettles had already begun to push their way up through the black earth, hooking themselves around the yellow warning signs that stuck out at intervals along the track. *Danger of Death. Private Property. Keep Out.* On the other side there was a tall wooden fence, a canopy of deciduous trees blocking out the light overhead, creating a sort of natural tunnel. A secret furrow carved into the flesh of the world. I ploughed deeper into the darkness, too cold to question the stacks of crushed beer cans littering the floor or the slashes of graffiti adorning the fence, the paint having run in rivulets before it dried, like melted candle wax, or blood seeping from a fresh wound.

I paused for a moment to take a drink. The tips of my fingers were almost completely numb, and it took a couple of second to unscrew the cap of my hip flask, the engraved inscription on the side glinting in the dim light. *Ultimate Sales Jedi 2008 — The force is strong with this one.* I grimaced and took a deep slug, the burning liquid chasing away the memories of monthly targets and office banter. I raised the flask to take another hit.

And then I froze.

Somewhere behind me I heard a noise. The wind agitating the trees. Or else someone fumbling in the folds of their oversized hoodie for a flick-knife. I started walking again, more briskly this time, my Oxford brogues struggling to find purchase in the mud. I was being paranoid, I knew it. Yet all the same, something felt very, very wrong.

The tunnel seemed to be narrowing by the second, the trees bearing down on me. There was another noise then, closer this time. Footsteps. I began to run, powering forward blindly, my heart threatening to unravel in my chest and choke me. Somewhere nearby a dog began to bark. I pictured myself punctured to death, a feral youngster making off with my terminally empty wallet. The police would come, the journalists and, eventually, Lydia. And then the horrible, heartbreaking truth of why I'd been down some scum-infested alley, rather than sat behind my office desk, would be out for the whole world to see.

I ran on, slipping and sliding in the muck until the alley tilted at an odd angle and I fell, sprawling to the floor. I lay there, winded, the sound of imminent assault ringing in my ears.

And that's when I saw it. A loose fence panel, right beside me.

I scrambled to my knees and hurled myself at it.

The wood gave without resistance, and I found myself tumbling down a steep bank on a tide of loose soil, rocks tearing at my skin and suit, the world a tombola of black and brown and green, until I was spewed abruptly into the light. It was over. I was alive.

I lay there for a moment, my eyes closed, listening to make sure I hadn't been followed. When I was quite sure I was alone I sat up and looked around. To my surprise I appeared to be lying in a large, open field, fringed by the dense woodland I had just fallen through, completely masking the alley above me. I climbed to my feet and brushed myself down. My coat had absorbed much of the damage to my torso, but my suit trousers were shredded. Still, aside from a few grazes and a gashed knuckle, I seemed to have escaped relatively unharmed. Instinctively I tapped at my breast and noticed the cold, damp patch spreading out from my inside pocket. Extracting the badly dented flask, I saw the lid was missing — lost in the chase. I held it up and drained the last few drops into my mouth before taking a step backwards and pitching the damn thing into the bushes. Then I started walking.

It took me about twenty minutes to realise that it was not a patch of wasteland, but a park. Or at least, it had been at one time, for it looked like it hadn't been properly maintained for decades. Gradually my eyes began to adjust. Here and there I spotted a rotting wooden bench or a rusting metal bin jutting out from behind an overgrown thicket, as if partially swallowed by some creeping, multi-tentacled monster. Further on I found an algae-choked pond that looked like it might have once been a boating lake; an old football pitch, the crossbars of the goalposts twisted and bent; as well as the skeletal remains of a children's play area, a length of chain dangling from the frame of a seatless swing, a perilous-looking slide leading to nothing but a sheer drop.

I explored for an hour or so before it began to get dark. I checked my phone — it was almost time to pick up Flynn. Realising I'd be unable to clamber back up to the alley, I instead began to make my way towards a gate I'd spotted earlier, hoping to find an alternate exit. Picking my way around the lake, I paused as two elegant swans emerged from the reeds and propelled themselves silently along the far shore, a dazzle of white in the gloom. As I watched them shrink into the distance, a slither of silver stirred beneath the surface of the water. I leant forward, struggling to make out anything in the murk beyond a skitter of pond skaters among the rushes. I turned to leave but then stopped, suddenly struck by the sensation I was being watched. I slowly straightened up, and scanned the nearby trees for signs of life, the earlier panic instantly reigniting in my chest. Though not yet five o'clock, the evening was folding in fast, the woods in the distance as dark and impenetrable as the surface of the lake. It occurred to me that somebody could be watching me from the trees and I wouldn't know. I'd never be able to see them. It was time to leave.

By the time I reached the gate I'd convinced myself I was being silly. I vaguely remembered reading somewhere that humans were hardwired to feel as if they were being watched, even if no one is paying them the slightest bit of attention. It's a sort of evolutionary reflex to keep us on our toes for predators, back before we were smart enough to shoot, poison or cage anything bigger or deadlier than us — the same prehistoric hangover that causes us to see snakes where there's only rope. Caveman thinking.

Easing back the bolt on the gate, I was faced with yet another alley, this time running between two low brick buildings. Seconds later I found myself standing in front of a row of dilapidated garages leading on to a small housing estate. It was unbelievable; from the patch of gravel where I stood, the park was completely invisible. Unless you knew it was there, you couldn't tell it existed at all. I peered back down the alley and noticed for the first time an ancient signpost staked into the ground near the entrance. I reached up and scraped away the layer of moss and dirt until at last a few faded words gradually appeared:

Welcome to Adenbury Community Gardens.

It was completely dark when I finally pulled up outside the house. Glancing in the rear-view mirror I saw that Flynn had jabbered himself to sleep in his car seat, his neck twisted at a wince-inducing angle. He stirred slightly as I lifted him but he didn't wake. I stood on the doorstep and took a moment to compose myself. I'd managed to wash away most of the dried blood from my hands with a bottle of mineral water, but my appearance had nonetheless provoked a look of panic from Flynn's teenage nursery teacher. "Heavy lunch," I'd mumbled, bundling the child into the car and driving off as fast as I could.

Lydia would be more difficult to convince. My trousers were shredded, my shoes caked in mud and I smelled like a distillery. Even with my well-honed powers of deception, this was going to be difficult to explain. My plan was to try and sneak in and bundle myself into the shower before I could be interrogated, but it was no good. Lydia was waiting for me by the front door.

"Hey, honey," I said, avoiding eye contact, I stooped forward to place Flynn down on the couch, keeping a tactical distance between us.

To my surprise, Lydia didn't comment on the way I looked. Or smelled. Or on the fact I was over an hour late.

"Adam, a man called today," was all she said.

I looked up, noticing for the first time the pained look on her face, her furrowed brow, her pinched mouth. Then I saw the red letters printed on the envelope she was holding in her hand.

"Oh?"

"Yes. About an hour ago. He wanted money. He said there's a problem with the car. Apparently we don't own it anymore."

CHAPTER
THREE

It wasn't just me. The whole world was at it. Politicians, bankers, brokers, all the way down to the little old lady scrabbling to find the three quid a week to pay the interest on her hire-purchase sofa. Everyone. Speculating, investing — gambling. Each of us blessed with the self-deluding arrogance of a drug addict that we could ride our luck until the end of time. That gravity had been permanently suspended just for us, history's golden generation; that things would just keep on going up, up, up forever. And why shouldn't they? After all, for seven straight years we'd all been partying in the greatest casino on Earth. *Spin the wheel and win a prize every time!* Buy high and watch it rise higher — you couldn't lose. And if you weren't quite in the position to bet, then no problem-o, Joe. Simply borrow your stake. *Don't put it off, put it on*, screamed the billboards. *Spend like there's no tomorrow.*

Which, as it turned out, was a pretty accurate summary of the whole sorry situation.

Like all the best disaster movies, it was born in America. However, what began with a monkey-bite of dodgy mortgage defaulters quickly spread with the ferocity of an apocalyptic virus, infecting an ever-widening circle of terrified consumers and replicating itself so that within mere months, half the planet was transformed into a horde of dead-eyed, slack-walleted zombies, each of us clutching our heads and groaning as we attempted to grapple with a brand-new vocabulary of horror: *Speculative bubbles . . . Subprime loans . . . Quantitative easing . . .*

Meanwhile the pyrotechnics department really began to crank up the special effects. Institutions that had stood for a century and a half padlocked their gates overnight. Generations of savings were wiped out in the time it took for a webpage to refresh. Whole high streets were razed to the ground, while a tsunami of debt and unemployment crashed into Europe, sweeping away with it the hopes and aspirations of an entire continent. It was a living, breathing, ever-mutating nightmare.

And for me, it had only just begun.

In the end I managed to convince Lydia that it was all just a silly mistake. A computer error. A clerical mix-up. I even went through the pantomime of pretending to call the repossession company, pacing up and down the hall and yelling at the dialling tone about how unacceptable everything was. After that I took the payment demand and tore it up in front of her, before scurrying up the stairs to change, brushing off her questions about my shredded suit with a dark "don't ask".

Thankfully she didn't.

That night I lay in bed until I heard Lydia's breath drop to a purr. I slipped out from under the duvet and quickly got dressed before tiptoeing downstairs. I let myself out and parked the car around the block. When I got back I went to the kitchen and poured myself a drink, pulling up a stool at the breakfast bar. I knew this was the end. Maybe not that night, or the next one. But soon. There were only so many buckets of water I could scoop up and throw overboard before I had to admit the ship was sinking.

I rattled the ice in my glass and sloshed in another slug of vodka, a familiar warm glow of self-pity already diffusing through my cheeks. It was a nice kitchen. A nice life. But it wasn't mine. None of it was. I was simply borrowing it for a while. And now the fuckers were coming to claim it back with interest.

I slammed my drink and poured another, my sorrow rapidly evolving into anger as I fumbled in my pocket for a tightly wrapped ball of film. Well, they could have it as far I was concerned. The car, the kitchen — the whole house. They were welcome to it all.

I chopped out a dual carriageway, two fat white lines running almost a third of the length of the counter. The same counter Flynn would sit at in eight hours' time and demand breakfast.

But I wasn't thinking about Flynn. I was only thinking about myself.

I bent my head forward and closed my eyes. Inhaled. There was a flash of green light followed by a constellation of stars, as if someone was attacking my eyelids with a pin. I tipped back my head, a bitter plastic taste dribbling down the back of my throat. Plastic and blood. I kept my eyes scrunched tight, trying to block out the light, before stooping forward again.

Whoosh.

This time I felt myself taking off, bursting through the ceiling, then the roof, my hair matted with splintered tiles and plaster dust and moss and bird shit, rising so quickly that within seconds the house was nothing but a vague rectangle of grey among a thousand other similar patches, higher and higher, until I could just about make out the bright silhouette of Britain, then Europe, the street lights of the cities and settlements glowing like a rash of orange liver spots; the motorways like infected wounds. Still I kept going, looking up just in time to see the faint blue glow of the ozone layer as I punctured it, sailing through the troposphere, stratosphere, mesosphere, and finally out into the endless, black void of space, the stars smearing as I sped ever faster towards oblivion.

A sharp coldness gripped me then, starting in my nose and spreading quickly down my spine, my limbs frozen by my sides as I slowly pirouetted through the nothingness all around me. As I turned I caught a glimpse of a small blue and green tennis ball. I tried to focus, to spot something I recognised, but it was too far away, and within seconds it had shrunk to a marble, and then I lost sight of it altogether, just one more speck among a billion points of light.

I kept going, deeper and deeper, leaving our solar system and the Milky Way far behind as I hurtled past a thousand other galaxies, some not even born yet — the pink-and-purple swirling clouds of nebulas rising up before me like the pillars of creation — until finally I saw it.

Or rather I saw him.

God.

He was wearing a shirt and tie and sat behind an enormous marble desk, his head bowed over a futuristic-looking laptop. I swallowed hard — or rather I would have if I hadn't been an inanimate block of ice. This was it, I realised. The moment of judgement. The divine balancing of the books.

I was screwed.

Then something strange happened. God yawned. He actually opened his mouth and yawned. Could it be that the Supreme Being was knackered? I guessed being both creator of the universe and principle object of human faith could take it out of you.

Only God didn't look tired — he looked bored.

At that moment he glanced up and, as if noticing me for the first time, he waved for me to come closer.

And that's when I realised it wasn't God at all.

It was my ex-manager, Dan.

Occasionally, another lifetime ago, I would sit in bars and listen to people moaning about their jobs. The hours of endless drudgery. The disrespect their superiors showed them. Their lack of career prospects. They would moan about it until they were too drunk to talk anymore, their misery and self-hatred spilling out over the sides and splashing over anyone sitting too close. They were like human vortexes, sucking the joy out of the room.

Whenever I heard somebody beginning one of these monologues I would reach for my beer and raise a silent toast to myself. Because I didn't just enjoy my work. I was in love with it. It was a thing of beauty. And the best thing of all was that I'd got there all by myself. I hadn't won the lottery or inherited it. No. I'd done this. The studying, the unpaid internships, the years of endless arse-kissing and networking, clawing my way over the desiccated piles of the weak and the old, until finally I reached a spot near the summit, my place in the sun. And once I got there I realised I'd found my calling. I wasn't just good at it. I was great. Even that asshole Dan admitted as much — right before he held a gun to my face and pulled the trigger.

Account manager. It's a dull job title to the uninitiated, as if perhaps I spent my day shuffling through dusty files or comparing spreadsheets. In truth, however, it's one of the most envied — and least understood — roles in advertising. Essentially, my purpose was to make sure existing clients were happy with all aspects of our work. More importantly, I needed to ensure that the big fat cheques they made out to us once a quarter, kept coming, and if possible got even bigger and fatter. One of the best ways to do that was to make sure the clients had access to everything they desired.

And I do mean everything.

The number one mistake most account managers make is to believe it's their job to sell the firm. They're the ones who turn up at the airport with a briefcase full of statistics. The ones who bore the visiting CEOs half to death with their scripted pitches about the company's core values. The ones whose idea of entertainment is a five-course dinner at a fancy restaurant while they rattle off half-baked Forbes quotes-of-the-day over seared foie gras and moules à la crème.

Those guys find they don't last too long — their clients mysteriously decide to take their business to another agency at the first available opportunity. No, in reality the job of a good account manager is not to sell their company, but to sell themselves. Because the truth is, when El Presidente of some FTSE 100 company turns up in town with his merry band of corporate flunkies in tow, he's not simply there to find an innovative way of selling yet more toothpaste or suspect financial products to the general public. No. He's there with a legitimate alibi to spend a couple of days away from the shareholders, wife and kids. In other words, he's on vacation. He's there to party. As a result, the account manager's job is to act as a sort of tour guide, or club rep. They need to be Mr Fun-Times; the 1,000-watt lamp every barfly in the room flutters to. The guy who can provide unlimited quantities of booze, blow and women — yet breathe not a word of it at the next morning's meeting. To smile and nod and lie with professional impunity.

Like I said, I'd found my calling.

For almost a decade I'd been the best account manager in the business. Not one of my clients ever left me. How could they? I knew the precise colour and splatter of the stains that smeared their dirty laundry. I was too dangerous to risk cutting loose. So they would keep the nibs of their fountain pens dancing along every dotted line placed in front of them, ensuring both my bonus and their good names remained intact. It was the perfect arrangement.

And then the bomb went off.

At first it looked like the advertising industry might escape unscathed. If anything I assumed the downturn might actually boost business. Surely if profits had dropped then the best way to resuscitate them was to scream a little louder? To come out guns blazing. And for a while that seemed to be the case. The whole world might have been under attack, but within my private principality the flags kept flying. The booze kept flowing. But slowly things were changing. A couple of our major clients folded overnight. Huge, centuries-old institutions. We woke up one morning and they were gone. Just like that. And with their deaths came fear. The newspapers — who of course were as up to their necks as the rest of us — started to point fingers. Austerity was the new buzzword and any show of excess was to result in extreme and sustained public humiliation. God forbid someone saw the size of your bonus, let alone found out about the harem of hookers you had charged to your company credit card.

It was at this point chief executives started jumping. Or were shoved. Overnight around half the pages in my contact book were irrelevant. And the new people who came in to replace them. Jesus. They were like monks. They'd turn up to business lunches and order tap water. They'd ask for a breakdown of every expense sheet. Every minute, every penny had to be accounted for. It was unworkable — something had to give.

And in the end that something was me.

Around ten months after the government announced that the UK was officially in recession, I was made redundant. Or rather, "my position" was made redundant, as Dan was at pains to put it. It was nothing personal. My firm had decided they no longer needed account managers. Dan had decided.

"The world's twisted on a notch, Ad," he said, flashing a smile from behind the security of his desk. "We're in evolutionary mode now. Adapt or die. It really is nothing personal."

And with the slash of a ballpoint pen it was over.

I was obsolete.

"Daddy?"

I opened my eyes.

I was lying face down on the kitchen floor. Next to me were two small feet, ten pink toes wriggling against the chill of the tiles.

"I'm thirsty," said the toes. "I want a drink."

I sat up, swallowed hard. My mouth was an open sewer, a dank cave full of sludge and broken glass. I tried to speak. "Ugh."

Flynn gave a sleepy smile. He wasn't really awake. "Silly Daddy. Did you fall asleep on the floor?"

I nodded. Silly Daddy. Staggering to my feet, I headed over to the tap, cupped my hands and took a long draft before pouring Flynn a glass.

"Time for bed, buddy," I croaked once he'd finished.

He came without a struggle. I hoisted him up into the crook of my arm, his head nestling into my chest. He was asleep before we reached the bottom of the stairs. I crept up quietly, wary of waking Lydia. My muscles felt hot and tingly under my skin, my back teeth clamped tightly together. I vaguely wondered if the coke might be cut with something. It wouldn't be the first time I'd ended up in a K-hole after buying a bad wrap. Whatever it was, it seemed to have mostly worn off. Despite the jitters, my mind felt sharp. In fact, things were a little too clear; dangerous, half-formed thoughts lurked at the periphery of my consciousness. I licked my lips. I needed another vodka.

As I reached the top step, Flynn shifted his weight in my arms, pushing his face into me, as if attempting to burrow into my chest. I planted a kiss in the mop of his hair, his scent sweet and buttery. I eased open his bedroom door and paused at the threshold. In the dark the room looked strange and unfamiliar. I scanned the walls, taking in the blotchy pictures he'd brought home from nursery, his shelves stacked with books and toys I hardly recognised. Like the rest of the house, his room was all down to Lydia. I'd input nothing but money. Now that had stopped I felt like an extra, wondering through the set of my own life.

Flynn stirred again, a bad dream playing on his lips. "No . . . "

"Shhhh," I said as I lowered him into his bed, drawing the duvet up around his tiny shoulders. I stooped to kiss him goodnight again.

"Goodbye," I said.

I froze. I'd meant to say *goodnight*. Now, however, the truth that had been hovering in the shadows for the last few weeks came hurtling out into the light. Goodbye. At that moment I realised I was going to leave. I was going to leave tonight.

I backed out of Flynn's room quickly, knowing that if I stayed any longer I'd change my mind. I crossed the landing, reaching for Olivia's door, pushing it open and slipping inside. Again I waited in the doorway, scared I'd wake her if I got any closer. Even in the darkness I could make out the features of my eldest child. She looked younger when she slept, the pre-teenage angst drained away to leave a softer expression. She looked happy. I studied her — the dainty curve of her mouth, the way her hair folded over her cheeks — trying to drink in the details of her form, storing them away deep inside me, as if they might sustain me later somehow. "Goodbye," I whispered, before I closed her door behind me.

I paused on the landing. Directly in front of me was Lydia's bedroom. *Our* bedroom. I pictured her fast asleep, oblivious under layers of duck feather duvet. She'd be frantic when she awoke to find me gone. But that was nothing compared to the fury she'd unleash when she finally discovered the truth. I couldn't win. Either way, I decided she deserved one last good night's sleep before her world fell apart.

I turned around and crept back down the stairs. I didn't take anything; no coat, no phone, no keys, no money.

And, just like that, I opened the front door and walked out on my life.

CHAPTER
FOUR

Everything was under control. Yes I'd been laid off, but it was a temporary measure. A snag in life's rich tapestry. A speed bump on the road to riches. There were plenty of other agencies out there. I'd interview for a new job and be snapped up by a rival company within a fortnight. Dan's loss would be someone else's gain. Meanwhile, I was on full pay for the next three months, and it seemed a shame to waste the chance to kick back a little. To relax and recuperate. To recharge my batteries.

Concerned husband that I was, I decided it would be cruel to burden Lydia with the details. Not when everything was definitely, positively, one hundred per cent under control. No, I decided I'd carry on as I always had. I'd leave the house at eight and be home for six. It was business as usual. Only with a little more free time on my hands.

Within a week things began to unravel.

As I've mentioned before, the problem with free time is working out how to fill it. Of course, this isn't such an issue when you still have access to a steady supply of hard currency to fund your secret all-day visits to the race course or casino. And when that runs out, you can always dip into your joint savings accounts and your children's ISAs while you wait patiently for the right hand or the right race to catapult you back into the black. You know your wife's PIN, you can pawn your wristwatch, borrow against your house and car, all the while chasing that one big win that will turn you around, that will make everything okay again.

By the time my losses were tallied up I owed more than the sum total of all of my assets. More than ten times the total. I began calling around the agencies, but by then it was too late. Dan was right — the world had moved on. Nobody was hiring. Or at least they weren't hiring me. They were like dogs; they could smell the fear. The desperation. I couldn't even get an interview. Of course I *thought* about confiding in Lydia. But where would I begin? And more to the point, where would I stop? A lifetime of little lies had snowballed and become an avalanche. There was no way of pulling out one or two details without the whole thing roaring into the open and burying me.

No, my only choice was to keep on running, hoping that my luck would change.

I was so cold when I reached Tamara's house that I couldn't feel my knuckles against her door. There was no answer. I kept knocking. Eventually I heard muffled footsteps from somewhere deep inside the building. I knocked again. This time the hall light came on. I dropped to my knees and hissed through the letterbox.

"It's me," I said. "Open up."

The footsteps got closer, followed by the pips of a burglar alarm. The rattling of chains and locks. I straightened up and took a step back as the door opened to reveal a slither of black hair and one furious eye.

"Adam? For fuck's sake. It's two in the morning. You don't text? You don't call? I've got a housemate you know. She nearly called the police . . . " She trailed off as she caught sight of my face. "Jesus. Are you alright? You look terrible. Where's your coat?"

I shrugged. "I've done it," I said. "It's over. I've left Lydia."

Tamara didn't move for a moment. Eventually she took a deep breath, her whole body sagging as she opened the door a little wider. "I suppose you'd better come in then," she said.

And so I did.

I didn't set out to have an affair. I'm sure a lot of married middle-aged men say that sort of thing — especially when backed against a wall by an apoplectic spouse brandishing divorce papers. But in my case it was true. Tamara had been my secretary for a full two years before anything happened between us, and even then it was she who'd chased me. Well, maybe we'd chased each other. But however it began, it was never a conscious decision on my part to cheat on Lydia. It's important you know that.

Of course I'd noticed Tamara. Everyone *noticed* Tamara. Yet the possibility that I might end up sleeping with her never crossed my mind. I was in my early twenties when I first started seeing Lydia and despite the money and relative power I'd accrued in the intervening decades, at heart I still thought of myself as this awkward, stuttering child. And so, when a late evening at work turned into an early, booze-fuelled morning and we found ourselves alone in the office together, I was shocked. Not only by the force of my own lust, but to find that longing reflected in her enormous green eyes. She wanted me. And not just physically either. Unlike the other women in my life she seemed genuinely excited by what I had to say. She was charmed by my bad jokes. She listened to my reheated anecdotes and ancient chat-up lines with the earnest reverence of a student, as if worried she might miss some small detail she would later be required to recall. As if she actually thought she could learn something from me. Me! Of course I was flattered.

And so, as my hands reached up and around to explore the taut angles of her young body, I knew that this would not be a one-off, a moment of drunken weakness. It would happen time and time again. I would devour her, until adultery became just another means of getting high, of escaping. And, just like every other drug in my life, I used it to excess, until it stopped being fun and became just another addiction to service.

And even then I couldn't get enough.

"Excuse the mess. I wasn't exactly planning on visitors."

I trailed Tamara through the squat chaos of her house. Though the majority of our time together had been spent in hotels around the city, I had still been here at least a dozen times before, and as I walked, the ghosts of our affair reared up around me, smearing like streaks of neon in the dark hallway. The places we'd fucked. The positions we'd folded each other into. The lies we'd told with our bodies. And later the arguments. I saw it all replayed in slow motion and from multiple angles, like the trailer for some low-budget erotic thriller.

"What the fuck do you want, Adam?"

Tamara stood facing me as I entered the kitchen. She looked tired. Older. I realised it was the first time I'd ever seen her without makeup.

"I thought we could start with a coffee?" I said, smiling weakly. "Or a beer if you've got one."

Tamara didn't move. "That isn't funny. You can't do this. I haven't seen you for two months and then you turn up stinking of drink, saying you've left your wife? I've got work in the morning."

"I know. I just . . . I needed to see you."

"Really? You needed to see me now? It couldn't have waited until tomorrow? You couldn't have called me first?"

"Jesus, Tammy! Didn't you hear what I said? I've left my wife. This is what we talked about." I took a step towards her, my arms encircling her waist. She tensed, but didn't push me away. "We can be together now," I continued. "Just the two of us. Like you always wanted." My lips reached her neck, the honeyed musk of her bringing me back to a hundred hotel rooms. I slid my hands lower.

"Stop," she said, gripping my wrists. "Ella's upstairs. It's not fair." She turned her back on me, filling the kettle, fumbling with cups and milk. Avoiding my eye. "So, how are you?" she eventually asked. Her tone was measured, unnaturally breezy. "How's work?"

She might as well have pulled a knife on me.

I'd only seen Tamara a handful of times since the afternoon I'd left the office; a shuffling cliché with a box file wedged under each arm and a string of incoherent threats on my tongue, all of them aimed at Dan. Each occasion had been more depressing than the one before, the memories of Michelin-starred restaurants fading in favour of frazzled liaisons in Holiday Inn car parks. After a while we'd stopped contacting each other altogether, the embarrassment and disappointment too much for either of us to stomach.

"I'm still looking. Things have been tough, you know? It's a difficult climate out there for everyone. But I've used the time constructively. I've done a lot of thinking. I've made some big decisions."

Tamara slammed a mug down so abruptly that a black wave of instant coffee sloshed onto the kitchen surface. "Look, there's something you should know," she said. "I'm seeing someone."

I tried to speak, but the words snagged in my throat, coming out somewhere between a growl and a cough.

"You don't know him," she continued. "He's my age. He works in IT. It's only been a few weeks but, well, it's serious."

"But . . . " I said, still choking. "But . . . "

42

"Oh, fuck off, Adam. You can hardly talk. We were never exactly exclusive."

Bile flooded my mouth. I swallowed hard. It was time to lay my cards on the table. "Listen, Tammy. I'm happy that you've met some kid. Really, I am. You deserve all the happiness you can get. But I'm in a bit of a spot. If I could just crash here for a couple of nights until I'm back on my feet. A week max . . . "

Tamara's eyes flashed from pity to rage. "So that's it? You have an argument with your bitch wife and you think you can just turn up here and stay? Did I miss the 'Vacancy' sign out the front?"

"No, of course not. It's not like that. I wanted to see you . . . "

"Well, I don't want to see you. Not ever."

I took a step towards her but she backed away. And that's when I saw it. Mixed in with the anger was fear. She was scared of me. Of what I might do. And without another word, I walked away.

As I reached the front door I turned. Tamara hadn't followed me into the hall. I opened the door, then paused. Slung over a coat peg was a handbag. Black. Expensive. I recognised it as Tamara's. In one fluid motion my hand dipped inside and fished out a purse, rifling through it to pluck a small bundle of notes. I let the purse drop back into the bag and then I was gone, a thief dissolving into the night.

It was past three by the time I arrived at the casino. Not that it really mattered. Time was irrelevant in these places. Actually, they deliberately tried to keep it from you. No windows, no clocks, no TV screens. Nothing to distract you from the serious business of losing money. I didn't have any ID, but fortunately the bouncer recognised me. He waved me through with a threat that I was to split my winnings with him. "No problem-o," I said. "Just make sure you've got a wheelbarrow handy to carry it all home."

Ho-ho-ho.

Once inside I went immediately to the roulette table. I'd taken six twenty pound notes from Tamara. Without hesitating, I put the lot on red.

Then I waited for the ball to drop.

Now some people will tell you that there's an art to roulette. They'll bore you half to death with their systems and strategies for beating the house. They'll insist that by sticking to the outside or by covering the middle and high numbers you can actually tip the odds in your favour. They'll advise you to double your stake every time you lose, or remind you to listen to the table for any irregular rattles that might imply a defection of the ball run. Or to watch the wheel for tilts or wobbles. Oh, and to always, always, *always* pick a European table over an American, so help you God. But these people are deluded. In truth, they have no more of an advantage than the old boy who picks out his grandkids' ages divided by the number of times he's beaten cancer. No, when it comes to roulette, there's no place for either science or superstition. It is the tossing of a coin, the throwing of dice. You are in thrall to the awesome forces of chaos. Which is precisely what makes it so irresistible.

"*No more bets please.*"

I watched as the wheel began to spin, the numbers blending to a blur of red and black before the dealer shot the little white ball into orbit. Nine, ten, eleven times it circumnavigated the rim before it gradually began to slow. My body throbbed with anticipation. The buzz was better than sex, better than drink, better than any drug. I held my breath until the centrifugal force acting on the ball abruptly lost its battle against gravity, watching as it was spat with a clatter into the waiting slot. I turned to the dealer for confirmation.

"*Red, Nine.*"

In less than an hour I had five thousand pounds worth of chips stacked on the table. Twenty minutes later it was more like fifteen thousand. A waitress appeared from nowhere, ferrying a constant stream of complimentary vodka tonics from the bar to my waiting hand, while a Ray-Ban-wearing manager hovered nearby, muttering darkly into a flesh-coloured earpiece. Every half an hour or so he would stride through the small crowd that had gathered around me and make a big show of ordering a change of dealer. But my luck held, regardless of who was spinning the wheel. Red, black, odd, even, I picked my bets at random, gambling with the confidence and complacency of someone unconcerned with petty human concepts such as winning or losing. I was operating on a higher frequency, in communion with the gods of chance and alcohol. It was the greatest streak of my life.

And then I began to lose.

I doubled down, trying to recoup my losses, but it was too late. By six in the morning I was down to my last thousand. By quarter past I had just two hundred left. The free drinks dried up. The crowd drifted away. The manager was nowhere to be seen. I placed my final bet. Everything bar one red chip.

"*No more bets please.*"

There was a small metallic chink as the ball came to rest, like the final nail being driven into a coffin. It was the loneliest sound in the world.

It was light when I got outside, the streets already filled with the first commuters of the day. They were business people mostly, the new plates of their company cars glinting in the breaking dawn. I wished nothing but pain and misery on each and every one that passed.

I still didn't have a coat, and even with the dozen or so vodka tonics inside me the wind was biting. I slipped into an alley and bumped the last of the coke — or whatever it was — from the back of my wrist, rubbing the plastic film around my gums afterwards. Then I carried on walking.

The morning edged on and my head began to hurt. My thoughts turned to Lydia and the kids. A couple of years ago I read about a salesman who'd hung himself in the building opposite ours. The paper explained how he'd broken into the office at night and locked himself in a janitor's cupboard. As it happened, the maintenance staff were in some sort of contractual dispute with the owners of the building at this time, and as a result his body lay undiscovered for over a fortnight. Now, this guy was married with three children, and so naturally the police wanted to know why nobody had raised the alarm to say he was missing. When they interviewed the wife, she explained how her husband had been working really hard lately — she'd just assumed he'd been putting in some extra overtime.

As I shuffled along the early morning streets I wondered how long it would take before my family realised that I'd left them. Aside from the school run, how much of a contribution did I really make to their lives? If it wasn't for that, they might not notice I'd gone at all.

After a while, steel shutters began to yawn open all around me as harassed-looking shopkeepers started to prepare for another day. I slipped into the first grocery store I passed and, with my final twenty pounds in the world, bought the biggest, cheapest, nastiest bottle of vodka I could afford. I cracked it open before I'd even left the shop.

From there on things became a little jumbled. With no more drugs to straighten me out, the booze dug its claws in, dragging me in staggered zigzags across the pavement. Car horns blared. School kids crossed the road to avoid me. The world became a stuttering mass of colour and confusion, punctuated by great black manholes that my memory simply refused to record. One minute I was vomiting a pool of bright red bile onto the steps of a library, the next I was lying on my back on the fringes of an old industrial estate. It was like teleporting from one nightmare to the next, the bottle acting as my demented tour guide.

Eventually I became aware of a stillness around me. I opened my eyes to find myself sitting on a rusted metal bench in some kind of field. It almost looked familiar, but I was too bent out of shape to make sense of it. It was nice though, the hard angles of the city replaced by soft green curves. I put the bottle to my lips and tipped back my head.

Hours passed. Or perhaps they didn't — it's difficult to tell. All I know is that at some point I became aware I was lying on the ground. Scattered around me were the crystalline fragments of a broken bottle, sparkling in light of the dying day. They were beautiful. I reached out to pluck a shard from the gravel, pulling my hand back in pain. A single drop of blood clung to the end of my finger. I pressed it to my lips and sucked. It tasted of salt and rust. I reached out my hand again.

This time I grasped the stubby neck of the bottle and held it to the light. I saw the world distorted through it, a vague smear of brown and green, and was suddenly aware of how drunk I was. So this was what the bottom looked like. I felt the weight of absence crush the wind from my chest. No job, no home, no family. No options. Everything was broken and dirty and destroyed.

And yet for all discord and dismay, one thing was suddenly blindingly clear. I won't call it a moment of clarity — my mind was far too sodden with vodka for that — but it was nevertheless a moment of decisiveness. Out of the haze emerged a plan. A way out. An exit strategy. I seized it without a second thought.

I took the broken bottle neck.

And dug it into the worm-like veins of my wrist.

I watched in fascination as my flesh ruptured, a crimson geyser erupting from the wound. I pulled back the glass. And then did it again.

And again.

Until I disappeared.

The best thing about being dead is that you are instantly absolved of all feelings of guilt and remorse. In fact, you are instantly absolved of all feelings full stop. There is nothing. Less than nothing. No hangovers. No to-do lists. No missed calls. You and everything you have ever worried about instantly cease to exist. And that's the way it's going to stay for ever and ever and ever. The end.

It's fucking great.

The only problem was, I wasn't dead. Not really. Because as I lay there — thinking nothing, feeling nothing, being nothing — I gradually became aware of a tugging sensation, as if someone was shaking me.

And then, before I had time to try and decipher what the sensation could mean, I heard a voice, calling to me from the darkness.

"Wakey-wakey," it said. "You've been a silly boy, haven't you, son?"

SPRING

CHAPTER
FIVE

Father Christmas was trying to kill me. That was my only thought as I hurled myself from the bench and attempted to scramble through the dirt to safety. The man launched himself at me, straddling my torso, his features lost among a mass of thick white beard.

"Now, you just wait there a minute," he said, shifting his bulk backwards so as to pin my legs to the floor.

I continued to thrash, my fists swatting pathetically at him as I attempted to free myself. It was no good though. He was too heavy. My arms grew heavy as I strained to get a better look at my assailant. It was still dark, and difficult to make out much apart from an enormous belly, which bulged grotesquely beneath the folds of his filthy red coat.

After a minute or so the adrenalin began to ebb away and I stopped fighting altogether. A jumble of fractured memories tumbled through my mind. The cold night, the abandoned park, a broken bottle of vodka. I raised my hands to my face and saw the jagged brown crust of dry blood around my wrist.

"Nasty," said the man. "Looks like you could do with a stitch or two in that."

As he shifted his weight I was hit by the rich, meaty tang of his body odour, causing my stomach to churn evermore queasily. Before I could attempt to wriggle free, however, I became aware of a rustling close by. I turned my head to see a monstrous German Shepherd darting from the bushes and bolting towards me, fangs bared, ready to rip out my throat.

I screamed, though the sound that came out of my mouth was little more than a dry croak. This seemed to amuse the man immensely, and he roared with laughter as he placed an arm around the dog's neck and jerked him away from me. "Oi! You big lump, Bruno. I don't think he wants you puffin' and pantin' your stinkin' breath all over him, do you?"

"Get off me!" I said, finally finding my voice. "I mean it. Get the fuck away from me!"

The man stopped laughing. "I'll get off you when I'm good and ready, sonny," he said. "But first off I need to make sure you're not going to do anythin' you'll end up regrettin'. Or rather I need to make sure you don't do anythin' *I'll* end up regrettin'. If you catch my drift . . . "

For a moment I thought about struggling again, but I knew it was hopeless. I felt weak, the first merciless thumps of a hangover threatening to stave in my skull. I looked from the man to the dog, and gave a small, painful nod before collapsing backwards in submission.

This seemed to be precisely the signal he'd been waiting for, and before I knew what was happening he'd eased his weight off me and yanked me to my feet.

"There we go. That's better, isn't it? Now, before we go any further down the wrong path, why don't I fix you up with a nice brew? You look like you could do with one, if you don't mind me sayin'. And while that's doin' I can see about cleanin' up that cut." He grinned broadly and stuck out a huge, paw-like hand. "I'm Rusty, by the way. And this here's Bruno. We're very pleased to meet you."

Over the next ten minutes or so, I sat and watched as "Rusty" built a fire while the dog lay dozing at my feet, lifting his head to bark a gruff warning every time I crossed or uncrossed my legs. Now that my eyes had adjusted to the light, I could see the man's beard was not quite as Santa-esque as I'd initially thought. While bushy enough to conceal his entire neck, up close I could see it was actually dirty grey rather than white, and seemed to be orange at the tip, as if dipped in paint. His forehead and cheeks, meanwhile, were as brown and weathered as a cracked leather purse, with deep creases etched around his watery eyes.

Once Rusty had built a sturdy-looking teepee of twigs, he held a match to the kindling, fanning the flames until they licked at the larger branches he'd placed on top. When it was crackling without assistance he disappeared into the trees behind us. Moments later he returned with a Y-shaped log, which he drove into the ground at an angle, so that it jutted out over the fire.

"Right-o, I'll get the kettle on," he said as he reached into one of the many pockets in his jacket and produced a small, stainless-steel bucket with a loop on the end. He hooked it over the branch, rummaged

55

around again, and then took out another container, this one a dented silver flask with a cork stopper jammed into the top. As he held it up, I noticed the inscription on the side: *Ultimate Sales Jedi 2008* . . .

"Found this one just yesterday." Rusty said when he caught me staring. "The things people throw away, huh? Nothin' but water in here now you'll be sad to hear." He pulled out the makeshift cork and poured liquid into the bucket with a sharp hiss.

"Right then," he said once he'd tucked the empty flask back into his coat. "We'll give that a few minutes to boil and we'll be cookin' with gas — or should that be wood?" He let out another hearty laugh.

"Be quicker with gas, that's for sure."

"Ah-ha. But then I'd have to worry 'bout my gas runnin' out, wouldn't I? Anyway, in case you haven't noticed we ain't exactly short on wood round these parts. Use what you got, that's what I say. Besides, you got somewhere better to be? Some urgent business meetin' perhaps, Mr Fancy Pants?"

I glanced down at my ruined clothes and shook my head. I didn't have anywhere to be.

"Well then. We can just sit here and enjoy the fire, can't we? You look like you could use a bit of heatin' up anyway."

He slumped down next to me and again I was hit by the smell of him. I slid down the bench, closer to the fire. As the warmth began to spread across my arms, I suddenly realised how cold I was. I leant closer still, rubbing my hands together in the amber glow of the flames.

"There you are. Nothin' a good fire won't fix," Rusty said, oblivious to my distaste for his personal hygiene. "Out in just your shirt? Catch your bleedin' death if you're not careful. Although from the look of things, that's the point, isn't it? Must've lost about a pint and a half of blood there. Plus, you stink of booze you do! Here, don't sit too close — you'll go up like a bleedin' can of petrol!"

I didn't say anything. The heat from the fire had made my wrists sting, and they pulsed in time to the spasms of nausea in my gut.

"Not that I've got a problem with suicide," Rusty continued. "Nope, I'm a big fan. Only way to protect the species, if you ask me. Too many of us as it is, using up all the food and dirtyin' up the air, without worryin' about people who don't even want to be here. And it's only goin' to get worse. No wonder they're plannin' to send a man to Mars. Only place that'll have enough room for us all pretty soon. No, if people want to kill themselves, that's fine by me. Hell, if I was the Prime Minister I'd put a bloody suicide machine on every corner. Press a button and that's it. Lights off. Quick and painless. Goodnight, Vienna!" He got up to poke the fire, still chuckling to himself. "Only thing is, you can't do it here."

"Huh?"

"Kill yourself, like. You can't do it here in the park. If there's a dead body, the police'll come sniffing around and then ... Well, it'll just be a big headache for everyone involved. 'Course you're welcome to do it outside the park. There's a nice secluded spot over by the railway lines. I can show you, if you like?"

"Look, I'm not going to kill myself, okay? I just had a little too much to drink and things . . . Things got out of control."

Rusty grinned. "Well, that's fine and dandy too. Glad to hear it. Whoops, looks like that water's finally boiled."

I watched as he used the stick to lower the bucket to the ground, wrapping his hand in the sleeve of his coat and pouring the steaming water into yet another container, this one a chipped ceramic pot.

"What are you putting in there?" I asked as he pulled a small packet from his pocket.

"Well, it's not Kenco I'm afraid, but it's not bad. We've got some chamomile, lavender, a bit of valerian root and . . . " he trailed off as he wandered back over to the bushes, returning seconds later with a handful of fresh leaves. "Nettles," he said as he stuffed them into the mug. "Great source of vitamin C, they are. That'll help with the hangover. Now, why don't I have a look at those cuts while that's steepin'?"

Even in the dark, I could make out the thick layer of ingrained dirt that covered his hands, his fingernails so caked in filth they were almost completely black. I hesitated, pulling back as he reached for my arm. "Why are you doing this?" I asked.

"Doin' what?"

"Helping me. You don't even know me. What's in it for you?"

Rusty shrugged. "You're in my park. I've got a whatchacallit? A duty of care. Besides, you know what I was saying about not killin' yourself in the park? Well, that goes for all sorts of dyin'. And, no offence, son, but you look like you're about to keel over."

I wasn't surprised. Now that the adrenalin had subsided I felt truly terrible. A deep chill had burrowed its way to my core, so that my whole body shook uncontrollably as I sat hunched in the dark. I nodded and let Rusty take my hand in his lap. Once again he excavated the deep pockets of his coat, this time dredging up a grubby-looking roll of bandage and a small brown bottle. "Iodine," he said. "Real strong stuff. Burns like bleedin' battery acid, but trust me, it's better than an infection. I seen a guy lose three whole fingers out here from nothin' more than a nasty flea bite. Now, you hold still."

The pain was unbelievable, a pure, white wave that crashed over me, strong enough to make me forget about everything else, so that I existed only in that moment — at least for a couple of seconds.

When I opened my eyes Rusty was bent over the wound. "See where you went wrong was your choice of instrument. Glass ain't no good. Sure it'll cut you up, but it's too imprecise. Won't know what you're hackin' at. That's why those poor old housewives always take a razor blade to the bathtub with 'em when they want to top themselves. You need something clean and sharp. And you gotta slice *up* the vein, not across. That way you'll really get em' squirtin'!"

He moved back, revealing the off-white bandage wrapped so tightly around my throbbing wrist that I could no longer feel my fingers.

"There," he said. "Good as new. Or at least, as close to new as you'll get until we get you to a doctor. Now, let's see about that tea, shall we?"

While Rusty began decanting the liquid from one container to another, I sat slumped on the bench. My head was swimming so much it was an effort just to stay upright. In the dim light the park looked soft and unreal. I had a powerful urge to sleep, and I was struck by the notion that if I could just crawl up and close my eyes then everything would be okay. I would wake up in my own bed next to Lydia. I would be Adam again.

"Ahhh, perfect," said Rusty with a loud slurp. "You know, I never used to be able to stand this muck. Espresso man I was. Seven or eight a day — doubles too. Soon as I woke up. Bang, straight down the hatch. Liquid cocaine I called it. Still, this ain't too bad when you get a taste for it. Don't give you the shakes neither. Here."

I used my good hand to take the cup from Rusty. The heat radiated through my fingers and, as the steam rose up towards my face, I caught a sweet, floral scent. It reminded me of Lydia. I lifted the drink to my lips and took a sip. At first the heat masked the flavour, but as I swallowed I caught a mossy bitterness. Instantly my mouth flooded with saliva. I leant forward and vomited into my lap, at which Bruno instantly leapt up and started barking.

60

"Ah, come on," Rusty laughed. "It's not that bad!"

I felt him take the cup from me, but I was too ill to sit up. I heaved again, a torrent of watery grey vomit splashing over my knees. I stayed hunched over for a few minutes, my throat burning, a sharp pain needling deep in my gut. It had been years since I'd been this sick, and with the vomit came a weird nostalgia. I remembered an illness I'd had as a child, my mother's hand stroking the back of my head as I retched into the bowl, my chin resting against the cool ceramic. Her words of comfort came to me again like a lifebuoy trailing across the stormy decades.

It will pass.

I clung to them with what little strength I had left.

When I finally straightened up, Rusty was staring at me. "You need to get home, sonny. Sleep it off. When the DTs kick in you'll want to be wrapped up somewhere warm. Trust me."

I spat on the floor, too weak to answer.

"I could call someone to collect you, if you like? I could walk you to the bus stop at least?"

I shook my head. "Nowhere to go," I said, my voice no more than a dull scratch.

We sat in silence while Rusty sipped his tea. "Well, this is a bit of a bloody mess, isn't it?"

I swallowed hard. "What's a mess?"

"This. You. I mean, you can't very well stay out here all night, can you?"

"I'm fine," I said, retching again as if to underline precisely how un-fine I really was.

Rusty knocked back the last of the tea and shook out the cup. He looked torn. "I suppose it wouldn't hurt. Just for one night," he said, more to himself than me.

"Huh?"

"Ah, blow it. You can stay here. With me, like. Just until you're back on your feet mind."

As sick as I was, I had to smile. The way he spoke, it sounded as if he was offering me his spare bedroom rather than a spot on a park bench. "What, here?"

Rusty stiffened. "Why, what's wrong with here?"

"Nothing. Here's great. Thanks," I said, wondering how long I should wait before I made my excuses and left this mad old bloke to his nettle tea and find a bench of my own.

He went over to the fire and kicked it out, scattering the ashes with a sweep of his boot. "Right then. Are you coming or what? I might be a big guy, but I ain't carryin' you. Not on your Nellie!"

"What?"

"Well, I don't know about you, but I ain't plannin' on spendin' the night on some bleedin' bench. What do I look like, a tramp? Now, come on."

And with that, he stalked off into the trees, Bruno tearing ahead of him.

For a moment I sat there. This would be the ideal time to lose him. I could simply get up and walk in the opposite direction, keep going until I'd left the park and the madness of the night behind me. But where would I go? Back to the city? To Lydia? With a heavy sigh I faltered to my feet, realising that following Rusty was the only real choice I had.

The ground lurched away from me with every step, my head spinning so violently I was forced to cling from trunk to trunk just to stay upright as I dragged myself deeper into the woods. After a couple of minutes, I caught a glimpse of a disembodied beard glowing up ahead.

"Come on," said the beard. "I haven't got all night."

I blundered after him as he turned again, following as he weaved between thick snares of brambles and beneath low-hanging branches, the undergrowth tearing at my exposed flesh as I did my best to keep up.

Eventually the trees began to thin out into a clearing and he came to a stop. I dropped to my knees, gasping for breath while Bruno butted up against me, almost toppling me over.

"Right then," Rusty said. "You can have my place for tonight."

I squinted in the direction he was pointing, confused for a moment. And then I saw it. Perched right on the edge of the clearing was a small, khaki-coloured tent, almost completely camouflaged by a thick layer of twigs and leaves.

"You comin' or what?"

I started to get to my feet again. This time my strength failed me, and I slid backwards into the dirt. Bruno was over me in an instant, his rough tongue scouring my face until a strong pair of hands clamped under my armpits and began to drag me across the clearing.

"Easy, son. It's okay, we're there. We're there."

I tried to speak but the words snagged in my throat, and so I allowed myself to be carried like a child, grateful to have finally ceded responsibility for my actions, to have all choice taken away. Seconds later I heard the sharp scrape of a zip and I collapsed into the warm shell of a sleeping bag. I felt Rusty rolling me onto my side and tuck something heavy over my shoulders, and then he was gone, pulling the zip behind him.

Even with my eyes shut tight I felt the darkness closing in around me. Not just the night, but something blacker. Emptier. As I teetered on the verge of oblivion, as the last trace of my consciousness ebbed away, I felt something pull me back. Somewhere, beyond the tent, I heard a noise. Or at least I thought I heard a noise. Low voices, talking nearby. Arguing maybe, though the words I couldn't grasp. Just urgent, angry whispers, rattling like the wind between the trees. And then they were gone again. Or maybe they were never there at all? Either way, I couldn't hold on any longer.

I let go of the world and allowed myself to fall.

CHAPTER
SIX

Lydia was already downstairs, swiping through the morning news, a fresh cup of lemongrass tea steaming beside a half-eaten bowl of granola. Flynn was nearby, curled up on the sofa watching his cartoons. Every now and then he called out for yet another bowl of cereal, mewling like a wounded kitten when he didn't get his way. Olivia was still in bed of course — like father, like daughter — although I hoped she'd slept better than me, tortured as I was by feverish dreams.

I burrowed down deeper under the duvet. In a minute or two it would be time to get up, to face the world. But for now I could forget about everything. Work. Responsibility. The thumping headache. I could simply snuggle down and deal with it all later. If only the bloody dog would stop licking my toes . . .

That's when I remembered.

We didn't have a dog.

I opened my eyes.

Imagine every hangover you've ever had happening simultaneously. Confusion. Guilt. Nausea. Panic. It was like an explosion. I sat up, struggling to make sense of my surroundings. The pain in my head was spectacular. I cupped my hands to my eyes and massaged my temples as the world slowly fluttered into focus. I was in some sort of tent, the green canvas walls slick with condensation. Below me was a thick khaki sleeping bag and roll mat, the sort you might find in a military surplus store, at the end of which was a dog's muzzle, poking through the bottom of the tent. Gradually, the night before came back to me. The park, Rusty — Bruno. I felt the dog's coarse tongue searching the crevices between my exposed toes, and instinctively I gave a sharp kick. There was a yelp and the muzzle disappeared. I was alone again.

I sat there for a moment, overwhelmed at the extent of Rusty's worldly possessions. Strewn along the side of the tent was an overwhelming array of boxes, tins, jars, cutlery, pans, clothes, water bottles, bundles of yellow newspapers, several bicycle pumps, a blunt-toothed hacksaw, a two-pronged trowel . . . the list went on. The ramshackle stacks seemed to be arranged by some indecipherable system, the carefully considered chaos of a junkyard or charity shop. A castaway's treasure, a hoarder's lot. Everything in there looked bent or rusted or broken in some way, the recovered garbage of the world, partially mended and catalogued according to usefulness. A mad museum of junk, everything coated in a fine layer of dust and hair and stinking of damp and dog and decay. I decided I needed to leave — immediately.

Before I could move, however, I heard a noise. Rusty appeared in the doorway, a grin on his face and a bowl of something steaming in his hands.

"Morning, sleepy head. Or should that be afternoon?"

As he manoeuvred into the tent, Bruno took the opportunity to make his return. He dived at me, forcing me onto my back and slobbering over my face.

"Get off me!"

"Ah, he's jus' happy to see you. Aren't you, boy?" Rusty laughed as he dragged him off me, so that his matted tail whipped my face. "I've brought you some breakfast, though it's more like lunch now."

I sat up and took the bowl he was holding out. It was filled with some sort of watery broth. The smell brought a surge of bile to my throat. "Thanks," I said, hoping desperately that he wasn't expecting me to eat any in front of him.

"Leek and onion. Not too bad neither. Here, get out of it, you!" Rusty yelled, bundling Bruno from the tent. "Dumb beast. Bleedin' allergic to onions too. He'll be spraying out of his back end for days if he gets so much as a sniff. Oops, sorry," he added as he noticed the look on my face. "I forgot you was eating."

I brought the spoon of mush to my face and stopped, letting it hover below my chin. "I'm not sure I can stomach anything right now. To be honest I was thinking of pushing off pretty soon."

Rusty frowned. "Nonsense. You're not goin' anywhere — you're as white as whipped cream. You need to line your stomach, sonny. Start getting' your blood sugar back to normal. That's half of the hangover that is. Hypergly-whatsit. Anyway, it took me half the bleedin' mornin' to cook that — didn't your mother teach you no manners?"

Seeing no way out, I raised the spoon to my lips. It took a minute or two to swallow the bland paste, which seemed to absorb what little moisture remained in my body. I managed two more spoonfuls before I began to sweat. "Mmmm, thanks. That's really good," I said, deciding to change the subject. "God, I was out cold last night. What time is it anyway?"

Rusty looked blankly at me. "Time? Well, I'll be buggered if I know! Late afternoon. 'Fraid I don't get much more specific than that. Light and dark — that's 'bout all I need to know. I don't even know what year it is. Mind you, I bet you don't either, amount you put away last night. How's the old head doin' anyway?"

"Not great," I admitted. "In fact, I'd say it's about one thump short of forming its own samba band."

"That's more like it! Samba band indeed! Listen, I tell you what. Why don't you stay here until you're feelin' a bit more like yourself? You can eat up the rest of that soup and then get your head down for a couple of hours. Come to think of it, I've got a little somethin' for that headache too."

I watched as he began to burrow through his mountain of supplies.

"Thanks," I said as I stirred the soup, which had already begun to form a skin. "Actually I'd murder an Alka-Seltzer if you've got one."

"Ah-ha. Here we are!" Rusty turned around and held up a bag of what looked suspiciously like pencil sharpenings.

"What's that?" I asked, struggling to hide my disappointment.

"White willow bark. There's one growing next to the lake. You probably saw it on your way in? It's a natural aspirin. It's the bee's knees when it comes to fixin' aches, pains and general maladies, though I have to admit it does taste like sawdust — which I suppose is exactly what it is. I'll whip you up a pot, if you like? It'll only take a minute or so."

I thought of the nettle tea he'd prepared the night before. "You know, I think I'll be alright for now. To be honest this soup has worked wonders," I said, hastily forcing another spoonful into my mouth.

This seemed to delight Rusty no end. "You see? That's what I was saying! You'll be right as rainwater in no time — you mark my words!" He dropped the bag of tree bark into his pocket and turned towards the doorway. "So I'll leave you to it for a bit, if that's alright?" he said, unzipping a corner of the tent. "If I was you I'd have a nap — before that bleedin' samba band strikes up again — I'll be back later so you can let me know if you change your mind about the tea. Oh, hang on, what's he up to now? Bruno! BRUNO!"

And with that he was gone.

I sat there for a minute and listened to him chasing after his dog, his hollers growing quieter as he moved further and further away.

As I slid the bowl of soup to one side and lay back down, an unexpected sense of loss settled over me. Rusty's presence — and his unprompted kindness — had helped blot out the reality of my situation. Now that I was alone again, my thoughts instantly turned to Lydia and the children. Maybe it wasn't too late to go back? I pictured myself wading through the ring of police cars that encircled the house and knocking on the front door. I saw the children run to me and decorate me with kisses as I fell to my knees and wept and begged Lydia for forgiveness . . .

The tent flapped in the wind and I snapped back to the present. How had I ended up here? It seemed impossible. I tried to piece together everything that had happened the day before, reliving every moment in reverse, as if rewinding an old video cassette. There was broken glass and gravel, the red lips of an open wound. I watched as my wrist healed itself, the flesh restitching, the blood flowing back into my veins. I saw the vodka bottle un-shatter as I put my mouth to its neck and tipped back my head, filling it back up with booze. I walked backwards out of the park and through the city until I reached the casino. The roulette wheel span anticlockwise and the chips spewed back out of the hole. I took my money and left, returning it to Tamara's bag before un-knocking her door.

And then I was back home, blowing powder from my nose onto the kitchen counter, un-drinking more vodka, creeping up the stairs and out of my clothes and sliding into the warmth of my bed, back into Lydia's arms. And it had all been a dream, some stupid story I'd made up to amuse myself. None of it had happened. Because who in their right mind would give up everything so easily? What kind of idiot would swap that life for this?

I pulled my knees to my chest and let the sleeping bag fall over my head.

When I woke again it was dark. There was no sign of Rusty. I moved my head slightly and found the pain had lessened a little. I sat up. Something was wrong. Things looked different. I scrunched my eyes and reopened them. Gradually the vague shapes inside the tent began to come into focus as my eyes adjusted to the darkness. The mountain of supplies seemed to have shifted somehow, though perhaps I was imaging it? It was difficult to tell in the dim light. I reached a hand towards the nearest pile and then froze.

aaaaWOOOOOOOOOOooooo

A shrill sound reverberated around the tent, the timbre and cadence of an old-fashioned air-raid siren. Or perhaps a howling dog.

aaaaWOOOOOOOOOOooooo

The noise came again, and this time I was certain it was animal in origin. I relaxed slightly as I remembered Bruno. Yet still, I was unsettled. This was like no dog I had heard before. It wasn't a pet inadvertently locked out overnight. No, there was something threatening about this sound. Something wild. Like a wolf calling its pack to hunt.

aaaaWOOOOOOOOOOooooo

Moments later a second howl started up, seeming to answer the first. This one sounded closer. I tried to stay calm, telling myself that Bruno had found a friend, that at any moment I would hear Rusty yell for the pair of them to shut up.

aaaaWOOOOOOOOOOooooo

I was surrounded by a chorus of wails, the notes clashing horribly and growing louder — and closer — by the second.

aaaaWOOOOOOOOOOOooooo

Fear shook me from my stupor. I threw the sleeping bag from my shoulders and began scrabbling around in the darkness for my shoes. I needed to get out. My hands shook as I dredged the floor of the tent, but it was no good. My shoes were gone. Someone had taken them.

aaaaWOOOOOOOOOOOooooo

Abandoning my search, I decided to make a run for it. I dived for the doorway and grabbed hold of the zip, only to find it jammed. I tugged at it with all my strength, but it was no good. Something was causing it to stick. I was trapped.

aaaaWOOOOOOOOOOOooooo

As more howls joined the cacophony, five, six — too many to count — I began to feel around the walls, desperate to find another way out. Just then something hit the tent. The fabric whipped and bulged alarmingly in one corner.

Whatever was outside, was trying to get in.

aaaaWOOOOOOOOOOOooooo

I tore at the tent, my fingers frantically pressing into the smooth walls for a way to escape. It was hopeless though. Without any sort of blade to cut myself free, I was imprisoned by a few millimetres of canvas.

aaaaWOOOOOOOOOOOooooo

As the baying circle closed in around me, I retreated to the centre of the tent. I felt throttled by panic, gasping shallow gulps of air as the tent shivered and shook under the assault. I curled tighter into myself, snatching up the sleeping bag and coiling it around me.

There were other sounds now. Hoots and hollers. Scratches and scrapes. Shadows flashed in the darkness, strange, monstrous silhouettes that reared up all around me, pummelling the tent from every angle.

aaaaWOOOOOOOOOOOooooo

Exhausted, helpless, I crumpled to the ground and plunged my fingers into my ears, attempting to block out the awful roar.

I closed my eyes and waited for the end.

CHAPTER
SEVEN

"You made it then?"

I opened my eyes. It was light. So light, that it took me a couple of seconds to focus. Slowly the world came into view. The fuzzy halo of Rusty's beard and hair framed a faceless void. I blinked a couple of times, then sat bolt upright. There were my shoes, at the bottom of the tent. Right where I'd left them. I spun around. The jumbled mass of supplies looked the same as before. Everything was as it was.

"You lost somethin', have you?" Rusty asked, watching me with a mixture of concern and amusement. "If you have, it's probably that bleedin' dog again. Eat anythin' he will, I swear. Wonder he didn't try and gobble you up in the night!"

There was a gruff bark outside.

"There he is. Protestin' your innocence, are you, boy? Even if you are guilty as sin! You alright? You look like you've seen a ghost. That storm put the willies up you, did it? I'm not surprised. Hell of a bad 'un to be fair."

"Storm?"

"Ah, come on. Don't try and tell me you slept through it? I was up half the night meself! The way that

74

wind came whistlin' through them trees I was half scared one of 'em was going to come down on top of me. You think you had a bad head yesterday? Try havin' a two hundred-year-old supportin' beam landin' on your bonce!"

I scanned the tent again. In the light it all looked so utterly innocuous — homely even — that with every second that passed, it became harder to remember what had terrified me so much only a few hours earlier. Could it all have simply been a nightmare, the last of the toxins offering a final, hallucinatory salute as they leached from my pores?

"Well, at least it seems to have blown some good weather our way," Rusty continued. "It's bloomin' gorgeous out now. Not a cloud in the sky. Sometimes I think we all need a good, strong blast now and then, just to shake off the drab and drizzle. Speakin' of which, why don't you come and get some fresh air? I was just about to fix us up a spot of brekkie."

Stomaching more of Rusty's soup was the last thing on my mind. Still, I was anxious to escape the confines of the tent. And so, with a tentative nod, I pulled on my shoes and followed him through the small flap of canvas into the world outside.

Rusty wasn't wrong about the weather improving. The air smelled sweet and earthy — fresh enough to loosen a rattle in my chest. I coughed hard and spat. Judging by the light I guessed it was still morning, the sun already sliding steadily upwards in the unblemished sky. I took a few more steps and then turned back, realising it was the first time I'd seen the tent in daylight. I was surprised to find that it was far smaller than it seemed from inside, the moss-green canvas ravaged by a series of dark scars and patches, marking what looked like decades of previous repairs. It almost resembled an organic being; as much a part of the landscape as the gnarled oak tree it nestled beneath. It blended so completely with its surroundings it would have been difficult to spot had I not been looking for it.

"You comin' or what?" Rusty called, by now already halfway across the clearing, Bruno trotting by his side.

I turned and hurried after them, hoisting up my trouser legs to save them from the misting of dew that clung to the long grass. As I picked my way through the foliage, I was struck by the lushness of my surroundings. From the purple and white flares of crocuses, to the blue dapple of forget-me-nots, everything looked crisp and hyper-defined in the sunlight, the colours rich and oversaturated — almost *too* real. My first instinct was to take a photograph, though a quick pat of my pocket reminded me I didn't have my phone. The realisation brought me sharply back to reality.

"I'll need to be leaving soon," I said as I caught up with Rusty.

He was kneeling beside an upturned log, next to which a small campfire had already burnt down to a glowing stack of embers. "Aye, of course you do," he said, without looking up. "But first — we eat!"

I watched as he retrieved a small canvas sack from behind the log and started digging through it, pulling out a small cast-iron skillet, a stainless-steel bowl and a fork. Setting the pan on the fire, he reached into his coat and, with a flourish, produced a mottled, white ball. He held it up for me to admire. An egg.

"Ta-dah!" he said as he cracked the shell on the rim of the bowl and let the insides slither out. "Bit better than bleedin' soup, eh?"

I sat in silence as he dipped his hands back into his pocket and produced another egg, the fork clacking out a steady rhythm as he beat them to a froth. Once satisfied with the mixture, he leant forward and spat towards the fire, leaving a brown stain sizzling on the surface of the pan.

"Ain't got no tomatoes I'm afraid," Rusty said as he poured out the mixture. "Bit early in the year for them. I have got a bit of this though." He held up a handful of sharp-tipped leaves, ripped them between his fingers and tossed them into the pan. "Wild garlic. Grows down by the lake it does. Not as strong as the bulbs, but it does the trick . . . NO! HOW MANY TIMES DO I HAVE TO TELL YOU?"

While we'd been talking, Bruno had crept round the back of the fire and now had his nose inches from the pan. At his master's roar he leapt back and dropped to the floor, cowering under his paws. I looked up, shocked to find Rusty's ordinarily genial expression replaced by an altogether darker look, his eyes flashing with menace. An awkward moment passed before he turned back to me. "That bleedin' mutt, eh? I swear he's got a death wish! Anyway, I think this one's just about ready." He reached into the bag and handed me a fork and a battered stainless steel plate.

"Cheers," I said, as he held up the pan and slid a surprisingly fluffy-looking omelette onto my plate. After eating so little for days, it tasted incredible, the wild garlic infusing the egg with just a hint of spice. "This is fantastic!" I said between forkfuls.

"Yeah, well. Be better with cheese. Cows are a bit of a bastard to keep though. I did think about getting a lamb or two, make some feta like. Could knit meself a nice woolly jumper for the winter too! But seriously, they're a pain in the wotsit. Foot rot and ticks and lice and all the rest of it? No thank you. I don't want to lose me eyebrows messin' about with sheep dip neither. At least the chickens more or less look after themselves. All I've got to worry about is the bleedin' foxes. That's where havin' a dumb brute like Bruno comes in handy."

At the sound of his name, Bruno looked up expectantly, having recovered from his scolding.

"Wait . . . So these are your eggs?" I said, pausing mid-mouthful.

Rusty smiled. "Of course! There ain't no Sainsbury's round here in case you ain't noticed. These are freshly laid about an hour ago. 'Bout as organic as they come I reckon!"

"So you keep chickens? Here in the park?"

"That's what I just said. I got a dozen or so in the back field. Thought they would've woken you to be honest. Noisy buggers they are. Still, I guess that's the price you pay for a half-decent breakfast. Now, if you've nearly finished I'll get a pot on. I like to have a cup of peppermint first thing in the mornin'. It ain't Colgate, but it'll freshen up your gob good enough."

I forked the final chunk of egg into my mouth and chewed slowly as I tried to digest this new piece of information. Was it really possible that Rusty was actually some kind of rebel agriculturalist? Growing vegetables, foraging for herbs, raising chickens — all under the nose of the local council? Part of me suspected this was all an elaborate joke. Any minute now he'd wink at me and slap his thigh and pull out a can of Special Brew.

I watched as Rusty fiddled with the fire. Just as before he'd staked a branch into the ground, over which the stainless-steel bucket had already started to steam. "Have you been here long then?" I asked.

"Where's that then?"

"Here. In the park."

He shrugged. "Oh, aye. We've been here a while, ain't we, boy?" he said, addressing Bruno.

I waited for him to elaborate, but instead he turned away to tend to the fire. It seemed for once the conversation was over.

A few minutes passed before Rusty handed me a warm mug of mint tea. I thanked him, before we again lapsed into a comfortable silence. Breakfast had provided me with a much needed bump of energy. In fact, I felt the best I had in days. Tucked away in the secret park, with sunlight spilling through the newly budding branches, I found it was almost possible to imagine my problems were happening to someone else, far, far away. I let my eyes fall shut for a moment and listened to the secret murmur of the woods.

Despite only the slightest of breezes, the trees stirred and groaned, their young leaves crackling like static. Elsewhere, invisible birds cackled a shrill call-and-response, trilling their gossip from vertiginous perches deep within the woods. Finally, so faint I could almost pretend it was my own pulse burbling in my ear, I detected a less welcome sound; the low mumble of distant traffic, dragging behind it the real world, and all of the unfinished business that lay there.

I swallowed a mouthful of bittersweet tea, determined to refocus my attention on this green pocket of serenity — at least for the short while I had left before I returned home to start picking through the wreckage of my old life for bits I could salvage.

"Listen, Rusty. I want to thank you for everything," I said, once I'd set my empty cup down on the tree stump. "You've been amazing. Seriously. I was in a bad way and you, well, you helped me out. I owe you one."

"You sound like you're leaving, sonny," he said, a hint of disappointment in his voice. "Got somewhere else you need to be?"

I shrugged. "I haven't decided yet."

"Aye. Well. You've got to do what you've got to do."

He stood up, shaking the remains of his cup into the fire. I followed suit, heaving myself to my feet and dusting myself down. As I did, I noticed for the first time the state of my clothes. I'd left the house in what I'd been wearing — just another high-flying corporate clone in a tailored suit and designer brogues. Now though, my trousers and shoes were caked in dark mud and my jacket was ripped along the seam of one arm. My shirt was smeared with various unidentifiable fluids. Stood next to Rusty, I realised that — aside from the beard — there was little to tell us apart.

When I looked up again, he was holding out his hand. I took it. His calloused palm engulfed my hand completely, crushing it slightly as he shook.

"So I'll be seeing you?" I said, wincing as I attempted to disengage.

Rusty gripped tighter though, pulling me closer to him, until my ear was level with his lips, so that I could feel the rancid heat of his breath. "I tell you what," he said, his voice little more than a growl. "Why don't I show you around the place before you go? I've got a few vegetables growing in the field back there. You can see the chickens if you like?"

I didn't answer.

"Ah, come on," he said, grinning now, but nevertheless refusing to relinquish my hand. "Won't you spare twenty minutes to humour a proud old fool? I hardly ever get any visitors. Besides, you said it yourself . . . You owe me."

It wasn't just a few vegetables Rusty wanted to show me.

It was a whole other world.

Once I had acquiesced to his offer of a guided tour, Rusty quickly packed away the breakfast things and then led me across the clearing to yet another section of woodland. As ever, Bruno charged ahead and was quickly swallowed by the undergrowth, his distant snarls and barks providing a ragged chorus to our own grunts of exertion. This time the terrain was almost impenetrable. Dense snags of brambles tore at my hands and face as we fought our way deeper and deeper into the trees. Rusty seemed unperturbed, however, chattering enthusiastically as he paused now and then to point out a particular species of edible herb, or to muse on the medicinal benefits of a variety of mushroom, the bulbous helmets of which erupted from the shadier patches of sodden earth.

After what seemed like hours of grappling with barbed tentacles of vegetation, we came upon a man-made fence; a rusting steel web that divided the woods. Scanning its length, I saw it was decorated with a selection of official-looking signs, warning that trespassers would be prosecuted.

Sensing my concern, Rusty paused to reassure me. "Ah, ignore all that. They're only there to deter the tourists."

We continued onwards.

Following his lead, I snaked my way along the fence until we reached a small breach, where it looked like a section had been snipped from the wire. The gap was just large enough for a person to squeeze through. I hesitated for a second. Somewhere nearby, Bruno was barking again.

"After you," said Rusty as he stood aside.

With a final look over my shoulder, I dropped to my hands and knees and began to crawl.

After another few minutes of walking, the trees began to thin out. Before long we stepped out into another clearing, this one three or four times larger than the field we'd been in earlier.

"Well, here we are," said Rusty. "What do you think?"

Ahead of me lay a patchwork of freshly turned earth, the land geometrically staked out and carefully segmented by crop. Here and there stood tall bamboo trellises, the first coils of beans winding around their ligneous frames. Elsewhere, recently ploughed furrows housed great leafy explosions of vegetables; wrinkled fans of rhubarb towering above fleshy pink stalks, while chaotic flops of spring cabbages cowered beneath the polythene parasols of poly tunnels. It was an allotment — but on a near industrial scale.

For once Rusty was silent, watching with evident pleasure as I strode around, trying to comprehend the size of the operation. A little further up the field I spotted an imposing wooden structure. Approaching, I realised it was an elaborate hutch, a dozen or so chickens strutting behind the crosshatch of a wire mesh fence.

"This is incredible!" I said once I'd eventually finished looking around. "You've got a whole farm back here. There must be enough to feed an army."

He flushed slightly behind his beard, scuffing the ground with his boot. He almost looked embarrassed. "Well, you wouldn't be far off the mark there, son."

I shook my head, confused.

"I have to admit, I haven't exactly been straight with you. You see, it's not just me that's here."

I followed Rusty's gaze to where his dog lay crouched, tongue unravelled from his jaw as he silently eyed up a fat hen. "What? You mean Bruno?"

Rusty chuckled but didn't smile. "No, son. I mean there are other people livin' here. Men. Workin' the land and that. We're a whatchamacallit? A community."

I studied the old man's face, trying to decide if he was joking or not. Over by the chicken hutch there was a sharp yelp followed by a panicked beating of wings. Neither of us turned to look.

"Well then," I said, having decided to call the old man's bluff. "Shouldn't you let them know I'm here?"

At this Rusty did laugh. A booming chesty convulsion, one that set his eyes streaming and doubled him in two. When he finally straightened up again his face was red and he was still smiling, though his eyes were once again sparkling with an unsettling intensity. "Oh, they know you're here alright," he said. "They know all about you."

CHAPTER
EIGHT

After we left the allotment — or "the farm" as Rusty now referred to it — I was led through to a small connecting field where forty or so large plastic water butts, stood in rows. These, Rusty explained, were used to capture rainwater. "You need to boil it up before you drink it though, else you'll be makin' a sharp dash for Squit Creek!"

I followed his finger to a narrow strip of marshland along the far edge of the park, surrounded by a wreath of wispy reeds.

"That's what we call the facilities here. You just dig a hole and off you go. Don't get much privacy I'm afraid, and it stinks to high-hell in the summer, but it's the best we've got at the moment. We have talked about buildin' somethin' more permanent, but we've never got round to it. Still, it does the job."

Since his revelation, he'd hardly paused for breath, so excited was he to reveal the history and details of his life in the park. He explained how he'd started sleeping rough on the streets at some point in the mid-nineties, after his wife had finally grown tired of his "monkey business" and kicked him out. For the first few years he'd stayed on the streets, but after taking one too many beatings from local thugs he started looking for somewhere safer to spend the nights. The local council was still maintaining Adenbury Community Gardens then, but it was nevertheless quiet enough that he could comfortably camp out without fear of being disturbed, and after a while he took to foraging for food in the woods to supplement what he couldn't beg or steal on the streets. As the years passed, others gradually joined him and they'd begun to actively grow their own food, to the point where they were now totally self-sufficient. "That's when I stopped being homeless," Rusty said with a chuckle. "Houseless, sure. But now I had somewhere I could call my own. Somewhere I belonged."

I nodded, still unsure of what to make of his story. On the one hand there was certainly enough food growing to support a sizeable community. There was no doubt that maintaining a plot of land that size would be a seriously big job. Despite Rusty's evident resourcefulness, I doubted he'd be physically capable of managing it alone. Having said that, we'd spent most of the morning wandering around the park and I'd seen nothing to suggest these other people were anything but the rambling figments of a wildly unhinged imagination.

As we left the water butts and "Squit Creek" behind us, Rusty led me to yet another connected field. This one, however, contained little but a steep depression ringed on all sides by tall trees; a sort of natural amphitheatre carved into the land.

"What is this place?" I asked as we began to slither our way down the topsoil of the slope, clinging onto tree trunks for support. "A bomb crater?"

"Nah. Though you're right, it looks like one. This place is an old marl pit. They used to dig the clay outta here and spread it on the land. Pre-industrial revolution, like. S'posed to be a good fertiliser. Probably explains why things grow so well out here. 'Course once they started buildin' factories and sprayin' around their chemicals they stopped diggin' up the marl. Now it's just a good place for the foxes to keep outta the wind. Well, it was until us lot showed up anyway."

Once we'd reached the bottom, I saw the pit did indeed make a good shelter. The steep sides created a sort of microclimate, both cooler and darker than the rest of the park. Gone were the rustle of trees and the birdsong — even the traffic — leaving nothing but the slight wheeze of my own chest as I fought to catch my breath. I stepped out into the clearing, and was once again struck by the pit's resemblance to an arena, a tight cage of trees encircled us on every side. In the centre of this circle was a dark patch where the grass had been scorched, the blackened cadaver of a log still smouldering slightly, as if only recently abandoned.

Puzzled, I turned to Rusty. A strange smile played on his lips, his yellow teeth just visible among the tangle of off-white hair. "They're here," he said, staring past me off into the trees.

I looked, but saw nothing. "Who's here?"

"Now listen, he can be a bit funny," Rusty said. "He don't mean nothin' by it. He just likes to let you know who's the boss. And make no mistake. He *is* the boss."

Bruno started barking at this point, an agitated snarl dampened by the dead air of the pit. At the same time, he backed closer to Rusty, the matted fur of his hackles arching along his backbone.

"Who's here?" I asked again, struggling to keep the panic from my voice. "Who are you talking about Rusty? Rusty?"

Then it happened. Out of the trees sprang another dog, a sinewy bolt of white. The dog charged and landed on Bruno, pinning him to the floor. Too startled even to yelp, Bruno looked up at Rusty, imploring his master for help.

Before either of us could move to separate the beasts, there was another sound. I looked up to see a man emerging from the trees, as bearded and filthy as Rusty. Tied around his head was a grubby red bandana, while in his hand he clutched what appeared to be a primitive spear, a shoulder-length branch with one end whittled to a sharp point. Moments later another man appeared by his side, then another and another, each of them similarly armed with wooden weapons: cudgels, slingshots — even a rudimentary long bow.

There was a rustling and three more men stepped into the clearing behind me, followed by another on the furthest side. This man stepped forward and approached us with long, deliberate strides. As he drew nearer I saw he was noticeably taller than the others, and wearing faded military fatigues: a camouflaged jacket and khaki trousers, a pair of black boots laced halfway up his shins. His eyes were hidden behind a pair of mirrored sunglasses. Like the other men, he was heavily bearded, though his glossy black facial hair was pulled into an elaborate plait that ended midway down his chest. The hair on his head was similarly dark, though most of it was stuffed under a green beret. He also had a weapon, though his was not made of wood. Rather, he held an air rifle with telescopic sight, the gleaming black barrel of which was levelled at my chest. When he was about fifteen feet from us, he stopped and bawled at the dogs. "ENOUGH!"

At the sound of his voice, the white dog instantly released Bruno and skipped to the man's side, leaving Bruno trembling at Rusty's feet. Satisfied, the man patted the dog roughly before turning to face us. He considered me with an expression that was impossible to read behind the shield of glasses and hair. Then all at once he smiled, his black beard cracking open to reveal a gaping red hole. The other men began to laugh, a gruff chorus echoing around the trees. Even Rusty let out a couple of obligatory snorts, though in truth he seemed just as uncomfortable as me.

"What've you brought me here then, Rust?" he said once the men had finally fallen silent. "Fresh meat?"

CHAPTER
NINE

His name was Marshall, and Rusty was right. He was the boss. At around six foot four he towered over most of the others. Yet it wasn't just his height — or even the gun — that marked him out as the leader of the group. The man had a presence about him, a natural authority in the way he held himself, so that all it took was for him to mutter "This feller looks like he could use a warm drink" for one of the others to scurry over to the charred logs and begin teasing a campfire into existence.

"This is the one I was tellin' you about, sir," said Rusty. Something about his demeanour reminded me of poor Bruno, who was still curled on the dirt, licking his wounds. "Adam's his name," he continued. "Adam, this is Marshall. Marshall is what you might call our . . . "

"That's quite enough, Rust," said Marshall, dismissing him with a curt nod of his head, before he turned to face me.

It was difficult to guess his age, though if I had to, I'd have put him somewhere between me and Rusty. Late forties perhaps. There wasn't much to go on though. Mostly I could just see myself, reflected in the silver lenses of his sunglasses. I looked small and dirty and scared.

Marshall smiled at me, a flash of red once again scarring the black forest of his beard. "Adam, is it?" he said, glancing down at my bandaged wrist. "I won't ask you what it is that brings you here. I'm sure the details of your personal circumstances don't differ greatly from those that delivered these other sorry souls to my charge. I have no interest in hearing yet another sob story."

At this there was another murmur of laughter from the men, though I was momentarily too distracted by Marshall's dog to pay them much attention. The animal was emitting a low, guttural growl as it stared up at me, an unmistakable glint of malice in its ice blue eyes. I took an involuntary step backwards.

"Nothing to be nervous about, Adam. That's just Tyrus' way of showing he likes you. Isn't it, boy?"

There was more laughter at this as Marshall stooped briefly to give the dog a couple of affectionate thumps. As he did so, I noticed a gold signet ring glittering on his little finger, looking strangely incongruous on the otherwise filthy shovel of his hand. Tyrus stopped growling but held my eye, staring until eventually I looked away.

"He's a good mutt, this one," Marshall continued. "Father was a husky, mother was a she-wolf. In other words, he's one mean motherfucker. As far as I'm concerned, you can take your pedigree pooches" — and with this he aimed a sneer at Bruno — "and make Chinese chowder out of them. Bunch of preening, inbred, disease-ridden, bourgeois bitches. No, give me a half-breed any month of the year. Better genes you see. Mix the blood and dilute the deficiencies, that's what I say. Get the best of every world that way. Sure, you might not see them on any podium with a goddamned rosette pinned to their breast, but you stick them in a one-on-one with any so-called thoroughbred and we'll see who comes out with both ears still attached. The mongrels will inherit the earth, Adam. Make no mistake about that. And speaking of mongrels, it's about time I introduced you to this motley bunch of strays and reprobates — what do you say?"

There was an anarchic whoop of approval as the men surrounding me shook their makeshift weapons in the air until Marshall raised his hands, instantly restoring order to the clearing.

"Right then, let's do a quick roll call, shall we? Now let me see. Fingers! Get your ignorant backside down here."

One of the men scurried forward to greet me, still clutching his spear in his hand. As he reached Marshall, he lowered the tip of his weapon and bowed his head, revealing a threadbare pate, scabrous with dandruff and dirt.

"Now, this here is Eric," said Marshall, as he slipped an affectionate arm around the man's neck, "but we all call him Fingers, on account of . . . well, why don't you show him yourself, Fingers?"

Without a word, the man lifted up his free hand, revealing a pair of shiny pink stumps, where his little finger and ring finger should have been. "Please to meet you," he said, the words leaking out through a row of brown teeth. I was struck by the ripe stench of halitosis.

"Seven years ago," Marshall continued, "Fingers here was some big cheese in the city. Le Grand Fromage as the French might say. I forget his exact job title . . . "

"Actuarial investment analyst," Fingers said.

"Precisely. An actuarial investment analyst. Whatever the hell they are when they're at home. And you were earning what a year?"

Fingers shrugged. "Fifteen hundred a day."

"Fifteen hundred pounds a day! And did you have a girl back then, Eric?"

Fingers smirked. "Several."

"Of course you did, you hound! A rich, young actuarial investment analyst like yourself? I bet you were beating them off with a stick. But was that enough to make young Eric happy?"

Fingers shook his head, his mouth crumpled into a guilty grin, like a toddler caught with his hand in the biscuit tin.

"No, it most certainly was not!" Marshall boomed. "Despite having all of the wealth and privilege and *pussy* any one man could reasonably expect to garner in a single lifetime, Eric here was miserable. He was jaded. He was *tumescent* with boredom. And so, like most moneyed people in his situation, he went and found himself a hobby. Which in Eric's case was . . .?"

"Methamphetamine," Fingers said, so readily that I wondered how many times this exchange had played out before.

"Ah-ha! And so of course the remainder of this tragic tabloid tale you can fill in for yourself. Smoking became snorting became injecting, and within a matter of months poor Fingers' world had contracted to the size of his next baggie of crystal. His life became an endless Friday night, a nightmarish tableau of anxiety, delusions, insomnia and violence. The luxury apartment, the monthly salary, all of those sexy wee birdies, all of it disappeared, replaced instead by a cold concrete bed in a piss-stained shop doorway. And then of course there was a misunderstanding about payment with your local distribution agent, resulting in a, ahem, double-digit fine."

Fingers gave his stumps a wiggle and grinned.

"But then something happened to change all that, didn't it, Eric?" Marshall said quietly.

Fingers nodded, his eyes shining with emotion.

"Why don't you tell the nice man here what happened."

"I was saved," Fingers whispered.

"Louder."

"I was saved!" Fingers yelled.

The crowd howled their approval.

"Next!" Marshall roared, giving Fingers a final, affectionate squeeze before releasing him to rejoin the ranks. "Who's next?"

On and on it went, as man after man came up to confess the sins of his former existence, before testifying to the salvation they'd found in the company of this terrifying yet oddly hypnotic man. There was

94

Hopper, a military veteran whose real name was Schwarz and who walked with a limp on account of his poorly fitted prosthetic foot; Ox, an ex-convict with a blue teardrop smudged across his cheek and whose rhinocerian physique dwarfed even Marshall; Al Pacino, an alcoholic quantity surveyor who claimed to be of Italian decent but bore only the faintest physical resemblance to his namesake; Butcher, who confusingly was actually a plumber, and had a penchant for prostitutes and prescription opiates; and Zebee, a well-spoken black man in a threadbare tweed jacket, who insisted he was only there on sabbatical until "I'm ready to be with my family again".

"Of course you've already met Rusty and myself," Marshall said, without further embellishment. "Which just leaves . . . Ah, Sneed."

I turned and saw the man who'd started the fire approaching us, a steaming cup of tea gripped tightly in his bone-white knuckles. He was a meagre, jaundiced-looking man, with a bald head and no beard. I thought he might have been younger than the other men — who without exception all looked somewhere between their early and mid-forties — though the dark folds under his bulging eyes made me less certain. His appearance brought to mind an ailing Russian spy I'd once seen on the news during the last days of the Cold War, whose defection to the West had resulted in a vicious radioactive reprisal.

Sneed held out the tea, observing me with a cold, reptilian gaze for a couple of seconds before slinking back towards the bushes.

"Well, that *was* Sneed," said Marshall with a rueful grin. "He's what you might call a work in progress."

There was a hack of laughter from the men, who by now had formed a loose semi-circle around Marshall.

"But we'll get there with him. We always do. Anyway, the point I've been trying to make, as I'm sure an educated man like yourself will have no difficulty grasping, is that each of these men came to me as little more than flotsam and jetsam; human excrement, tossed overboard and washed up on the dankest shores of society. Junkies, winos, perverts" — he paused to wink at the man he'd introduced as Butcher — "derelict shells bereft of virtue or grace. Scum to give scum a bad name. No present, no future, no hope. And yet . . . And yet."

Marshall took a step forward. I could smell the fresh perspiration beating through the layers of camouflage as he towered over me, so strong that it stung my nostrils.

"And yet they were good men," he continued, his voice quivering with emotion now. "Or at least, there was still a kernel of goodness at their centre, buried beneath the calcified layers of abuse and bad decisions. And I saw that goodness in each and every one of these motherfuckers. I understood that, underneath all of the *diabolical shit* life has hurled at them, these men are as soft and as pure as newborn babies. That all they needed was for someone to reach down into their chests and scrape away the stone from their hearts for them to be able to start over again, fresh. That's what they find here. A new beginning, away from the greed and excesses of the outside world. Here they find food, shelter, kinship. That which is essential. All I ask in return is three simple things. Firstly, there is to be no intoxication of any kind. That means no booze, no pills, no sniff, no needles. Nothing. No coffee. No cigarettes. And no sex. There should be absolutely nothing to distract you from the ongoing project of your salvation. Number two: We do not leave the park. For any reason. Ever. Everything we need is here, growing under our boots or above our heads. Outside is for outsiders as far as I'm concerned, so if you leave — and you are of course free to do so at any time — then you'll not be welcome back. Finally, and of all I ask, this is the most important. You must do what I say. You do not question me. You do not disobey me. Now, I know there's plenty of poncey leadership skills *some* people like to employ, participative, delegative transformational and what have you, but they're of no interest to me. I'm as autocratic as they come. I'm a goddamn tyrant and proud of it. As far as I'm concerned it's my way or the highway. God knows, I've seen enough good men lose a limb or worse after defying a direct order out in the field. Am I wrong, Private Schwarz?"

"No, sir!" cried the man known as Hopper.

Marshall reached up and removed his sunglasses, revealing for the first time the dark circles around eyes that shone with a startling intensity. Around him I felt the crowd stirring, drawing closer.

"And so, my friend, the time has come for questions. And I'm sure you have many. But first of all, I'd like to ask you one."

He leant forward, so close that our foreheads touched and his eyes became one giant black hole in the centre of his face, a bottomless pit from which no light could escape.

"Will you join us, Adam?"

I stared back into that single black eye, and felt something inside me shift. I thought about Lydia, waking up alone in our bed. The panic she must have felt. The confusion and dread. And then there were the kids. Had she told them the truth? That she simply didn't know where I was? Or was she more brutal? Sorry, darlings, but Daddy didn't love you enough to stick around. Daddy was an addict and a liar and a thief. Christ, even my old man had the courage to be there while I was growing up, even though it drove us, and most likely him, halfway round the bend most of the time.

"Will you join us?"

The question burrowed deep down through my flesh, dislodging the layers of ice that had hardened within me over the days and months and years even. The men drew their breath. In the silence I imagined I could hear a creaking as my defences began to thaw. Then suddenly I cracked, sending everything I'd sought to conceal and control surging towards the surface. I attempted to speak and discovered I was crying.

"Yes . . . Yes . . . "

I felt a heavy hand on my shoulder as Rusty took a step forwards to reassure me. "It's alright, sonny. Everythin's gonna be alright now."

98

I stifled another sob as Marshall pulled me closer to him, as if trying to absorb me. More hands reached out, the circle collapsing in on itself as they fought to get nearer, drumming their support along my spine. I felt Marshall's grip slacken as he guided my head down towards his chest, his powerful arms embracing me.

A cheer went up from the crowd as the circle stooped as one to catch me, grabbing me by arms and legs and hoisting me skywards.

And then they were carrying me, back up the steep banks of the pit and through the wood, the trees shaking as if offering their applause as I was thrust ever forwards. Carried on a sea of love.

Eventually we came to a stop next to the lake where I had stood days earlier — another lifetime ago. It still felt late. The sky above me was already blistering pink and purple, the sun preparing itself to set on yet another day. I swayed uneasily on the platform of hands, the men evidently tired of carrying me, though not one of them said a word. It seemed they were waiting for something.

Somewhere below me there was a thrashing of water, and I managed to turn my head just enough to glimpse Marshall wading into the lake, closely followed by Bruno and Tyrus. There was a beating of wings as across the lake a pair of swans darted for safety, a disgruntled blur of white against the turbid black murk.

Marshall raised his arms to speak, his booming voice ringing out around the park. "Gentlemen. We gather here today to welcome Brother Adam into our fold. We are here to give him a second chance, another shot at the life he has so wantonly destroyed. We are here to offer redemption . . . "

As Marshall spoke, the hands that held me began to sway to and fro, almost imperceptibly at first, but gathering pace, as if mirroring the rhythm of Marshall's words.

"Just as the body is purified by water, so then the soul is purified by this *blessed* act, allowing Brother Adam to be reborn into the world . . . "

"No!" I managed to shout out as I realised too late what was about to happen.

"I call on him to banish all darkness from his heart and to step out into the light . . . "

"No!" I cried again, helpless as the men continued to swing me higher and higher in an ever-widening arc.

"To repent to whatever-the-fuck higher power he deems worthy and to rejoice in the knowledge he is free from the burdens of the past. A-fucking-men!"

There was a lurch and I was free. For a moment I hung suspended in mid-air, neither flying nor falling as the early evening sun emerged from behind a cloud, momentarily dazzling the world white.

And then I plummeted, hitting the surface of the lake with a colossal splash. And instantly sinking to the bottom. The water was so cold I felt scalded. I scrambled to get my head above the surface, my feet slithering in the sludge of the lakebed until eventually I was sitting upright.

The water was shallower than I'd expected, only reaching my shoulders. I gasped for air, gradually aware of the crowd that had formed around me. A hand reached out from the haze and pulled me to my feet. It was Marshall. He was smiling. He pulled me closer to him and grabbed my head, landing a single, tender kiss on my forehead.

"You made it," he said. "You're home."

SUMMER

CHAPTER
TEN

The first day was the hardest of my life.

After my impromptu baptism in the boating lake, I was led to yet another section of woodland, where a ragtag assortment of shelters was scattered among the trees, resembling a sort of rustic shanty town. Unlike Rusty's tent, which I later learnt was usually only used to store supplies, each dwelling was wide enough to accommodate at least three or four standing adults — though each man appeared to have his own home. They were haphazard affairs, constructed from large strips of weather-worn canvas strung between trees and weighed down with rocks and boulders. Most looked like they'd been extended multiple times, with long branches propping up porches and awnings, their modest boundaries marked out with wooden stakes and chicken wire fencing.

Dotted between the tents were larger communal areas covered by marquees. In one, several splintering fence panels had been balanced on a base of grey milk crates to create a table, its surface strewn with the detritus from an earlier meal. Elsewhere an improvised punchbag dangled from a tall branch, stiff needles of straw protruding from its tattered corners. There was also a rudimentary football pitch with a set of traffic cones for goal posts, and even a ping-pong table, its green playing top warped and blistered with age.

In the very centre of the camp stood an enormous gnarled oak tree, at the top of which sat something that looked like a cross between a tree house and a bird's nest, a dense knot of reeds, twigs and wire that was so well-hidden it might have gone unnoticed were it not for the rope ladder snaking down the nearest side of the trunk.

"Who sleeps there?" I asked Rusty.

"That's the gaffer's place," he said. "But nobody goes there. At least they don't if they know what's good for 'em! Right-o, this one's yours," he said, gesturing towards a teepee-like shelter, which consisted of little more than a blue sheet of tarpaulin lashed to a tripod of branches.

"It's not much to look at, but it'll keep you dry and warm for now. Just make sure you get out of those wet things before you catch a cold."

I nodded my thanks as I slithered into the dim shelter, using the last of my energy to shoo out Bruno before peeling off my damp clothes and collapsing into the soft pile of bedding that lay on the floor. Though not yet fully dark outside, I craved sleep, both my body and mind too exhausted to process everything that had happened to me.

"So I'll be seein' you in a bit," Rusty called from outside. "My place is the green one on the other side of the tree. Just yell if you need anythin'!"

I grunted my response, my eyes already fluttering shut. And then I was gone, plummeting into a darkness so absolute that it felt like death, the tarpaulin above my head the lining of my sarcophagus, quivering gently in the breeze.

I woke to the sound of thunder. I opened my eyes. It was still dark. I pulled the covers over my head. The thunder sounded again, closer this time. I sat up. My mouth was dry and my head was still throbbing, the last traces of alcohol in my bloodstream still potent enough to make my stomach clench. Then it happened. The entire structure of my tent began to shake with such force that for a moment I feared it might become untethered from the earth. I thought back to my nightmare the previous night, but before I could react, a familiar gruff voice rang out.

"Right then, you good-for-nothing maggots! Time to rise and shine!"

I poked my head out of the tent and squinted. I was just able to make out Marshall's silhouette as he marched towards the next tent, banging a saucepan with a wooden spoon. As I groped around for my clothes, I was amazed to find my wet things gone, replaced instead by a fresh vest, fleece, trousers, along with a pair of boots and a bottle of water. I took a long draught and splashed a little on my face before I reached for the clothes. Although clean, there was nevertheless a smell to them, a bitter mustiness that led me to suspect they might once have belonged to Rusty. Too cold to care, I quickly dressed, then hurried out into the night, stumbling in the direction of Marshall's cries.

"I see you decided to grace us with your presence?"

The men were already stood in a line before Marshall, who was wearing a stained string vest and shorts, his sunglasses still clamped firmly to his face, despite the poor light. Nearby, Tyrus lay chained to a tree. He sniffed the air menacingly as I arrived.

"You're just in time to welcome in the morning with us," Marshall continued, gesturing up towards the night sky.

"Yoga," Rusty hissed. Like Marshall, he'd swapped his jacket for a vest, though thankfully he was still wearing his cargo trousers. "The boss is mad for it, rain or shine. Now, you just do what I do and you'll be right — ain't nothin' to it but a bit of stretchin'!"

At this, the men began to spread themselves apart, unravelling small patches of tatty-looking carpet and kicking off their shoes.

"Remember men, bendiness is next to godliness," Marshall said, aiming a sharp slap between my shoulder blades as he passed me a roll of carpet of my own.

I got in line as he raised his palms and addressed the group. "Now, seeing as we've got a guest today I want you all to show him a good example. I don't want to hear any excuses from anyone, else you'll have Tyrus to answer to. Understood? And breathe, two, three, four . . ."

By the time we'd finished, the first rays of sunlight had slashed the sky red, banishing all but the brightest stars.

108

I lay on my back and gasped for breath as I stared up at the bloodshot dawn. My entire body ached from an hour or so of punishing contortions. While I'd recognised many of the moves from years of Lydia "downward dogging" in my peripheral vision, in Marshall's hands the practice was twisted into a relentless drill of squats, lunges and high kicks. Now, it more closely resembled a martial art than meditation, a masochistic assault on my knees, spine and hamstrings. Gone were Lydia's placid mumbles about chakras and energy, replaced by a constant refrain to "Put your fucking *arse* into it!" If it was possible for yoga to be violent, this was a case in point.

"Enjoy that, did ya?" Rusty asked, appearing above me.

I groaned, unable to muster a response.

He reached down and grabbed me by my fleece, dragging me to my feet. I felt clammy and sick, uncertain of whether my legs would hold without his support. Around me men were rolling up their mats and slipping on their boots as they disappeared into the woods.

"Good," Rusty said. "Cos that was just the warm up!"

Before I could reply, Marshall plucked me from Rusty's grasp. By his side stood Tyrus, now freed from the tree and straining against his master's muscular grip. "And how's the new recruit doing?" he said, beaming at me from behind his mirrored sunglasses.

I eyed Tyrus warily. "Okay, I guess. I mean, I'm a little tired."

"Nonsense! Like Rusty here just told you that was just a little morning stretch. Now, you'd better get a move on, else you'll never catch them up."

"Catch them up?" I said. "But where are they going?"

Marshall grinned. "Why, for a little jog of course."

To my surprise, Rusty quickly sped ahead, leaving me at the back of the pack, flanked by Marshall and Tyrus. While the dog growled and snapped at my every juddering misstep, Marshall seemed oblivious to my discomfort, cheerfully pointing out features along the route as I struggled to suck enough air into my lungs to remain conscious.

"I think we'll just stick to one lap this morning. It's six and a half kilometres around the perimeter — or four miles in old money. And oh, did you see that? The little fellow with the black feathers and the white belly? That's a house martin. First I've seen this year."

I didn't answer. Couldn't answer. As we continued on our tour of the park — past the old marl pit, down through the farm and out into the playing field — all of my focus was on putting one foot in front of the other. I hadn't run since my school days, where the miserable weekly ritual of a compulsory, all-weather cross-country run had been enough to ensure I'd never take part in any kind of competitive sporting event again. Now, as then, my legs cramped and my muscles screamed. There was a stitch in my chest so severe that I was convinced one of my ribs had punctured the skin. And yet I kept going, the ever-threatening presence of

110

Marshall — or more specifically, Tyrus — providing enough motivation to keep putting one leg in front of another.

After running for what felt like hours, I spotted someone sitting on a bench up ahead. As we got closer I saw it was Hopper. He had one leg up and appeared to be battling with his prosthesis.

"Bloody hell," he called. "You look worse than me — and I've only got one foot! Jesus, are you okay?"

As we passed level with him, my legs gave way, sending me crashing to the ground. Instantly Hopper was up from the bench, limping towards me with his hand outstretched, before Marshall yelled for him to stop.

"He'll get up by himself, Private. Every man here needs to stand on his own two feet . . . " he paused, throwing a glance towards Hopper's exposed stump. "Or however many feet they have."

I looked up at the two men and the dog standing over me. I barely had enough energy to lift my head, let alone start running again. My lungs felt like they were bleeding. My back ached. Everything hurt. I was ready to collapse, to roll over and let them do whatever they would with me, when I happened to glance over at the bench where Hopper had been sitting. It was the same spot where I'd first met Rusty a few days earlier, the ground around it still littered with crystals of shattered glass. It seemed another lifetime ago now. Instinctively I glanced down at my wrist. The bandage was still there; my arm stained orange from where the iodine had run. For some reason, the sight of it stirred something inside me. I'd been on that ground before. I didn't want to be on it again. I took a deep breath and, drawing on reserves I didn't know I had, pushed myself into a crouching position.

And then, I stood up.

"Fair play, mate," Hopper said. "That looked like a bad one from where I was sitting. I thought for sure you'd broken something."

I turned to Marshall.

He nodded.

We started to run.

By the time we made it back to the camp I was drenched in sweat. My eyes felt raw from the salty streaks that ran down my forehead and I was desperately thirsty. So much so, that as we'd passed the boating lake it had taken all of my self-control not to veer away from Marshall and dive open-mouthed into dark water.

As I came into the home straight, I fantasised about a cold drink in almost pornographic detail: beads of condensation sliding down a frosted glass, ice cubes the size of golf balls chattering against the sides. Yet as I stumbled to a stop among the trees, I saw at once that I had about as much chance of getting one as I did a hot shower.

The other men were lined up as they had before yoga. Only this time they were each naked and cupping themselves, their clothes stacked in neat piles besides half a dozen plastic buckets. I turned to Marshall, who gestured for me to join the line. I squeezed in next to Rusty, who was grinning with an unbearable enthusiasm.

"Best bit this," he whispered. "You'd better get your kecks off quick mind. Here, I'll give you a hand."

Without the slightest hesitation, he reached up and started tugging at my vest, exposing the gnarled slump of his genitals. Too tired to resist, I submitted to his fumbling paws, watching with the detached obedience of a toddler as he slipped off my boots and slid my trousers down my legs.

He'd just managed to strip me of my damp clothes, when the first bucket was thrown. There was a collective huffing of breath as the men at the other end of the line jumped around on the spot. Marshall staggered towards me, grey water sloshing over the side of a second bucket, a sadistic smile stretched across his face. Even in my exhausted state, I noted he was still wearing his shorts and vest. I took an involuntary gasp, before the cold stole the air from my lungs. Next to me, Rusty squealed with delight, scrubbing at the matted bramble between his armpits and legs before another torrent came crashing down on us.

I stood shivering while Zebee came walking down the line, handing out the rough strips of cotton towel, along with a dark brown square of what looked like burnt flapjack.

"What are these?"

"Potato fritters," he answered with a smile. "Rusty cooked them, but they're my wife's recipe. Best breakfast a man could ask for!"

Although I wasn't hungry, I took one of each, cloaking myself in the towel, grateful for what little warmth it offered.

"Right then!" Marshall said, still shouting despite being less than six feet from us. "Now that you're all nice and *awake*, it's time to hand out today's rota. Zeb and Al, you're on maintenance. Hopper, Rusty, you're on dinner duty. And not another one of your curries, Rust — I'm not spending two hours crouched next to you lot at Squit Creek tomorrow morning. Butcher, you take surveillance with me. Adam — you're on farming with Ox, Fingers and Sneed."

Around me the others began to reach for their clothes, dressing quickly and dispersing in different directions. I took the opportunity to pull Rusty aside.

"What does surveillance duty entail?" I asked.

"Ah, nothin' worth worryin' about," he said. "The gaffer likes a couple of people patrollin' the park. Just to keep an eye on who's comin' in, and make sure no civvies come sniffin' around too close."

"And what happens if they do?" I asked.

"What's that?"

"Other people. What happens if they accidentally stumble across you. What do you do then?"

Rusty let out a long laugh and shook his head. "Well, let's just say it'll be the last bit of stumblin' they ever do, eh?"

Before I could question him any further, Marshall interrupted. "Hey! That means you too, soldier," he said, flinging one of my shoes at me. "There aren't any free rides here!"

114

I snapped into life, scurrying forward to retrieve the rest of my clothes. "Sorry, I'm just a little tired."

Marshall began to laugh, quietly at first, but growing steadily louder. He bent over, clutching his knees so that his glasses slipped down his nose and his temples throbbed purple with amusement. The remaining men stopped what they were doing and joined in, until finally Marshall straightened up and wiped the spittle from his beard. "Tired? But we haven't started yet . . ."

I spent the rest of the day on my hands and knees next to Fingers, who helped point out the weeds from the newly sprouting vegetables. While my clumsy hands burrowed beneath the hard soil to search out the stringy roots, he rabbited on about his days as a high-functioning meth addict, his stories punctuated by accounts of OD'd prostitutes and loan shark-shattered kneecaps. Considering how much he claimed to regret his old life, he certainly seemed to relish telling me about it, becoming particularly animated whenever describing moments of either sex or violence.

Meanwhile, Ox spent the morning digging irrigation trenches, his shovel a metallic blur that only stopped while he sprinted across the field with a soil-laden wheelbarrow. He worked with a ferocious intensity, his vest sodden with a dark Rorschach test of sweat, and hardly spoke other than to tell Fingers to "shut the fuck up" whenever his stories became too loud or colourful.

As the day wore on, I was surprised to hear the occasional snatch of music drifting over the field. I was so absorbed in my work that I initially forgot about the

115

lack of electricity and assumed it was a radio. It was only later that I realised it was Ox, crooning to himself while he worked, classic rock standards delivered in a surprisingly tender baritone.

Sneed meanwhile kept to himself. Skulking at the very edge of the farm, it was difficult to see what he was actually doing, other than avoiding us. As the hours passed, my fingers and back began to cramp painfully, and I found myself increasingly resentful of him. Part of me longed for Ox to lash out, to send a well-timed insult, or even a boot, in his direction. The others seemed infuriatingly oblivious to his lack of work, however. Realising no one was going to say anything, I turned my attention back to my own patch of dirt, making a point of working twice as hard as before.

When the sun reached the centre of the sky, Rusty and Hopper appeared, dropping off a large jerry can filled with fresh water and a couple of flasks of tepid soup. Once they'd left, Fingers and Ox slurped greedily at the grey mush. On the other hand, I found I was almost too tired to eat, struggling through only a few spoonfuls before I gave up, though I drank deeply from the can. While the others finished eating, I took the opportunity to grab a short rest, lying on my back and closing my eyes. As my spine settled into the earth, my entire body seemed to vibrate slightly, my muscles struggling to adapt to the strain of manual labour. I lay there for perhaps a minute or two, aching in places I hadn't thought about since I was a child, before Ox stood up and clapped his enormous hands together, signalling the break was over. It was only much later that I realised Sneed hadn't joined us to eat.

The rest of the afternoon passed in a haze of soil and sweat. When we'd eventually finished weeding, we switched to planting, dropping partially sprouted seed potatoes into carefully spaced holes before raking over a fine layer of compost. For a former actuarial investment analyst, Fingers seemed remarkably knowledgeable about potatoes, explaining in detail about the importance of keeping the soil slightly acidic and bemoaning the misery of ring rot, powder scab and blight. For my part, I kept quiet and concentrated on digging the holes. It had been a long day.

It was getting dark when we finally downed our tools. Sneed had disappeared hours earlier, and so the three of us traipsed back to the camp without him. We arrived to find a roaring fire, the other men already sitting around the rickety table in the dining area. A huge pot of food lay before them, which Rusty proudly declared to be a broad bean risotto, accompanied by a salad of wild herbs. While it was certainly better than lunch, I again found I was too tired to eat much. Thankfully, the other men were more concerned with their own gripes — the lack of meat or the size of the portions — to pay me much attention, and after half an hour or so I was able to shuffle off to bed without anyone noticing.

As I collapsed into the dank sanctuary of my tent, I realised just how broken I was. My limbs cramped in painful revolt. Too exhausted to move, I sank into the pain, grateful to sense sleep already sucking at the edges of my consciousness. Slipping deeper into the darkness, I was subjected to a tumble of nightmarish visions. At first I saw the disembodied heads of Lydia, Olivia and Flynn, swooping above me like bats, strafing me with a machine-gun fire of demonic laughter. After that, I saw my body like a rusting car, stripped for scrap metal by unseen hands. My breastbone was cracked and parted as one by one my ribs were wrenched from my chest. My kneecaps and elbows were prised away, my ligaments pulled and severed, my organs plucked from their cavities, until finally there was nothing left of me, and for a split second I experience the sheer bliss of oblivion . . .

Until a rumble of thunder brought me thrashing back into existence.

I opened my eyes and waited.

Then it came again.

"Right, you good-for-nothing maggots! Time to rise and shine . . . "

CHAPTER
ELEVEN

For six days our routine didn't falter. We woke in darkness, practiced yoga until sunrise, ran — or in my case, stumbled — around a circuit of the park, before stripping naked and being doused with freezing water. Breakfast consisted of a single potato fritter and a boiled egg, before our chores for the day were handed out. While the other men seemed to enjoy some variation, for me this inevitably meant being put to work on the farm.

Most days were spent weeding beds, or sowing and planting new crops, though occasionally other jobs took precedence. One day I spent an entire morning with Hopper performing "pest control". As we were forbidden by Marshall from using any artificial chemicals, this consisted of scouring the strawberry patch for flies, squashing them between my thumb and forefinger and scraping the residue onto my vest. Another afternoon I worked alongside Butcher and Al Pacino, digging out an old tree root that Ox had uncovered a few days earlier. We each took turns to attack it with a pickaxe, sliding a fork underneath it and working it to and fro as we attempted to lever it out. It was dark by the time we eventually managed to wrench the ancient stump free, leaving behind a ragged, knee-deep abscess in the earth.

Towards the end of the week, I was woken not by Marshall's usual insults, but by the sound of a fierce storm lashing my tent. Marshall's only concession to the increasingly inhospitable conditions, however, was to distribute faded waterproof ponchos ahead of our run, as well as allowing us to forgo our usual morning "shower" before we started work on the farm. The rain refused to let up all that day, so by the time I squelched back to the camp at dusk, my fingers were numb and my arms were caked in a thick, clay-like sludge up to the elbow.

In the evenings we sat together and ate whatever combination of vegetables Rusty had prepared for us. Before each meal commenced, Marshall would make a speech, extolling the virtues of our home-grown fare.

"Back in the bad old days," he began one evening, "when I used to read the newspapers, I read a report from a scientist who'd analysed a frozen pizza and found it contained ingredients from over sixty countries. Sixty! Across five continents! There was cheese from China, salt from Siberia, pepperoni from Poland. You wouldn't believe the sheer number of people who'd had a hand in constructing this Franken-snack. It must have been in the hundreds when all was said and done. Yet the thing that really stuck in my mind was that it was on sale for less than two quid. Two quid! It doesn't make sense. Even if they sold a million of the fuckers, there's no real profit for anyone once you take into account the time and cost of producing and shipping each component. Unless" — and here Marshall paused theatrically — "unless of course they used the cheapest, nastiest, laboratory-engineered ingredients they could lay their money-grabbing hands on. Unless they used illegally irradiated tomatoes that you could leave out in the sun for a month without them ever going soft. Unless they used mechanically harvested herbs which included traces of arsenic, mercury and lead. Unless they used festering factory-farmed poultry, diced and bleached to hide the pus-filled tumours on their rotting underbellies. Unless they pumped it full of all manner of chemical fillers and firmers and flavours, until that final 'oven fresh' extra value pizza has more in common with a rubber car mat than anything you might want to actually put inside your body. *Then*, and only then, might there be a few coins for somebody in the whole sorry enterprise."

There was a loud cheer from the men, though Marshall held his hands aloft. He wasn't finished yet.

"But it's not just pizzas, is it?" he continued. "We live in a world where eight out of ten children can't draw the line between the cow and the milk. The pig and the ham. The chicken and the nuggets. A world where fish have fingers and potato comes powdered in a packet. And yet this is the very stuff we are made of! Our blood cells, our bone marrow, our brain matter, all of it is literally manufactured from what we shovel into our gobs. So is it any wonder then that we have become a nation of wheezing, obese, diabetic slobs? It's a goddamn tragedy is what it is . . . Though one that, thankfully, we no longer have to worry about."

He spread his fingers towards the food on the table, the venom draining from him as he reached out to pluck a slither of courgette from one of the dishes.

"No, boys, I think it's safe to say that we're building our bodies on strong foundations. While those suckers on civvy street might be content to fill themselves up with a chemical slurry, we've got the real deal. And thanks to Rusty here, it doesn't taste too bad either. So enjoy the fruits of your labours. And remember — you are what you eat!"

Despite Marshall's sermons, in those early days I would give up after a few mouthfuls, my eyes so heavy I could hardly keep them focused. After the plates were cleared away, a fire would be teased into life and the men would sit around, talking and telling stories. Although I enjoyed the warmth, I tended to slip away at the earliest available opportunity, collapsing into an exhausted coma before the whole thing started again the next day.

At the end of the sixth day, Rusty cornered me on my way back to my tent. "You shootin' off early again, sonny?"

I felt my cheeks flush with guilt. "Just a little worn out," I mumbled.

"Ah, but that's to be expected," he said, placing a hand on my shoulder. "Tomorrow's Sunday, so it should be better."

"I thought you didn't keep track of the days?"

"I don't," he said with a mischievous wink, "but the gaffer does, and if he says it's Sunday, then that's alright by me. Day of recreation, innit? Says so in the Bible."

"Isn't it the day of rest?"

"Ah, same thing, more or less. Anyway, you'll have a good time tomorrow. Trust me!"

I nodded and turned to leave, when I felt a tug at the back of my jacket.

"Oh, Adam, there was one other thing. Sneed. You've been workin' with him down on the farm, haven't you?"

I shrugged. "I don't know if you'd call it working. He pretty much keeps to himself."

Rusty took a step towards me. He wasn't smiling anymore. "Yeah, well, you just make sure it stays that way. I'd give him a wider berth if I was you. No good'll ever come of gettin' mixed up with a man like that. You mark my words."

"Oh, I don't think there's any danger of me getting mixed up with him. Like I say, he pretty much keeps himself to himself. I've never even heard him speak. What's his story anyway?"

Rusty leant closer still. "All you need to know is that he's trouble," he said, before quickly straightening up, the storm having apparently passed. "Right-o, I'll let you get off, shall I? You'll want to get some kip. Especially once you see what we've planned for you in the mornin'!"

The next day I again woke to the sound of Marshall yelling. After yoga, we ran and washed as usual. Rather than being allocated jobs however, we were divided into two teams — blue and red. I was in the blue team, which meant that, along with Marshall, Fingers, Ox and Butcher, I was to spend the morning practicing hand-to-hand combat. This turned out to be a particularly aggressive derivative of ju-jitsu, of which Marshall claimed to be both the founder and highest-ranking practitioner. Within ten minutes I was nursing a nosebleed, having fallen prey to a vicious roundhouse kick from Ox during my first sparring session. As I sat with my head between my legs, pinching my sticky nostrils together, Marshall left the men and squatted down beside me.

"You don't look like you've done that many times before," he said, leaning forward to inspect my injury.

"What, get kicked in the face? Can't say I make a habit of it, no."

"Fighting," Marshall continued, ignoring my sarcasm. "Then again I don't suppose there was much call for it in your old life. Tucked away in your private office with its security cameras and burglar alarms. Probably had a couple of guards on the doors downstairs to keep the wolves out, right? Then you'd jump into your car at the end of the day and drive away in your hermetically sealed, climatically controlled bubble-mobile. You'd do your shopping online, get your groceries delivered, only ever view the world through the pixelated window of your TV or smartphone. Am I ringing any bells?"

"I used to go to the gym sometimes," I protested. "There was a boxercise class I signed up to a few years ago."

Marshall's laughter was like a dog choking on a chicken bone. "Boxercise? That's a good one. Goddamn it, I can't tell you how grateful I am to have

124

left that stupid fucking world behind me. Did it ever occur to you how ridiculous it is that we live in a world where gyms need to exist? All those guys in their tight vests and shorts, lifting things and putting them back down again. Sweating over their rowing machines and treadmills. Treadmills! Running fast and getting nowhere. And for what? So you can kid your body that it's being used for what it was designed to do? So you can keep guzzling refined sugar and saturated fat and sit stationary behind a fucking *desk* all day? It's not even funny. It's just sad. We are living, breathing miracles, each and every one of us. We are the apex predators on this planet. Top of the food chain. And yet this is what we've been reduced to. Bloody gyms." He paused to spit in disgust.

"And the way they make you look! Not like a human being, that's for sure. Six-pack abs and over-defined traps? Could someone please tell me what activity on earth would ever give rise to a physique like that? Hunting? Gathering? Do you really think our caveman ancestors were equipped with roaring glutes and killer pecs? Their biceps so bulbous and distended that their arms looked like the permatanned shaft of some prehistoric hippopotamus' cock. Brother, save me from the bronzed he-models, for they know not what they do!"

I sniffed hard, my mouth filled with the salted-rust of fresh blood. "At least boxercise you don't get walloped by guys twice your size . . . "

"Ah-ha!" Marshall cried. "So that's what you're bitching about. You didn't think it was a fair fight? Well, let me tell you something. It's got nothing to do with size. Jesus, when I was in the forces I put down guys far bigger than Ox. Not that I'm particularly proud of it. If you actually listen, you'll see that fighting should only ever be a last resort. That's what I teach all the guys. You should always try and resolve conflicts with psychology first. Detect and de-escalate. That's my motto. Only when all else fails should you fight. And even then, you'll want to get in and out as quickly as possible. Hollywood would have you believe that most guys can go more rounds than Mike Tyson. Well, that's a load of crap I'm afraid. Most fights last as long as it takes to throw the first punch. Or kick in your case . . . "

I gave a resentful sniff. "So what, I should have just decked Ox? Because I might not know much about physics, but I'm pretty sure I'd come off significantly worse."

"God, you like to whine, don't you? This is just training. Sure you're going to take a knock now and then. But out there?" He nodded vaguely in the direction of the bushes. "You need to understand it's a matter of life and death. No one's going to give you a cosy couple of minutes to mop up your nose. You need to get in and out. Anyway, who said anything about punching?" He paused to shoot me a conspiratorial grin. "There are plenty of other areas you can target. Genitals are there to be yanked, eyes gouged, ears bitten or twisted." He reached up and pinched my earlobes between his thumb and forefingers. "They're not as well attached as you might think. All it takes is a quick tug and . . . "

"Ow!" I recoiled, a searing pain shooting through both ears.

"Ah, grow up. I barely touched you," Marshall grinned. "Besides, this is self-defence. It's worth hurting for. I teach all the men this stuff. You were the one who wanted to live in the wild. Well, the first thing you need to learn is that there are no rules out here. Survive, no matter what. Even if it means fighting dirty. Hell, even if it means fighting *filthy*. And I'm telling you, if you tear a guy's ears off and hand them back to him, you won't have to worry about him chasing you anymore. I don't care how big he is."

With that, Marshall straightened up, raising his voice so that the rest of the men could hear him. "Now back on your feet, soldier! I want to see you back in that ring, or it won't just be your nose bleeding. COME ON!"

Following Marshall's "pep talk", there was another hour of ju-jitsu, where I added a split lip and a black eye to my growing list of injuries. Following that, we were tasked with fashioning bows, picking out long, springy branches of elm and birch and stringing them with twine, coiling it around the end until it pulled taut. For arrows we whittled lengths of ash to a point, attaching chicken feathers to the ends to serve as flights. Again, I was invariably terrible, my arrows trembling gracelessly through the air, falling far short of their target every time. Finally, we reconvened at the camp for a heated game of five-a-side football. Here I fared a little better, though I soon hobbled off when Al

Pacino caught me with a knee-crunching slide tackle. The blue team eventually conceded victory in my absence, a humiliation Marshall took so personally that he decided to treat the five of us to an extended afternoon run, allowing Tyrus to run off the lead as a way of providing us with a little extra "encouragement". By the time I limped back to my tent and collapsed that evening, I was mentally and physically exhausted. I couldn't wait to return to the farm the next day.

So why did I stay? It's a reasonable question, one that I've asked myself countless times in the year that has passed, especially when I think about the nightmare that eventually engulfed us all. I suppose I have to admit that I enjoyed it. Or at least, I enjoyed part of it. Sure there were hardships, but in a way they only added to the strange pull of it all. Each scrape and bruise felt like a battle scar, something I'd earned. I learnt to relish the pain, not only as a reward, but also as punishment for all of the shitty things I'd done in my life up until that point. I guess I saw it as a penance of a sort, a way of paying my dues, though perhaps I am being overly sympathetic as to my real motives. There was of course also the fact that I truly believed I didn't have anywhere else to go. And if this was to be my lot in life, I was determined to make the most of it.

Aside from physical challenge and the convenience of a dry bed and a warm meal each night, there was also the pull of the men themselves. The longer I stayed the more I discovered a sense of camaraderie that I hadn't experienced since my school days. I found that despite our different backgrounds, we nevertheless managed to find some common ground as we huddled together among the budding vegetable patches.

Then of course there was Marshall. It's embarrassing to admit it now, but there was something about him that turned me into a five-year-old child again. I felt an irrational urge to please him, to impress him somehow, despite my ineptitude at the simplest manual task. I was the fawning puppy to his alpha dog, ever eager for his praise, fearful of his bark. My only defence is that we all acted that way, competing with each other for his time and approval. It was only later that I saw just how much he revelled in the attention.

The only one I remained wary about was Sneed. Though I saw very little of him, whenever our paths did cross, he would fix me with bulging insect eyes, neither frowning nor smiling. Rather, he simply observed me. He reminded me of a scientist in a vivisection lab, examining his subject with a cold detachment before slicing through its skull and poking around in its brain. Rusty was right, no good would come from getting mixed up with a man like that.

As the weeks rolled by, the days became warmer and the trees grew plump with foliage. It wasn't just the environment that changed. I discovered that my body too began to adapt to my new daily routine. My muscles hurt less at the end of each day, the jiggle of my belly replaced by an unfamiliar tautness beneath my vest. As my strength and stamina increase, the work became easier to manage. I got better at gardening, no longer relying on Fingers or Butcher to help me distinguish crops from weeds. I even managed to knock in a goal or two during our Sunday football matches.

With the mornings growing lighter by the day, I found myself waking long before Marshall came to rouse me. Back in my old life, the first thing I would do when I opened my eyes was to reach for my phone. I'd check the weather, the news, the stock markets. I'd deal with text messages from my secretary, or compose an email to a client, all before raising my head from the pillow. Those days were long gone. Now when I woke I'd lie very still and stare at the roof of my tent, listening to the sounds of the new day as it broke overhead. As the birds screeched and chattered all around, it occurred to me that I had no idea what was going on in the world beyond the park. The Russians could be dropping bombs on London and I wouldn't know. The Chinese stock market could be crashing to its knees. It didn't matter.

I wondered if it had ever mattered.

CHAPTER
TWELVE

It was the warmest day of the year so far. At this point I'd lost track of how long I had been in the park, though it was definitely a case of months rather than weeks. I woke to find myself clammy with sweat, the early morning sun turning the inside of my tent into a sauna. I dressed quickly and then fought through the folds of tarpaulin into the cool air outside. I was still standing there twenty minutes later when Marshall arrived. He looked vaguely disappointed to have missed out on the chance to wake me, but didn't say anything as I followed him and Tyrus to the centre of the camp. Despite the heat, he insisted on an unusually long yoga practice that morning. We held the impossible positions until one by one our legs buckled beneath us and the clearing was filled with our combined groans. Satisfied we had suffered enough, he gave us permission to roll up our mats and retrieve our shoes. It was time to run.

By this point, my fitness had improved enough that I was no longer confined to the back of the pack, though I was by no means the fastest. Surprisingly, that honour belonged to Sneed. Despite his ungainly appearance, he would run alone upfront, propelling himself forward with an unexpected agility. That morning however,

Sneed was nowhere to be seen. I'd noticed he had a tendency to disappear for days on end, not that anyone seemed particularly saddened by his absence. Without him to set the pace, we ran slower than usual, bunching together to moan about the weather, cracking bad jokes whenever Marshall was out of earshot.

As we reached the lake, we all paused to catch our breath.

"Alright then, fellers, I've got one for ya," said Rusty. "What's orange and sounds like a carrot?"

We all gave a loud groan.

"Bloody hell, Rust, where did you dig that one up from?" said Fingers. "A Victorian Christmas cracker?"

"Right, forget the jokes. I've got a true story for you," said Butcher, licking his lips and dropping his voice. "There were these two Polish slags, right? Proper dirty bitches . . . "

Before he could finish, Marshall appeared round the corner. "We seem to have come to a standstill, boys. Did you have something you wanted to share with the group, Butch?"

Butcher gave a non-committal snort. I glanced over at Tyrus, who was doing a good impersonation of an enraged bull, scraping the earth with one enormous paw as he huffed indignantly in the heat.

"Well, I don't blame you boys for not feeling particularly energetic this morning. Day like today? I'd rather be sprawled out with a cold beer and a plate full of barbeque chicken wings than busting my ass out here. Are you with me?"

132

This time Fingers took the bait. "Well, seeing as you're offering . . . "

A couple of the guys sniggered at this.

"But then again, that's how most of you sorry bastards ended up here in the first place, isn't it? Sitting around on your bone-idle backsides, swelling your guts and your livers. Or maybe you've forgotten all that?"

He wasn't smiling anymore.

"Okay then," he continued. "Seeing as we're all here because we're committed to being better people, what say we pick it up a little? In fact, I think we should make it interesting. Why don't we say the first one back to camp gets double portions tonight?"

There was a murmur among the men.

"And the last one. Well . . . Let's just say you can save your excuses for Tyrus. That goes for you too, Hopper. I don't want to hear any excuses. Now, on your marks, get set . . . "

And with that he started to run.

At first we stuck together, puffing out our cheeks as we scrambled after Marshall. I figured nobody would exert themselves for an extra bowl of curried vegetables. I'd underestimated our capacity for competitiveness though, and within a matter of minutes the pack became stretched. At the back, naturally, was Hopper who with only one working leg at his disposal was at a major disadvantage, whatever Marshall said. Not far in front of him was Rusty and Zebee, the combination of their age, weight and the hot conditions proving too much for them. Next up, the heavier men in the group, namely Ox and Butcher, staggered together, their faces flushed with exertion, their huge arms pumping hopelessly back and forth. Finally, there was Al Pacino, Fingers and me, splashing through stagnant puddles and tearing our way through the dense patches of bramble that had enveloped much of the park during the last few weeks. No matter how fast we ran though, we never seemed to be able to close the distance between us and Marshall, who maintained a lead of around three hundred feet, leaping forward with an almost superhuman agility while Tyrus galloped alongside him.

As the race intensified, I stopped looking behind me to check on the others and focused entirely on trying to catch Marshall. Fingers had long ago pulled up with a limp, leaving just Al Pacino and me in contention. We ploughed onwards, neither of us talking, our footfall synchronised to form a splattered trill that after a while morphed into a looped mantra in my mind:

Yes-you-can-yes-you-can . . .

When we reached the top of the playing field, I saw Marshall turn abruptly and dive into the woods — he was on the home stretch. I powered on. Next to me I felt Al strain to keep up. Seconds later he disappeared, doubling over and gasping for breath. I slowed for a split second to see if he needed help, but he raised one hand and waved me on.

It was just me and Marshall now.

As I entered the woods, I felt a sharp stitch needling into my side. A steady trickle of sweat ran from my hair down my forehead and into my eyes, almost blinding me. My teeth ached and my ears rang. I couldn't go on.

Just then, there was a flash of white up ahead. I squinted in time to see Tyrus crashing through the trees. Next to him, holding onto a branch to steady himself, was Marshall. It seemed impossible, but the gap between us had closed to little more than a hundred feet. What's more, it looked like he'd stopped. I willed myself on, cupping my ribs with my hand in an attempt to block out the pain. The foliage in the woods was almost impenetrable. Barbed branches tore at my skin, but still I blundered forward, closer and closer to the finish.

At the sound of my approach, Marshall looked round and began moving again. He was less than fifty feet ahead of me now, and I could see from his movements how badly he was struggling. Along his back was a series of lacerations where he looked like he'd been caught by a trailing branch. It wasn't just the cuts though. His whole body looked exhausted, each stride forward as though he were wading through tar.

"Hey!" I called. "Are you okay? Do you need a hand?"

He turned again, and this time I saw a look of resignation on his face as he stumbled to a stop. He leant forward, breathing heavily while Tyrus sat patiently at his feet. For a second I thought he was going to be sick, but instead he turned and spoke, his words spilling out in a series of angry gasps.

"What . . . the fuck . . . are you doing?"

I didn't move. I didn't understand the question.

"This . . . is . . . a . . . race."

I still didn't move. "Do you need a hand?" I asked again.

This time I was sure he would hit me, the veins in his neck swelling purple. A plume of nesting birds erupted from the nearby trees, briefly turning the sky above us grey.

"I SAID IT'S A RACE!"

His meaning finally clear, I leapt into action, brushing past both him and Tyrus as I belted towards the finish line — *yes-you-can-yes-you-can* — onwards, onwards, towards victory.

I don't know how long it was before everyone finally made it back to the camp. The moment I arrived, I immediately crumpled to the floor. I was still lying there when Fingers and Butcher finally showed up, looking hot and tired. Neither of them could speak, though Fingers did give me a congratulatory thumbs up before collapsing next to me. The rest of the group trickled in one by one, everyone dripping with sweat. Last of all, came Marshall, just behind Hopper and Rusty. He looked like he had fully recovered, a broad grin on his face as he opened his arms to address us.

"Leave no man behind, that's my motto!" he said, thumping Hopper and Rusty on their backs, before striding up to me.

I sat up just in time to catch his hand as he reached out and hoisted me to my feet. Behind him I caught Rusty glaring at me, but Marshall's smile didn't flicker.

"Right then, *ladies* . . . I declare Adam our winner!"

There was a half-hearted round of applause as Marshall thrust my arm into the air.

"Now, as promised, Adam here will get double portions tonight . . . "

"Really, it's fine," I said. "I'm happy with the usual amount."

"Nonsense!" Marshall cried, gripping my hand tighter. "You won the race. You get the reward. That's how it works round here, isn't that right, Rust?"

Rusty gave a terse nod. "I guess so, boss."

"Ah, come on now, Rusty. There's no need to look so pleased about it. I'll personally guarantee that Adam's hard earned reward won't mess up your carefully measured rations. You see, with him having double, I thought everyone else could have half. That's only right and proper, isn't it?"

There was a loud groan from the men. A couple of them glowered menacingly in my direction.

"Don't worry, fellers," Marshall continued, raising his hand to quell the noise. "I'm sure you'll all find a way later on to show Adam your appreciation. Right now, however, there's a bit of company business I'd like to discuss. As you may or, more likely, may not be aware, this weekend officially marks Midsummer. That's the longest day of the year to you heathens," he said, turning pointedly to me. "Now, throughout human history, it's been traditional for people to celebrate the solstice and make merry. The Romans did it. The druids still do it. It's a good excuse for a knee's up basically, and God knows the world could do with a few more of those. Which is why this weekend we will mark the occasion with a Midsummer feast. And what does that mean, men?"

"Bonfire," called Fingers.

"Singing," yelled Ox.

"Meat," shouted Butcher.

"Meat," cried someone else, before the chant went up.

"Meat, meat, meat, meat . . . "

Marshall held his hand up for silence. "That's right," he said, licking his lips. "We like to mark the occasion by helping ourselves to a little treat from Mother Nature's bountiful pantry. Maybe a squirrel or two. A rabbit if we're lucky. What you reckon, Rust? Could you do something with those?"

Rusty gave an eager nod. "Oh yes, boss. Nice bit of squirrel kebab'd go down a treat!"

"Good. Well, that's settled then," he said. "I'm sure with your help Rusty it'll be the Midsummer Feast to end them all."

There was a final cheer before gradually the men began to drift away, chattering excitedly to themselves.

"Oh, there is one last thing," Marshall called.

Everybody froze.

"I thought as a centrepiece, we could go and bag ourselves one of them fat white birds moping around on the lake. Must be enough eating on those things to feed us for a week, eh, boys? You think you could rustle us up a nice plate of swan goujons to go with that squirrel, Rust?"

The men had fallen silent now, their eyes gleaming, a ravenous expression on each of their faces. This was something new, I sensed. Something dangerous and exciting.

Rusty scratched his beard in consideration. "I would have thought so. I mean, it's just like a big chicken, ain't it?"

Marshall clapped his hands together. "Excellent! Swan surprise it is. Oh, and seeing as Adam here is such a *persistent* fellow. I reckon he should be rewarded with the honour of fetching us the swan."

He turned to me, his grin even wider now, revealing two rows of rotting teeth.

"Don't you think?"

CHAPTER
THIRTEEN

I'd been crouched among the trees for so long I couldn't feel my legs. Overhead, sunlight streamed through the canopy, dappling the undergrowth with a bullet-spray of gold. Kneeling next to me was Marshall, a pair of binoculars clamped to his sunglasses, his air rifle by his side. Fingers and Ox were also close by, having volunteered to make up numbers for the "hunting party", although for once Tyrus was absent from his master's side, having been deemed too likely to try and eat our potential quarry.

Following Marshall's announcement about the feast, the three of us had been led to the "armoury". In reality this turned out to be little more than a small tent at the far end of the camp. Once there, we were kitted out with a motley assortment of wooden weapons, with Marshall keeping the gun for himself.

"A dozen kills," he said once we'd finished arming ourselves. "That's what I expect as a minimum. When I was in the forces we used to go out for an hour each morning and come back with enough breakfast for the whole platoon. And that was in the desert, dammit."

"Yeah, but I bet you all had guns?" Fingers mumbled.

"A good soldier doesn't need a gun," Marshall snapped back. "I've snared rabbits with nothing but a coat hanger. Skinned and gutted 'em with a nail file too. Only reason I'm bringing this baby," he said, tapping the barrel of the rifle, "is for insurance."

"Insurance?" Fingers asked.

"For when you clowns shit the bed," Marshall said. "Besides, I bet Adam here can't wait to show us all what he can do. I'll be surprised if there's anything left for the rest of us to shoot once he's finished . . . "

I didn't answer. If I'm honest, the whole hunting expedition had caught me off-guard. Aside from eggs, the menu had been almost exclusively plant-based since I'd been at the park. As far as I was aware, even the dogs were vegetarian. And while there was admittedly the occasional grumble about the lack of meat in our diet, it was never argued with any real conviction. The one time I'd tentatively suggested to Rusty the possibility of eating one of the chickens, it had been met with something approaching outrage.

"Why the bleedin' heck would I want to eat one of 'em for? So I could swap a single roast dinner for a year's worth of omelettes? Use your noggin, son."

Sensing I wouldn't bite, Marshall eventually grew bored of baiting me and instead returned to the tactics for the morning's hunt, describing the type of animal tracks we should look for, explaining the importance of staying downwind of our quarry. It was the most excited I'd seen him in weeks, and his enthusiasm was infectious. Feeling courageous, I decided to take the opportunity to try and find out a bit more about him.

141

"So did Rusty do much hunting back in the old days?" I asked.

At the sound of Rusty's name, Marshall snapped around. "The old days?"

I swallowed hard, instantly regretting starting the conversation. "You know? Before you arrived here."

"I'm not sure I understand the question," he said, his words leaking through gritted teeth.

"I just mean . . . well, Rusty said that he was living here for a few years before the others came along. I just wondered if he, er, hunted much before?"

"Living by himself? Listen, I don't know what you've heard, but Rusty and those other bums weren't living before I got here. Sure they might have *survived*. In the sense that a rat survives. Feeding off garbage. Nothing but parasites. They weren't living in any real sense. Ox was there. You ask him what it was like. Were you doing much hunting before I arrived, Ox?"

Ox shook his head, not lifting his eyes from the ground.

"Of course you weren't."

"I heard old Rust was still on the bottle when the boss first got here," Fingers added, winking at me. "Of course, I'm not one to judge . . . "

Marshall gave a satisfied nod. "Anyway, we'll have no more talk about the past. We've got more pressing things to focus on. Like catching us some dinner. Now, let's get shooting, shall we?"

As the hours wound away, however, Marshall's enthusiasm for the hunt began to wane. We had caught

142

nothing, the only potential target being a small blackbird that had swooped down about twenty feet from us to pluck at the desiccated corpse of a worm. At Marshall's insistence I had taken aim with my bow, only for my arrow to fall embarrassingly short. His yells had been loud enough to ensure no other animals had been seen since.

While Marshall's sulk hardened into a frosty silence, I found I had time to pay attention to the changes in the woods around me. The transformation that had taken place over the last few months had been astonishing. Where once there had been only the faintest fringing of green shoots, now a tangle of foliage blocked every path. Where months earlier there was nothing but dead sticks and cold earth, now clouds of midges swarmed among a riot of wild flowers that sprang from every dimple in the dirt. Everywhere I looked there was life. Even in the apparently deserted clearing, you only had to lift a stone or lean against a tree stump, and the floor would suddenly writhe with the panicked scuttle of liquorice-coloured woodlice, or the scattershot waltz of befuddled ants. At one point I watched as an injured bee attempted to fend off the advances of a marauding spider. I sat there in a trance, the whole drama of life and death unfolding among the detritus of decaying leaves, until Marshall abruptly turned around and hissed something at me, unwittingly sweeping aside the miniature gladiatorial battle with a flick of his boot.

"What?" I asked, still scanning the ground for signs of either the bee or the spider.

"Two o'clock," he repeated through gritted teeth.

This time I followed his extended finger to a patch of bracken on the other side of the clearing. At the foot of the bush, a plump grey squirrel sat erect, tumbling a purple berry between its paws. Instinctively I raised my bow, only to have Marshall instantly slap it down.

"I think I'd better take this one," he said as he shouldered the rifle. "We can't afford any more fuck-ups."

I watched as he peered down the barrel of the gun, lining up the sights with the grey fuzz of the creature's ears.

"It's important you get a clean shot, else you'll spoil the meat," he said, not taking his eyes from the animal. "If you hit it in the bladder or the gut, you can forget it. That's a quick way to poison yourself. No, you want to clip it . . . right . . . between . . . the . . . eyes."

There was a sharp crack as Marshall squeezed the trigger.

The squirrel looked up from his berry, considering us for a moment, and then darted for the nearest tree.

"Damn it!" Marshal roared, before rounding on Ox. "You goddamn oaf. You knocked me."

Ox stared at Marshall, his big, dumb eyes widening in confusion. "But I didn't move."

Marshall spat. "So you're going to contradict me now? Just get back to the farm, will you. I'm sure there's a hole that needs filling somewhere. That's if you think you can handle the responsibility?"

Ox didn't move. "But . . . "

"JUST GO!"

Ox stared for a moment longer before he finally clambered to his feet and trudged off into the trees.

Fingers muffled a small cough.

"Jesus! Don't you start!" Marshall snapped, before raising his binoculars. "Right, you two idiots better keep a look out. We're not going home until we've bagged ourselves at least a dozen of the little fuckers, so you can get comfortable. And if anyone even *thinks* about knocking me again they'd better hope they can outrun a bullet."

The day was almost over before Marshall finally called time and we were allowed to return to the camp. The hunt had not gone well. Neither Fingers nor I were anywhere near proficient enough with a bow to come close to hitting anything. As for Marshall, there always seemed to be a problem whenever it came to shooting. The barrel was bent, or the sights were off. Or, more commonly, one of us was putting him off. In the end, all we had to show for our sore knees and aching backs was three sparrows (which, as Marshall himself put it, was hardly enough for a starter for Tyrus), as well as a fat brown rat that Fingers had somehow managed to spear — though once we'd examined it, we decided against bringing it back with us, reasoning the tiny amount of meat it would provide wasn't worth the risk of contracting whatever diseases the miserable creature was carrying.

Marshall's mood was so bad that he couldn't even bring himself to insult us, storming ten paces ahead

145

and lashing out at any bramble or branch that dared to cross his path.

"Guess the pressure's on you then, eh?" Fingers whispered as we traipsed back to the camp.

"What do you mean?" I asked.

He smirked. "I'm just saying, there's a lot of bellies to fill now. I'd be surprised if he doesn't have you fetch both of those birds . . . "

The swan. With the disaster of the morning's hunt I'd almost managed to forget about it. "It'll be fine," I mumbled.

"Well, rather you than me," Fingers sniffed. "They can break a man's arm just by beating their wings."

"I'm pretty sure that's an old wives' tale," I said, before Marshall shot a reproachful glance over his shoulder.

"Christ! You girls reckon you could make a bit more noise back there? I reckon there's still at least one damn animal you haven't managed to frighten off yet!"

With that, the three of us lapsed into silence.

We returned to the camp to find the other men already finished work, a pot of stew steaming in the centre of the dinner table. Our arrival diverted their attention from the food however, and within seconds they had abandoned the table to crowd around us, peppering us with questions about the hunt. Marshall quickly shut them down by raising the sack of carrion into the air. Though mostly empty, it was enough to stop the men in their tracks. A shiver of anticipation fanned out through the mob as they each eyed the hessian sack,

146

licking their lips even as they wiped fresh stew from their beards.

"Now, I have some great news for you gentlemen," Marshall began, joggling the bag for effect. "Despite the *inexperience* of our shooting party, we nevertheless managed to bag ourselves a few choice morsels for tomorrow night."

At this, the men began to mutter, an excited rumble that quickly grew in fervour as they began to speculate on the potential menu for the feast.

"Rabbit," said Al Pacino, his hands pressed together in prayer. "Please let there be rabbit."

"We had wood pigeon last year," said Hopper. "A nice fat one."

Marshall once again shook the sack for silence. "All will be revealed in due course, though needless to say your unrefined palates are in for a treat. Especially once Rusty's had his wicked way with our haul. However, all of this is nothing but an appetiser, an amuse-bouche if you will, when compared to the big, juicy bird our newest recruit is planning to fetch us . . . Isn't that right, Adam?"

Instantly I felt every eye on me, the men's faces glowing with a mixture of envy and expectation. Unable to speak, I responded with a small but definite nod. The crowd exploded into a rapture of whoops and cheers.

"Well then," he continued, leaning closer to me so as to be heard over the din. "Let's go get ourselves a bird, shall we?"

CHAPTER
FOURTEEN

I stood alone at the edge of the lake, peering out over the slate grey expanse. Though still light, the sun slunk low in the sky, causing dark, distended shadows to jut out at strange angles over the water. Behind me, I could hear a few of the men debating the legalities of the act I'd been chosen to perform.

"It's treason, whichever way you look at it," Hopper was saying. "We'll all be up for the chop if anyone finds out."

"How do you work that one out?" asked Butcher.

"They're Her Majesty's, ain't they. Every single one of 'em belong to her. So in other words, you're vandalising sovereign property. Stealing too I wouldn't wonder. In the eyes of the law that's the same as bending the Duchess of Cambridge over the throne and slipping her your crown jewels. Either way, your head's ending up in a bread basket."

"Bollocks," said Fingers. "They abolished that law years ago. Round the time they stopped dunking witches and burning Catholics at the stake. Christ, Hopper, how old are you? Besides, even if was true, so what? What have the royals ever done for us? Bunch of inbred, silver-spoon-sucking, tax-dodging perverts. If the people are starving, let them eat swan, I say. As far as I'm concerned the Queen can go fuck herself."

"Fuck the Queen!" yelled someone else in support.

The cry went up then: "*Fuck-the-Queen, fuck-the-Queen, fuck-the-Queen . . . "*

I stared again at the two white birds gliding along the opposite side of the shore. Even from a distance they looked enormous, their necks like a pair of muscular arms reaching out of the water, their sharp beaks flashing hazard-sign orange — a warning to keep well away. In my hand I clutched the crude wooden spear Marshall had provided me with. Initially I'd asked for the gun, but this only provoked a derisory snort.

"I've seen you with a bow, sunshine. You reckon I'd let you loose with this thing?"

I felt a sharp nudge in my back. "Well?" Marshall asked. "Are you going to go in there and get us some dinner? It'll be dark soon and the men won't wait for ever."

I looked past him at the assembled mob. There was something vaguely sinister about their enthusiasm, a palpable blood-lust stretched across each of their faces — though whether it was swan's blood or mine they were after remained to be seen. Only Rusty seemed unmoved. He stood slightly off from the rest of the pack, his old face more creased than ever. I tried to catch his eye, but he wouldn't lift his head to meet my gaze.

"Well?" said Marshall again.

I didn't answer. Instead I hitched up my trouser legs, raised my spear, and waded into the lake.

* ★ * ★ * ★

The water was freezing, far colder than I remembered from my initiation several months earlier, and even with the early evening sun on my chest, it was almost too much to take. By the time I was halfway across, the water was up to my waist. My teeth chattered violently in my jaw and I could no longer feel my toes. Several times I nearly went under, a thick layer of mud sucking at my boots. With each slip I felt the crowd's eyes burning into me. Without looking back, I willed myself on, deeper into the lake.

As I inched closer to the birds, they began to grow uneasy. The one closest to me puffed out its feathers and aimed a furious hiss in my direction. Huddled together they looked vaguely comical, resembling a single, two-headed beast, something between an angel and a dinosaur. Still, even antagonised, they were astonishing things to behold, their albino plumage and elegant curves a marvel of evolution. It was hardly surprising the Queen had called them for her own.

With less than twenty feet between us, I stopped dead, realising for the first time just how difficult a task I was facing. In my whole life, I'd never killed anything bigger than a housefly, and though I had no moral problem with the concept of meat, I was unsure about the practicalities of dispensing death, especially to a creature who, with the benefit of being able to float on the water, was able to look me square in the eye.

As I inched forwards through the icy water, I thought back to *Seventy-Seven Steps to Sterling Success*, desperately trying to positively visualise the killing. It

150

was hopeless. While I could easily imagine myself wading ashore, a successfully slaughtered swan slung triumphantly over my shoulder, the details eluded me. There was an established method to these procedures, that much I knew. Critical veins to sever. Organs to target. For instance, was a swan's heart on the left or the right? Did a swan even have a heart? I clutched my spear ever tighter, hoping that when the time came I would be able to channel my inner caveman and tap into some long-dormant hunting instinct.

Glancing over my shoulder, I saw that the men had crammed along the edge of the shore to get a better view of the action. Marshall was shouting something to me, and though his words warped in the wind, their meaning was clear enough. It was time to act.

Dipping my hand below the water line, I reached into my jacket pocket and teased out a mass of gelatinous brown mush. Along with the spear, Marshall had given me a wedge of potato bread with which to lure the birds. With no better plan, I plucked off a chunk and tossed it in their direction. It landed with a fat plop beside them. The swan nearest to me — the one that had hissed — looked in the direction of the bread, and then back at me. It didn't move. This wasn't going to work. I took a deep breath and threw another piece. This time the swan took the bait. Its neck darted down and struck the surface of the water. As it straightened up, it tilted back its head and I watched the powerful muscles of its oesophagus force the bread down the thick white branch of its throat. I tore off another piece.

Little by little the swan began to drift towards me, leaving its partner to watch from the safety of the bank as it followed the trail of breadcrumbs out into the open water. When it was just outside of arm's reach, however, it stopped and eyed me warily. Up close, it looked even bigger. I held up the remains of the bread for it to see, extended my arm and then dropped it. The swan considered the bread with its brown-marble eyes. Still it didn't move. It didn't trust me.

There was a faint sound behind me. I glanced around to see Marshall gesticulating wildly. He was miming something with one arm, using an invisible spear to stab an invisible swan. In contrast, the rest of the men remained perfectly still, perched on the edge of the bank. They were waiting for something to happen. Waiting for the violence they were certain was about to erupt. I turned back to face the bird. The bread still floated between us, bloated in the dark water.

I raised my spear.

The swan looked from me to the bread.

From the bread to me.

And then it pounced.

I moved before I had time to think, plunging my spear into its side the moment it snatched at the bread. There was a sickening crunch as the spear penetrated a layer of feather and bone, a flash of dark red seeping through the pure white. And then the swan was rearing up at me, its wings fully extended as it honked and howled in rage. I braced myself as it attacked, beating out a violent rhythm on my chest, face and arms, the world around me a blur of water and pain. I held onto the spear as best I could, but it was hopeless. Even wounded, the bird was too strong for me, and with a sudden lurch I felt it break free. I held up the spear and saw it had snapped in two, the other end still protruding from the gash in the swan's side. The bird seemed to pause, weighing up its odds, and for a moment I dared to hope it might have the sense to fly away. But then it was back on me, redoubling its efforts, its beak jabbing at my face, its wings beating so powerfully that I feared my arms would actually break.

Terrified, I began to retreat, doing my best to protect my head with my hands. At that moment there was a crash of water behind me as the second swan decided to join its ailing partner. I tried to turn away, hurling myself in the direction of the shore, but it was no good. Within seconds I was overwhelmed.

Both of them towered over me now, each blow of their wings like a hammer to my spine, until suddenly I was under the water, gasping for air while the swans thrashed above me, forcing me deeper and deeper into the lake, drowning me.

I was going to die.

Even in my wretched state, my skin lacerated, my muscles pounding, my lungs bursting, I could see how ridiculous it all was. *Murdered by swans.* Those were the words the coroner would scratch onto his report. That was if there even was a report. After all, I couldn't see Marshall wanting to draw any unwanted attention from the authorities. No, far more likely I would find myself composting at the bottom of an unmarked pit, fading from the narrative, unnoticed, unmissed. I felt hope seep from me with the last of my air, the frozen filth filling my eyes as the swans churned their frenzied dance above me.

And then something unexpected happened.

A human hand reached down through the sludge and grabbed me by the chest. And through the warped prism of the surface I saw a lizard-eyed man, his sallow face framed by angel's wings. He was pulling me up, up, up towards the light.

It was Sneed.

As I spluttered my way back into the world of the living, I saw I wasn't the only thing he was holding. Clutched in his other hand was the body of the wounded swan, its crumpled frame as limp as a discarded carrier bag, its neck tilted at an impossible angle. Its partner was nowhere to be seen. Without a word, he handed me the carcass, before he turned and paddled away toward the bank.

Still coughing up water, I glanced back to see the men celebrating on the far shore, waving their arms and cheering wildly. A few of them had even jumped into the water and were splashing their way over to meet me. As they drew closer, the chant went up again: *"Fuck-the-Queen, fuck-the-Queen, fuck-the-Queen . . ."* and then suddenly we were all celebrating together, their arms joining mine as we hoisted the dead bird in the air.

And it was only then that I noticed Marshall, his hands buried deep in his pockets, his body hunched. Without so much as a glance in my direction, he turned and walked away.

154

CHAPTER
FIFTEEN

The story of my exploits on the lake grew wilder with each telling, so that by the time we began our preparations for the feast the next morning a bystander might have been forgiven for thinking I'd battled a man-eating tiger with my bare hands, rather than the truth, which was that I'd very nearly been finished off by a temperamental swan. Oddly, nobody mentioned the role Sneed had played in my rescue, though there was no doubt they'd all witnessed his surprise appearance. I guess his intervention — and the fact he still hadn't surfaced since he'd waded from the lake and disappeared into the woods — was a little inconvenient for the narrative. In the end, it was far simpler to edit him out altogether.

For my part, I did nothing to correct them. Truth be told, I still felt confused about the incident. While on the one hand I was grateful that Sneed had stepped in and, in all probability, saved my life, on the other, I couldn't suppress my irritation that he had swept in uninvited to steal my thunder. It just didn't seem right somehow. There was also the issue of how he'd managed to appear right on cue. Impossible as I knew it was, I felt like he had stage-managed the whole thing.

At the very least, the thought that he'd been spying on me from some unseen vantage in the bushes was unsettling, if not downright creepy. With all that in mind, I was content to keep my silence and enjoy the backslaps and well wishes that were bestowed on me by all except Marshall, who instead focused his energy on bellowing insults at us as we scrabbled to meet the evening deadline.

It had been decided that the festivities were to take part in the shelter of the marl pit, and there was no shortage of tasks. Much of the day was spent lugging tables, chairs and supplies across the camp and down the steep sides of the pit. It was gruelling work. The sun beat down hotter than ever, and my palms quickly grew tacky with sweat. Numerous times I found myself tangled in the thorny stems of brambles, great bushes of which choked the gaps between trees, forcing us to take the longest possible way down to the clearing. On one occasion I actually took a fall, losing my footing among the loose soil and tree roots. I tumbled backwards down the slope, sending birds shrieking from the bushes until eventually I came to a halt in a springy web of nettles, leaving me stung but otherwise unhurt.

Despite these hardships, the break from routine sparked a child-like excitement among us. As we staggered across the fields we cracked jokes and sang songs, our anticipation of the evening's entertainment so infectious that even Marshall's constant criticisms couldn't put a dent in it. At around midday Rusty arrived, enlisting Ox, Butcher and Zebee to help in the makeshift kitchen he had set up. The rest of us were to spend the afternoon gathering wood for the bonfire, which was to provide the centrepiece for the festivities.

Thanks to the fine summer, there was no shortage of dry firewood, and within a matter of hours we had stacked a towering pyramid of branches in the middle of the clearing. It stood at least twice as high as any of us, and five times as wide. As we stepped back to admire our handiwork, Fingers piped up.

"You know it's only missing one thing, right?"

We all turned to him, confused.

"It needs a Guy, doesn't it?"

"Bollocks," said Al Pacino. "That's only for Bonfire Night."

"Says who?" Fingers snapped back. "We're having a bonfire, ain't we? Seems a shame not to burn *something* on it."

We considered this for a minute. The more I stared at the fire, the easier it was to imagine a man perched on top of it, his straw hair alight, his eyes aglow. In fact, now that he'd mentioned it, the stack of wood almost looked unfinished without one.

"But we haven't got a Guy," said Hopper eventually.

"Exactly," said Al. "Unless you're offering to make one, that is?"

Fingers grinned. "I am, as it happens."

For the next hour or so we raced around the camp, gathering materials to make our straw man. As it was his idea, Fingers offered to donate a spare jacket to the cause, though he was less enthusiastic about giving up his only pair of trousers.

"Quit moaning. Have you seen the weather?" Al said as he rifled through Finger's scant possessions. "I'll make sure I leave you a pair of shorts."

"I don't see you volunteering to give up your clothes."

"My friend, I'm doing you a favour burning those grotty old rags," Al said, holding up one of Finger's threadbare vests. "I'm serious — just because we live in a park, doesn't mean we have to dress like tramps."

For my part, I offered a pillowcase and a pair of gloves, while Hopper provided socks, boots and an old handkerchief. With the help of a roll of duct tape we lifted from Rusty's tent repair kit, we set about assembling our Guy, stuffing his body and limbs with dry grass and leaves until he began to take shape. Once finished, Fingers took the pillowcase and stuffed that too, slicing a wedge out of the bottom and pulling some of the vegetation free to create a beard. He added a few more leaves for a hairline and then tied a handkerchief into a bandana to complete the effect.

"So, what do you think?" he asked, holding him up for us to inspect.

"Hmmm," I nodded.

"Yep," said Hopper.

Al Pacino shook his head. "He's not quite right. I don't know what it is, but he's missing something . . . Ah!" He stopped mid-sentence and sprinted off in the direction of his tent, reappearing a few minutes later with an old pair of sunglasses. One of the arms was missing, but Fingers used the tape to secure it to the pillowcase all the same, stepping aside when he was done.

"Well?"

It was perfect.

"So shall we go and stick him on now?" asked Hopper.

"No," said Fingers, a mischievous twinkle in his eyes. "Let's wait until later and then bring him out as our surprise guest of honour. That way he'll be sure to get a real *warm* welcome."

At last the preparations were ready and, as the sun began to dip below the tree line, Rusty arrived with Bruno, who darted straight for me, his tail a matted blur of excitement. Behind them Rusty's kitchen assistants carried several huge serving boards, each piled high with an assortment of extravagantly presented salads. Carrots, celery and cucumber symmetrically sliced and fanned across plates. Charcoal-blackened skewers of wild mushrooms. Courgettes and baby tomatoes. Bowls of boiled potatoes dressed with shredded leaves of basil and mint. There were steaming pots of soup and curry, bowls of roasted root vegetables and loaves of freshly baked potato bread. At the back of the procession, Rusty cradled a large ceramic serving dish covered over with a mismatched silver lid, which I presumed contained the swan.

Although we'd arranged the tables to face the bonfire, there was so much food we were forced to make up another table to accommodate it all. We were still laying out the plates — the ceramic dish naturally taking pride of place in the centre — when a loud shriek from somewhere above us caused everyone to stop what they were doing and turn towards the trees.

*aaaa*WOOOOOOOOOO*ooooo*

The sound came again. This time the men answered in kind. Rusty was first, cupping a hand to his lips as he let out a high, extended howl. The rest of the men joined in then, creating a discordant cacophony that rang out around the clearing until the world itself seemed to vibrate and I found myself compelled to join them, raising my mouth skyward and adding a thin wail to the chorus.

*aaaa*WOOOOOOOOOO*ooooo*

Just as the sound began to die down there was a shaking of branches, and Marshall stepped into the clearing, his beard freshly plaited, a clean bandana tied around his head, his hands raised like a champion boxer as he swaggered into the clearing with Tyrus at his side. We fell silent as he strode around the clearing, his eyes narrowing as he examined everything for signs of cut corners or sloppy workmanship. Finally, he returned to the table, stooping over to inspect the spread, before plucking a carrot stick and crunching it deliberately between his teeth.

We held our breath, waiting for his judgement.

"Well then," he said, chewing the carrot around his mouth before swallowing. "Are we going to get this fucking party started, or what?"

Now, I've been to my fair share of parties. Including the ones I've attended in a professional capacity, it

160

probably ranks in the hundreds, if not thousands. And the thing about parties is they all tend to track along the same graph. They begin slowly, people exchanging small talk and pleasantries, before the booze starts to take hold. The music gets louder, the voices growing rowdier as they compete with the throb and creak of relentless basslines. The lightweights, those decaffeinated tea drinkers and designated drivers, tend to fall off around this point. They make their excuses and hurry home to their beds and their well-adjusted children and their fog-free mornings. But for the rest of us, things are only just getting started. Beer becomes wine becomes tequila. Then somebody breaks out the blow and things really come to life. We start talking to each other's mouths, necks, chests; words and meaning ceasing to matter as the subtext for the gathering — which of course, is always sex, sex, sex — is brought to the fore. We dance slowly, chew our cheeks, grind into each other, find a room . . .

It was fair to say, however, that this party was unlike any other I'd attended before. The lack of either booze or women saw to that. Yet despite this, there was a certain giddiness to proceedings, a sort of innocent excitement I recognised from Flynn's birthdays, when something as simple as a plate of sausage rolls or a game of pass the parcel was enough to send him and his friends into a fit of hysteria. For one thing, we made a hell of a racket for nine, sober, middle-aged men, especially once the singing began. Ox started us off, belting out the introduction to Bon Jovi's "Livin' on a Prayer", before we all joined in on the chorus, some of us hopping around as we played air-guitar solos, while others beat out a rhythm on the table with their knives and forks. More songs followed: Meat Loaf, Black Sabbath, Boston, plus a whole host of ones I didn't know. With each song we became more and more boisterous, a few of us clambering onto chairs and dancing, others wrestling and getting each other in headlocks, a spirit of abandon sweeping our little group until eventually Marshall brought a temporary halt to the revelry.

"I think it's time we take a breather and get some grub. What do you say?"

A cheer went up as we took our places at the table, followed by a gasp as Rusty finally removed the silver lid from the dish containing the swan. Plucked and roasted, it had shrunk considerably in size, and resembled on first glance a slightly deflated, brown leather football, nestled between the incinerated bodies of the three tiny sparrows. Nevertheless, Rusty had done a good job at presenting it. A sprig of white feathers decorated the dish, along with an elaborate patchwork of greens. There was a moment of reverent silence as Rusty carved, before everyone eagerly began to fill their plates.

Marshall stayed on his feet however, a glass of freshly made apple juice in his hand. "Before we fill our faces, I want you all to take a couple of minutes and give thanks for that which we're about to receive," he said. "I'm not just talking about thanking Rusty for preparing this glorious feast. Or even Adam, for the blood, sweat and tears he put into catching it. Even if he did have a little 'help' along the way . . . "

An awkward chuckle went up as the men turned first to the swan, then to me, and then finally to the one vacant seat at the table.

"No, I want you all to give thanks to the park itself," Marshall continued. "Now, I know that all of us have lived through times of famine and thirst one way or another. Lying on the streets with our bellies rumbling and our wallets empty, wondering where the next meal will come from. Or more likely where our next drink — or line — is coming from . . . "

A few of the men shared an embarrassed smile.

"Or perhaps it wasn't a physical hunger, but a spiritual one. An emptiness in our centre that couldn't be filled with all the food or drugs in the world?"

More of the men nodded now, myself included.

"Regardless, the important thing is that we give gratitude for what we have now. For these are the times of plenty, my friends. We have everything we need, and no one to take it away from us. And so, on this Midsummer's Eve, I propose a toast to the park. For all that it has given and for all it still has to give. From now until the end. The park."

We raised our glasses dutifully.

"The park," we cried. "The park."

In the event, the swan was an anticlimax. Once the meat was carved from the bone there were only a few measly mouthfuls each. What little we had was tough and greasy, a weird taste of mud permeating the entire

163

dish. Still, nobody complained, with people seeming to enjoy the novelty of the meat if not the flavour itself. Besides, Rusty's other offerings more than made up for the disappointment. He'd outdone himself, having apparently saved his finest, juiciest crops for that night, every bite revealing new and unexpected flavours and textures. Even the standard dishes seemed to be imbued with an extra attention to detail; the curry seasoned with finely chopped coriander, the potato fritters lighter and fluffier than ever before. Everyone agreed, it was the best food they had ever eaten.

It was almost dark by the time our bellies were finally full. We sat there for a few minutes once we'd finished, quiet save for the odd contented belch, before Ox once again staggered to his feet and began to sing. While the others joined in on the chorus of "We Are the Champions", I volunteered to help Rusty clear the table. As I began to scrape the leftovers into a bucket to feed the chickens, however, he pulled me aside.

"So, has the gaffer said anythin' to ya yet?"

"About what?" I asked, leaning closer to be heard above the caterwaul of the men straining to hit Freddie's high notes.

"'Bout that business at the lake yesterday. That bloody freak stickin' his oar in where no one asked for it."

"Who? Sneed? I think he was just trying to help, you know? You might not have noticed, but I was having a bit of trouble there," I said, trying to lighten the mood.

"Aye, well. No one asked him for help," Rusty snorted. "He wants to stay out of it. The boss might

164

think he's harmless, but I know better. You can't change a man like that. And where is he now, huh? He'll be creepin' around up to no good — you mark my words. Nah, it's not right. If I was the gaffer, I'd bloody well . . . "

Rusty trailed off as the singing stopped abruptly. I turned to see Marshall stood before the men, once again gesturing for silence.

"I thought this was supposed to be a party?" he roared. "Yet for some reason I find myself standing in the dark with goose pimples on my nutsack."

Nobody moved.

"Come on then!" Marshall said, clapping his hands together and pointing at the bonfire. "Are you gentlemen going to get that fucker lit? Or do I have to do everything myself?"

There was a whoop of approval from the men as Fingers, Hopper, Al and I leapt into action, scrambling towards the giant mound in the centre of the clearing.

"You guys better stand back," Fingers called over to them. "This baby's going to go up like a petrol station once she catches!"

We'd stashed the Guy in a bush behind the fire, and we giggled among ourselves as we raced to retrieve it. In the dark he looked eerily realistic, his neck lolling to one side as if recently broken.

"This is going to be a fucking blast!" Hopper said with a grin.

Sticking to the plan we'd agreed earlier, Al waited out of sight while we began to light the fire, striking matches and touching them to balls of kindling we'd

165

placed within the cage of branches. The wood was dry, and within seconds the flames took, licking higher and higher, until the entire structure was an amber blaze, the air filled with sweet-smelling smoke.

"Now!" Fingers called.

I stood back and watched as Al launched the Guy into the air. It was a good throw, and our man landed square on top of the pyre, his legs snagging on a branch. He immediately began to smoke.

We sniggered among ourselves as we walked back towards the others, waiting for someone to notice our surprise guest.

And then it started.

Even above the sizzle and pop of burning leaves I could hear the gasps as one by one the men began to point at the fire. We began to laugh openly then, slapping palms and backs as we congratulated each other on our excellent prank. Until we got close enough to see the look of horror on their faces as they turned from the flames to Marshall, who was staring open-mouthed at the fire.

We stopped laughing and high-fiving and backslapping. Something was wrong. I turned back to the inferno. It was really burning now, red and orange flames forking up towards our Guy who sat there smouldering, not quite yet alight.

Confused, I turned back to Marshall, who was by now clutching his head in despair. "After all I've done for you bastards," he roared. "After everything I've done."

166

And with that he turned and stormed off in the direction of the camp.

I felt a hand on my shoulder. It was Hopper. "Oh, shit," he said.

I looked again at the fire. The Guy had finally caught, the inferno reflected in his sunglasses as his grass beard burned down to a fine black stubble. And then I saw it.

On top of the bonfire, unmistakable now that it was fully engulfed in flames, was an effigy of Marshall.

The four of us sat huddled around the remains of the fire. The Guy had long-since burned away to nothing, leaving a crackling dance of orange-tipped embers. Though everyone agreed it was all simply an unfortunate misunderstanding, Marshall's exit had effectively pulled the plug on the celebrations, and one by one people had begun to drift into the night.

As Rusty stood to leave, he called me aside. "Don't go blamin' yourself, sonny," he said, resting a paternal hand on my shoulder. "Everyone knows the gaffer can be a little . . . sensitive. He's just got the wrong end of the stick is all. It'll be forgotten in the morning, you'll see."

I'd nodded and strained a smile, but didn't feel any better. With everything that had happened at the lake the day before, I felt cursed, as if I was simply lurching from one disaster to the next. I thanked Rusty and waved him goodnight.

At last it was just Fingers, Hopper and Al left. None of us spoke, each of us lost in our own thoughts as we stared entranced at the ever-shifting patterns of the ashes. I've read somewhere about the effect an open fire has on the human brain, about how the flicker and spark speaks to our deepest genetic memories of millennia spent camped out in caves, where the light and warmth of the campfire was the only thing between our ancestors and the saw-toothed nightmares that lay waiting in the darkness. The popularity of the television in modern homes, so the theory goes, is an attempt to recapture that ritual, the smokeless shimmer of quiz shows and soap operas echoing back through the ages to an altogether simpler time, when we would stare into the flames and make the pictures ourselves.

Of course in the park we had the real thing. I'd always found zoning out to the soothing glow of a fire to be one of the most enjoyable aspects of outdoor living. That night, however, all I saw among the embers was portents of misery; a human skull, a dying swan, a burning man. I'd had enough of fires for one evening. As I prepared to bid the others goodnight, I became aware of a rustling in the bushes behind us. They heard it too, turning in their seats towards the source of the noise. It grew louder, and at once we were on our feet, staring wildly into the darkness.

"Who's there?" Al called, already gripping a branch to protect himself. "Show yourself."

There was no response. The noise came again, even louder this time. There was a tumble of grey and we all leapt back in fright as a rock rolled into the dim circle of light. Then the rock stuck out its snout and sniffed at us. We laughed. It was nothing but a large hedgehog.

168

"Jesus!" Hopper said as he nudged the beast with his boot, causing it to transform into a hissing ball of prickles. "I thought it was a . . . I don't know what. Something bad. Or *someone* bad."

We all laughed again, the thought an outsider might somehow intrude on our private world too outlandish for us to take seriously. Just then there was another sound from the bushes, something louder — and bigger — than any hedgehog.

Before any of us could react, Rusty crashed into the clearing, his face contorted in agony. "Help! Help!" he cried, struggling to catch his breath. "He's gone bleedin' mental. It's a massacre back there!"

"Slow down," I said. Even in the dying firelight I could make out the splashes of red that speckled Rusty's top. "Who's gone mental? Marshall?"

Rusty shook his head. "No, no. It's that damn bug-eyed freak is who. It's Sneed. He's killed them all."

CHAPTER
SIXTEEN

Everywhere I looked there were signs of violence: smashed flowerpots, uprooted saplings, snapped trellises. And of course, the corpses strewn indiscriminately in the dirt, the ground sticky with blood. Rusty wasn't wrong about it being a massacre. The farm looked like a war zone.

I waited for Al, Fingers or Hopper to say something, but they all looked too shell-shocked to speak.

"And there are definitely no survivors?" I asked, finally breaking the silence.

Rusty shook his head. Even in the dark I could see the tears brimming in his eyes. "He murdered every last one. Poor bastards never had a chance."

The silence stretched on, until at last Fingers knelt to inspect one of the bodies. "Well, this is going to stuff breakfast up a bit, isn't it? I could've gone for a nice bit of scrambled egg too."

Rusty was on him in a flash, his hand closing around Finger's throat while Bruno leapt up and began barking. "You think this is bleedin' funny, do you?" Rusty yelled. "They might have jus' been chickens to you, but as far as I'm concerned they was part of the

170

family. I swear if I get a hold of that little freak I'll string him up from the nearest tree and . . . "

"WHAT THE HELL'S GOING ON HERE?"

We all turned to see Marshall marching towards us, his rifle raised to his chest. As he drew closer he froze, turning slowly to survey the carnage all around. It was a clear night, and the moonlight leant the entire scene a surreal quality, the scattered feathers like snow on the ground. When Marshall finally spoke, his words dripped with bile. "You Judas bastards . . . "

We all cowered as Marshall waved the gun towards us.

"First the fire. Now this. So it's a war you want, is it?"

At this, Fingers took the opportunity to wriggle free of Rusty's grip, his hands held in the air as he approached Marshall. "Nah, boss. It ain't like that at all. Rusty reckons Sneed's gone and flipped his lid. Look." He paused to nudge a mutilated chicken with his boot. "Everyone of them's dead. Throats slit from the looks of it . . . Ow!"

Before Marshall could respond, Rusty leapt forward, driving a finger into Finger's chest. "You listen here, you. I don't *reckon* anythin'. Of course it was Sneed. Who else could it have been? The sicko's got a taste for blood after that business with the swan, hasn't he? We need to get after him now, before he does any more damage. Who's to say it won't be one of our necks he goes for next, huh?"

Hopper piped up then. "What do you say, boss — shall I go and raise the alarm? Boss?"

171

Marshall didn't answer immediately. He was still staring at the ruin of the farm, his face wearing the same, helpless expression as when I'd beaten him in the race.

"You say you *saw* Sneed do this?" he asked eventually. He didn't look at us when he spoke.

"I didn't need to," Rusty said. "It was him alright. Got his grubby little fingerprints all over it."

"Rust raised the alarm as soon as it happened," added Fingers. "It's just terrible, isn't it? And we were having such a lovely evening too."

Ignoring him, Marshall turned to Rusty. "So where were you when all this happened?"

"Me? I was jus' takin' Bruno for a piss, weren't I? Save him scratchin' at the tent door all night. I was over in the bushes when I heard a right racket. Thought a fox might've got in 'ere. I came as soon as I could. But . . . " Rusty's voice cracked. "But I was too late."

Marshall nodded, pursing his lips. "I just can't imagine him doing this," he said, more to himself than to us. "I mean, he's always been a bit . . . funny. But this?" He shook his head. "What do you think, Adam?"

Everyone turned to me. It was the first time Marshall had spoken directly to me since the mix-up with the Guy. Despite everything that had happened since, I was still embarrassed.

"He was pretty helpful yesterday," I mumbled. "At least, he didn't seem like he wanted to hurt anybody."

"Except for that bleedin' swan, you mean?" Rusty snapped. "He was quick enough to come flyin' out the bushes to wring that poor thing's neck, wasn't he? Creepin' up on people. Sneakin' around. It's not right."

Al, Hopper and Fingers all nodded in agreement.

"You have to admit, he sure looked like he knew what he was doing out there on the lake," Fingers added as he tugged at his beard. "I reckon he's killed a few birds in his time."

Everyone nodded again except Marshall, whose only response was to send a missile of spit streaking through the moonlight. We each shuffled uneasily on the spot, waiting for our next instruction. For the first time that night, I became aware of how cold it was, our breath joining together to form a single gossamer cloud, drifting off into the night.

"I know you thought you could tame him, boss," Rusty said, his tone softer now, though his eyes were still blazing. "But the boy's not right. Never has been as far as I can see. Some people just ain't meant for savin'."

Marshall shook his head, but wouldn't meet Rusty's eye.

"Either way, he's gone too far this time," Rusty continued. "He's turned on you. Turned on us all. And when a dog bites the hand that feeds him? Well . . . " Rusty swung a leg out and clipped Bruno's hind leg, causing him to let out a shrill squeal and dart off towards the trees. With that he began to walk towards the camp.

He was halfway across the farm before Marshall called out.

"Wait."

Rusty stopped but didn't look back.

We all turned to Marshall. Maybe it was just the lack of glasses, but I thought he looked older, black ink spots bleeding out from under his eyes.

"Wait," he said again, and this time I saw the pain in his face. "We'll come with you."

Nobody slept that night. After rousing the others from their tents, we made our way to the armoury. The details of Sneed's betrayal spread throughout the camp with the enthusiasm of ripe bulrush seeds, so that by the time we arrived, each man was bristling with outrage. As Rusty handed out weapons, Marshall talked us through the plan, explaining in a dull monotone how we should split into pairs and comb the park from the outside in, with the aim of flushing Sneed back into the camp. What would happen once we got him there was less clear, though as we filtered out into the night, Marshall did bark one last ominous command.

"Take him alive."

"Only if he's willing to come quietly," Rusty added. "After all, we know what he's capable of."

We looked to Marshall for confirmation, but all he did was scowl and stalk off towards the trees, his gun slung over his shoulder.

In the event, there was no need to worry about what we'd do with Sneed once we found him. I was paired with Butcher, and though we spent the whole night silently trudging through the dark undergrowth, the most interesting thing we spotted was a pair of fox cubs scampering across the deserted playing field, their amber hides flecked with golden moonlight. Butcher, meanwhile, seemed more interested in telling me about romantic — and not-so-romantic — conquests from his old life, turning the night air blue with his graphic recollections of his former lovers' anatomies. By the time the sky had blushed with the first rays of sun the next morning, I felt bludgeoned by both the lack of sleep and the endless tawdry tales. I was glad to return to camp, where we found the other men already sprawled out on the floor, red-eyed and weary. Only Marshall remained absent.

"So what now?" Hopper asked as we arrived.

The question hung in the air.

"Well, I for one wouldn't mind forty winks," Butcher said at last.

"And I wouldn't mind some breakfast," Fingers added. "What say we fry up them chickens before they turn bad? Bit of KFC, eh, lads?"

There was an enthusiastic murmur, until Rusty stepped forwards, his face folded into a furious scowl. "You boys disgust me!" he yelled. "There's a mad man on the loose and all you lot can think about is your beds and your bellies? Those poor chickens represent an act of vandalism against this community, and you want to eat 'em? Shame on you. I wouldn't eat 'em if my life depended on it. Wouldn't feed 'em to Bruno neither. Nah. We'll give those birds a proper burial like they deserve. It's only right."

With that, he stormed off in the direction of the farm, Bruno racing off into the bushes ahead of him.

We hung our heads, tired and embarrassed.

"I was only saying . . . " Fingers mumbled, rubbing his cheeks as if Rusty's words had been a physical attack. "Don't know who he thinks he is anyway. Going on like he's the bleeding gaffer."

"At least he's doing something," said a gruff voice.

We all turned, shocked to hear Ox speak.

"What do you mean?" aked Al.

"Well, where is Marshall now?" Ox continued, his words slow and deliberate, as if the act of talking took an immense amount of concentration. "Hiding I bet," he continued. "He doesn't want to show his face because he invited Sneed to stay. It's his fault this happened. But I don't see him coming to help clean up, do you?"

The silence crashed over us. I'd never heard anyone criticise Marshall so openly before. To hear it from Ox, who hadn't previously shown any interest in the internal politics of the group, was doubly startling.

"Ah, shut it you lot," said Butcher finally. "You know Rust had a hard on for them fucking chickens. He'll get over it soon enough. The boss too. As for Sneed, well, that's the last we'll see of that mad fucker. He's long gone, I reckon. Everything will be back to normal in a day or two, you mark my words." With that he stood and dusted himself down. "Now, let's go and get that farm cleaned up before we get another ear bashing."

It took us the rest of the day to get the farm straight. We worked in silence, sweeping up fragments of terracotta,

176

mending fences and replacing bamboo canes, replant-ing or re-staking the crops we could save and tearing out those we couldn't. By the time we'd finished, the place looked almost as good as new, except for the small hump of freshly turned earth next to the empty chicken run, marking the mass grave of its recently departed inhabitants.

There was no sign of Rusty or Marshall when we finally staggered back to camp. With all that had happened, it seemed no one had thought to prepare a meal for us. Instead we were forced to make do with a small bucket of fruit we'd managed to scavenge from the farm, a handful of blackberries and a bruised apple helping to stave off the dull pain in my gut.

"Am I missing something?" I said as we huddled round the empty dinner table.

"Probably," said Fingers.

"I mean, it's not like we're in the wilderness here. What's to stop us from going and buying some new chickens? There's a pet shop about half a mile down the road from here. I'm sure they'd . . . " I trailed off as I noticed the blank faces staring back at me.

"What are you talking about?" said Butcher roughly.

"Getting new chickens," I answered slowly. "I was just wondering why can't we just hop on a bus and buy some new ones?"

"Hop on a bus?" Hopper repeated.

"Buy some?" said Butcher.

I looked around the table, trying to work out if they were joking or not. "Come on, guys. They didn't just appear by themselves. Marshall must have got them from somewhere originally."

Zebee smiled politely. "I think you're forgetting something, young man."

"What's that?" I asked.

"The rules," he answered.

"Yeah," said Butcher. "The rules."

"The rules," Hopper nodded.

"The rules say we can't leave the park," said Al Pacino, holding out his fleece for me to inspect. "You think I'd be wearing these rags if I could just pop down the shop any time I fancied it?"

"But you could!" I said with a laugh. "The shops are literally just down the road. If you go to the top of Squit Creek, you can see them through the trees. We could be there and back in about ten minutes flat."

Ox let out a huge sigh, his barrel chest bobbing up and down. "If you don't like the rules," he said, "maybe you should speak to the boss."

I nodded. The conversation was over. We chewed our fruit in silence and were in our beds before darkness fell.

The next morning I woke to the clanging of metal. Marshall was back, and from his cries it seemed he was ready to resume our daily routine. I dressed hurriedly and made my way to the camp, relieved that things were at last returning to normal. When I arrived, however, I was surprised to find Rusty standing before the assembled men, a saucepan and wooden spoon dangling from his filthy fingers.

"Ah, Adam," Rusty said as I took my place in the line. "As I was just explainin' to the boys here, there's been a change of plan this mornin'. The boss got back real late last night, so he's asked me to pass on his orders."

"There's still no sign of Sneed," blurted Fingers.

Rusty glared at him for a moment before continuing. "It's true there's still no sign of the coward Sneed. Which is why Marshall wants us to do things a little differently this mornin'. We've been asked to form a security detail around the perimeter. If that little beggar shows up again, we'll show him how we treat murderers around here."

Nobody spoke for a moment.

"Does that mean we're not running?" said Hopper eventually.

"Boss says the defence of the camp is to take priority over all other activities," said Rusty, before winking at Hopper. "So I guess that means you're off the hook."

There were sporadic chirrups of excitement as we gathered our weapons and fanned out into the woods. None of us were quite able to believe the stroke of good fortune that meant we were able to miss out the early morning exercise regime. Indeed, I myself was so pleased that it wasn't until much later, while I stood guarding the entrance to Squit Creek, that I realised we'd also missed out on our shower and breakfast too.

CHAPTER
SEVENTEEN

In the weeks that followed, a new pattern replaced our old way of life. Every day we would arm ourselves with wooden weapons — in my case a spear I'd fashioned from a length of ash — before taking up our perpetual patrol of the park. The security measures didn't stop there, however. After the first few days brought no sign of Sneed, we were informed that, in order to ensure our safety, night patrols were to be instigated. A roster was drawn up and each evening three men were nominated to stay awake, watching over the rest of us while we slept. Those nights I was unfortunate enough to be selected as watchman were some of the longest of my life, my nerves chafed raw by the unfamiliar crackles of the undergrowth, along with the constant feeling I was being watched from just beyond the fringes of the camp. I was always glad when morning finally broke and the other men began to stir, their idle chatter chasing my nightmarish imaginings back into the shadows for another day.

With Marshall still absent, Rusty seemed to have been promoted to acting leader — a role he undertook with great gusto. Indeed, there was hardly a day that went by during which he was not heard to bellow an elaborate new set of instructions at us, designed to capture Sneed once and for all. As Marshall's sole confidant, these pronouncements came rubberstamped with the weight of his authority, something Rusty was keen to point out if ever challenged. "I'm just readin' from the big man's script," he'd say if anyone dared complain about the double night shift they'd just been given. "Don't shoot the autocue operator!"

Not that Marshall had disappeared from view entirely. I'd still catch sight of him now and then, usually at the very end of the day as he went out for the night, or first thing in the morning as he returned to his tree house. Or else he'd come stalking from the bushes with Tyrus at his side, his rifle trailing over his shoulder, his brow knitted with worry. It seemed that the stress of the attack had manifested itself physically, his black hair and beard suddenly speckled grey, his head stooped forward, resolutely avoiding our gaze or questions. I couldn't be certain, but I thought he looked smaller, his cheeks hollow and drawn behind his sunglasses, his coat seeming to hang limply from his shoulders.

Marshall wasn't the only one to have lost weight. Since the new regime left little time for cooking, formal meals had been reduced, with the men gathering together only once in the evening to eat a simple broth, or more likely a selection of raw fruit and vegetables roughly chopped and tossed into a bowl. Rusty's fritters, curries, stews — and eggs — were now nothing but a distant dream.

Of course, there was nothing stopping us helping ourselves to whatever we could scavenge from the park

181

on our daily patrols, though as the summer wore on, pickings became noticeably slimmer. The apples I'd relied on for breakfast soon lay mouldy and crawling with wasps, the berries shrivelled to hard black stones — even the wild salads, the sorrel, goosegrass and dandelion leaves that had up until recently sprouted in abundance, now retreated to inedible clumps of brown straw.

Still, after a week or so I found the hunger pains began to recede into the background, as easy to ignore as the swarms of fruit flies and midges that fogged the sky at dusk and dawn. And whenever my stomach did occasionally cramp, I did my best to remember there was still much to be grateful for. For one thing, the security patrols provided a welcome break from the endless toiling on the farm. It felt nice to give my muscles a rest, my back no longer hunched over a barrow, my fingers no longer cramping in the dirt.

My good mood was further bolstered by the weather, which for weeks remained fine and dry, providing excellent opportunities for illicit sunbathing. Indeed, whenever the boredom of standing guard over the empty playing fields became too much to bear, I would set my spear aside and snatch a few joyful hours lying in the long grass, my thoughts as meandering and insubstantial as the handful of wispy clouds that scuffed the otherwise perfect blue sky. Yes, I thought to myself during those long afternoons, there was much to be grateful for.

One afternoon, perhaps five or six weeks after the security patrols first began, I was standing in the thin copse of trees that divided the old playground and the football field. It was a scorching day, too hot even to stretch out and enjoy the sun. My tongue felt heavy and swollen in my mouth. Along with the reduction in food, the lack of rain meant our water reserves were running dangerously low, to the point where we had recently been forced to dredge up buckets from the lake. The murky water left a residue of brown scum around the pan when it was boiled, along with a bitter aftertaste of chalk and silt that even Rusty's herbs couldn't mask.

I stood motionless, propped against the trunk of a wide pear tree. Already the leaves above me were beginning to change colour, from a lush green to a jaundiced yellow, the dead fruit at my feet now only fit for the wasps that bobbed drunkenly around my ankles. Although it was still light, I was debating calling it a day, the combination of hunger and heat sapping my energy and leaving me craving my tent — though I knew the airless fug of the canvas would provide little relief.

Just then a sharp cry rang out around the trees. I turned quickly, peering through the splayed fingers of branches for the source of the sound. It was likely a bird, I told myself. Either that, or one of the domestic tabby cats that occasionally strayed into our territory. Even still, I found myself gripping my spear more tightly, a vision of Sneed throttling a swan swimming before my eyes.

A few minutes passed in silence, and I was ready to dismiss the sound as a figment of my sun-addled imagination, when it came again, far louder and closer than before. There was no mistaking it this time. It was a scream. It was a person.

Instinctively I dropped to my knees, the hours I'd spent training with Marshall kicking in as I found myself crawling commando-style towards the cries, which grew louder by the second. Picking my way through the dense undergrowth, I at last came to the edge of the trees, affording me a wide vantage over the old playground. Being careful to remain concealed, I scanned the landscape for signs of life. My head was hurting, my temples thrumming with adrenaline, making it difficult to concentrate. Any second I expected Sneed to descend on me, his mad eyes rolling in his head as he thrust a blade under my chin.

Suddenly I spotted something. A flicker of movement in my peripheral vision. Turning slightly, I spotted not Sneed, but two small figures, ambling away from me in the distance. It had been so long since I'd seen anyone other than a member of the tribe that it took me a moment to recognise the figures as a pair of schoolgirls. I watched as they crossed towards the park entrance, shoving each other tipping back their young heads as they shared some unknowable joke.

I let out a deep breath. It was just a couple of school kids messing about. Nothing more dangerous than that.

Then the cry came again.

I whipped my head back towards the play park. It was a girl's voice, that much I could tell. She seemed to be screaming.

"Help!"

184

I followed the sound, and this time I saw her, a shrunken figure slumped against the rusting frame of the swing. Being careful to remain within the cover of the trees, I crept closer, trying to get a better look at her. Like the other girls, she was wearing a school uniform, though it was stained and dusty, as if she'd recently been rolling in the dirt. Though her long hair was loose and covered most of her face, there was something oddly familiar about her. I could see now she was struggling with something. Moving closer still, I spotted the loop around her wrists. The other girls must have tied her up.

"Help!" she cried again, the words little more than a mangled sob now. It was a sound I knew well — the sound of someone out of hope.

I froze, uncertain of what to do next, when the girl abruptly flopped forward, as if fainting. I made up my mind. Abandoning stealth, I charged from the trees towards her. At the sound of my footsteps the girl looked up, the hair falling from her face. And at that moment the world seemed to wobble and then topple completely from its axis.

For tied to the swings, not fifteen feet in front of me, was my little girl, my only daughter.

It was Olivia.

AUTUMN

CHAPTER
EIGHTEEN

"Get off me, get off me!"

Olivia was hysterical, her tiny body writhing in panic, her bound hands straining uselessly behind her back as she lashed out with her legs, aiming spindly kicks at my shins. "Get the hell away from me, or I swear . . . I swear . . . "

As appalled as I was to see her in this state, part of me was proud to see how much fight she still had left in her. She might have been tied to a rusting swing while being assailed by a spear-carrying stranger, but my daughter was nobody's victim. She wasn't going down without a fight.

"Shush, Ollie! If you just calm down for a second then I'll . . . Ow!"

I'd pressed my palm to her mouth in an attempt to pacify her, receiving a painful bite in response.

"OLLIE, IF YOU DON'T STOP THIS INSTANT, YOU'LL BE IN A WHOLE WORLD OF TROUBLE, YOUNG LADY!"

Olivia's head jerked up in sudden recognition, the damp storm of her fringe parting to reveal not a wild animal, but a confused and frightened little girl.

"Dad?"

I nodded slowly as she searched my face for something familiar, for something to hold onto as the world crumbled beneath her. Her gaze darted from the gnarled tangle of my beard to the grey knot of my hair, before settling on my eyes. Something passed between us then — telepathy, electricity — and I watched as the understanding finally dawned behind those bottomless green eyes. We each stayed perfectly still for a second, an eternity; a father and daughter trapped in amber, permafrozen in time.

And then she exploded.

"You fucking, fucking, FUCKING . . . bastard!"

This time I took her kicks, absorbing each blow until finally she was spent. She slumped forward, sobbing.

"I'm sorry," was all I could say. "I'm so very, very sorry."

She didn't immediately run when I untied her. I took this to be a good sign. The girls had used a school tie to bind her hands, and when I eventually got it loose she stood there, rubbing at her raw wrists and staring at her feet, no longer able to meet my eyes.

"Listen, Ollie — " I began, before she cut me off.

"Flynn stopped talking."

"What?"

"After you left. He wouldn't speak to anyone. Not a word. Mum took him to the doctor, a psychologist. He was like it for months."

"Ollie. It's complicated."

"He thought you were dead," she said as she finally looked up at me, her eyes brimming with tears. "We all did."

It was my turn to fall silent then. I shrugged helplessly. Olivia kept staring, examining me in the way a detective might study a particularly brutal murder scene, her expression a mixture of revulsion and professional fascination. Gradually, something began to soften in her, the corner of her mouth twitching in amusement.

"You smell like you're dead, anyway," she said at last, scrunching up her nose. "When's the last time you had a bath? Seriously, you're rank."

Instinctively I turned my head to sniff myself, and was greeted by a vaguely musty aroma. "I'm not that bad, am I?"

"Ugh! Have you lost your sense of smell as well as your mind? You're making my eyes sting. And what's with the beard? You look like a serial killer or something."

She was teasing me now. This was good. This was progress.

"Shut it," I said.

"You shut it."

"No, you shut it. Don't think you're too old for a smacked bottom, missy. I'm still your father."

A misstep. She recoiled at the word, the thin slither of her smile shrinking away, replaced by a quivering bottom lip.

"Oh, Dad . . . "

I stepped forward to embrace her, but she swatted me away, trying to mask the smear of snot and tears.

"Honestly, honey, I'm fine. Really. I'm doing okay."

"Jesus! I know *you're* okay. What about us? How could you just leave like that? Weren't we enough for you?"

"Olivia, please. Of course you were enough. I told you. Things were complicated. Adult things . . . "

"What, so I'm old enough for you to abandon but too young to get an explanation? Jesus, Mum was right about you."

My stomach shrivelled at the mention of Lydia. "Why? What did she say?"

"What do you think she said? You disappeared in the middle of the night. She tried calling your work and spoke to that guy. The creepy one you brought over a couple of Christmases ago . . . "

"Dan?" I breathed, my mouth almost too dry to speak.

"Yeah, that's him. Dan. He told Mum you hadn't worked there for months. And then those men from the bank turned up at the house and everything just went crazy."

I felt the blood drain from my face, my legs threatening to buckle. "The house? Jesus. And now? Where are you living now?"

Olivia shrugged. "At home. After you left, Mum called a solicitor and they worked something out. They took your car but the rest was fine. She's started selling her art online now. Do you remember the big red one? With the fabric attached?"

I shook my head feebly.

"*Seriously?* It took up like half her study. Anyway, some American guy bought it for a butt-load and then ended up commissioning three more. She's got her own website and everything. She's doing really well." Olivia paused to dig around in her blazer pocket to produce a mobile phone. "Or at least she was. I swear, she's going to flip out when she finds out you're back."

I was instantly back in control, my hand swooping through the air to grab her wrist before she could dial.

"Ow, get off! You're hurting me."

I loosened my grip but didn't release her. "Put the phone down, Ollie."

"What? Why?"

"Just put it down and I'll explain."

"God, you're such a . . . Anyway, how am I supposed to put it down if you won't let go of me?"

I sighed. With my free hand I removed her mobile phone, before letting her wrist drop.

"Hey!" she yelled, trying to snatch the phone back "Give it to me!"

"I will in a second," I said, holding her phone out of reach. "First, I need you to promise me something. You can't tell Mum you saw me here, okay? You can't tell anyone."

Olivia stopped jumping and stared at me. "What do you mean? Aren't you coming home?"

I didn't answer.

"You can't just . . . I mean, what are you even doing here?" She waved a hand towards my spear, which lay abandoned a few feet away. "You're running around playing cavemen now? Is that it? That isn't normal, Dad. That's messed up. Look at you. You stink. You're dressed like a tramp. What do you even eat? You look like you're lost about six stone. Please don't tell me you're eating out of bins or I swear to God, I'll never speak to you again."

"I'm doing fine. I promise," I said, ignoring the swish and grumble of my hollow belly. "Anyway, from the looks of those wrists it should be me who's worried about you. Who were those girls, Ollie?"

Her scowl deepened. "You always do that."

"Do what?"

"Change the subject. Well, guess what — you don't get to ask me questions now. Not while you're running around a park pretending to be Bear Grylls."

"Ollie . . ."

"Don't 'Ollie' me. I mean it. Don't say my name. It's not yours to say anymore. If you're not coming home, then just forget the whole thing."

She reached down for her bag and slung it over her shoulder.

"Wait . . ." I held out her phone for her to take. "Here."

She took it from me, slipping it into her pocket without glancing at the screen.

"You aren't going to call Mum?"

She shrugged. "I've got to go."

"I will come home," I said as she turned her back. "I've just got a few things to sort out here. But I will be back. Soon. I promise."

Her little shoulders twitched dismissively. "Sure."

"Oh hey, Ollie," I called as she skulked towards the gate. "I meant to say. If those girls start giving you grief again. Just . . . Just . . . " I stumbled, searching for the right words, the perfect piece of parental advice.

This time Olivia did stop, looking back and fixing me with an expression that was so like her mother's it was frightening. "What?" she said, her eyebrow arching cruelly. "Run away?"

And with that she was gone.

It was dark when I made it back to camp. Butcher, Fingers and Al Pacino sat muttering around the faint glow of a campfire, the feeble flames kicking out little in the way of light or heat. Like most other jobs, gathering firewood had been neglected in the wake of our beefed-up security patrols, meaning there was little to burn besides the dry leaves and twigs that lay around the edge of the camp. Still, the evenings were mild. These days we lit the fire more out of a sense of ritual than of any need to keep warm, the reassuring smell of smoke an attempt to convince us that everything would go back to normal soon enough.

Though I wasn't hungry, I made my way to the deserted dining table. I'd felt dazed ever since my encounter with Olivia, my head heavy with the weight of a million stunted possibilities. Should I have followed her home? Or sent her back to Lydia with a message? *Hi. It's me. I'm alive.* Instead I'd simply reverted to type. Hid. Lied. Ran. I guess no matter how much Marshall liked to speak in terms of our "salvation" or "personal betterment", the project was a failure. I was still at heart the same chickenshit con-artist I'd been when I'd sat down at the park bench to cut my wrists

195

all those months ago. I didn't deserve Olivia. Perhaps I never would.

Strewn across the table were the remains of a paltry evening meal consisting of a handful of raw potatoes, along with a few other tragic-looking vegetables. I reached for a carrot and bit into it. There was no crunch.

Tossing it aside, I began to head in the direction of my tent when a fragment of the men's conversation drifted over to me from the fire, the unmistakable sneer of Butcher's voice ringing out in the warm night air.

". . . tight arse on her. Little bitch looked like she was gagging for it."

I froze, every molecule of my being suddenly alert.

"So did you give her one then?" Fingers was asking.

"Nah. She looked like she was in a hurry."

"Probably off to go and meet a real man," Al laughed. "I can't see a girl like that going anywhere near a scruffy *finocchio* like you."

"And you think she'd touch a wop like you?" Butcher spat, jumping to his feet.

"Hey!" said Fingers. "Take it easy, girls. Now, why don't you tell us more about this little cutie-pie again so we can *all* go to bed with sweet dreams."

I swallowed hard as the men sniggered, already knowing what Butcher was about to say.

"Well, alright then," he said, sitting back down and leaning in towards the men. "Just as long as the greaseball here keeps his mouth shut long enough for me to get to the juicy bits."

Despite the darkness, I could hear the leer on his face.

"So, like I said, I was out on patrol, looking for that boggle-eyed bastard. Not that I was likely to find anything, eh?"

"Amen to that, brother."

"I'd been out there for hours. Bored shitless, I was. Anyway, I was thinking of calling it a day when I got a sniff of something on the breeze. Something sweet that I half recognised. Like sour honey it was. I haven't smelled it for years, at least not round here . . . " He paused to let a throaty gurgle escape from his mouth, more like a growl than a laugh. "Then I realised what it was. Pussy. I could smell pussy."

The other two joined him then, letting out a low mechanical grunt of laughter, like a broken car straining to start.

"I looked up and there she was," Butcher continued. "Little strip of a thing. Like Bambi. Big eyes, brown hair. No tits to talk about. But that arse. Looked like she'd been round the block a few times, if you know what I mean. She had this little skirt on . . . "

"Yeah?" breathed Al.

"Yeah. It was so short you could see her white panties peaking out underneath."

"Fuck yeah!" said Fingers.

"Less than twenty feet away she was, but she couldn't see me. Like I say, she was in a rush. Half running for the park gates. But before she disappeared she turned and looked back. That's when I got a proper look at her. Little slut was all dressed up. Wearing this tight school uniform she was. Fuck me, I felt like bending over the bench and giving her one right then and there."

As the men howled their approval, my fear bloomed into an all-consuming hatred for Butcher. I saw myself striding over to the fire and forcing the ball of my fist into his mouth. I would shatter those pointy yellow teeth, then tear out his tongue. And then I'd turn on the other two cackling morons and gut them like the pigs they were.

I saw myself doing it, and yet I didn't move.

A second passed, an hour. I still didn't move.

And then, through the seething fog of my rage, I once again caught the thread of Butcher's voice.

". . . if she does come through this way again, I won't make the same mistake. She'll be getting exactly what she's asking for. And once I'm done, I'll bring her back to camp and I'll pass her around so you can all get a turn. You mark my words, boys. They'll be nothing left of her by the time we've finished."

CHAPTER
NINETEEN

That night it began to rain, a violent downpour that hammered my tent like the sticks on God's snare, an endless drum roll with no punchline. I lay awake and stared up at the sagging membrane of canvas above me. My gut bubbled with anger, as all the things I should have said to Butcher echoed in my ears. I would leave, I told myself as I twisted my blanket into a thick rope between my thighs. I didn't know where I would go, but I would leave. I would leave and I would never come back.

As the night wore on, however, my resolve began to dissipate, my rage giving way to fear and uncertainty. After all, it was my recklessness that had landed me here in the first place. Besides, just because Butcher was a bad apple, it didn't make the rest rotten by association. No, I decided, the best thing to do was to wait. I would be calm and rational. I would bide my time until . . . Well, until I worked out what I was going to do.

By the time I began to drift off, the night had already cracked open, a thin grey light seeping through the gaps in my tent. Outside, the rain continued to bounce. My dreams were filled with hideous, disjointed visions of sinking boats and drowning men. I woke a few hours later to discover I was wet. The canvas had sprung a leak. As I wrung out my clothes, a blast of thunder detonated overhead. Moments later there was a cry from outside.

Time to get up and out. Time to find Sneed.

At first I assumed it was Rusty.

Then the cry came again.

This time I realised it wasn't Rusty, but Marshall. What's more there was something in his tone I recognised but couldn't place. Something that sounded an awful lot like . . .

"Help! Help!"

Fear.

Without pausing to dress, I rushed from my tent. The rain had turned the ground to slush, and as I slipped and skidded my way towards Marshall's screams, thick, dark mud splashed up and coated my bare legs black. I kept running, my thoughts once again filled with lizard eyes and throttled swans.

"Help! For the love of God, help!"

The closer I got the more desperate Marshall's cries became. He was being murdered, of that I had no doubt. I ran faster, terrified that I would be too late. That he would already be dead.

When I finally found him, the sight that greeted me seemed to confirm my worst fears. Marshall was lying in the clearing, his jacket spread around him like a black puddle. He was no longer screaming. In fact, he wasn't moving at all. Ox, Zebee and Butcher stood above him, each of them grey and brittle with shock.

Before I could ask what had happened — or where Sneed had escaped to — there was a rustling of branches behind me. I turned to see Rusty storming into the clearing, his face as red as the tip of his beard.

"What the bleedin' hell is goin' on," he asked, his gaze settling on our fallen leader. "Boss? Boss? Why are you lot just standin' there? Do somethin'!"

As he rushed to Marshall's side, I watched in amazement as the crumpled figure on the floor groaned, and then sat up. As he did, I saw for the first time what he was concealing beneath his jacket. It was Tyrus, his big head twisted at an awkward angle, his lips drawn tight to reveal a pink slither of tongue poking from between his teeth.

Marshall let out a groan. It was so weak that it took me a moment to realise he was using words. "It's too late," he said. "It's too late."

I leant closer, spotting the small pool of blood around Tyrus' snout, the white foam around his muzzle.

"He's fucking dead," Marshall cried, his voice ragged with emotion. For once, he wasn't wearing his sunglasses, and as he turned to look at us I saw his eyes were swollen and raw. "I found him here, shaking. Convulsing. His breath was shallow. I thought he was choking on a bone or something. But then he . . . he . . . "

As Marshall choked out another cry, I glanced down and saw the pool of brown beneath Tyrus, mingling with the rain and running in rivulets towards our feet. I took a step backwards.

201

"How old was he?" Zebee asked. "I remember when my wife's golden retriever passed. Devastated we were. The vet said —"

"Shut it, you old fool," Rusty snapped. "This weren't no natural death." Leaning closer to the dog, he jammed one of his crinkled fingers towards the dog's muzzle and into Tyrus' mouth, before retracting it and sniffing at the residue. A grim expression creased his face. "Just as I thought."

"What is it?" Marshall demanded. "What's happened to my dog, Rust?"

Rusty held his fingers out for Marshall to smell. He took one sniff and recoiled his head to spit on the floor. "Hemlock?"

Rusty nodded. "There's no doubtin' it. Poor Tyrus here wouldn't have stood a chance. Your dog's been poisoned, boss."

He turned then, still talking to Marshall, but looking at us.

"Or rather, *someone's* poisoned your dog."

Weeks passed, and still the rain didn't stop. Tyrus' death had been met with yet another round of defensive measures designed to put an end to Sneed's reign of terror. All non-security related jobs — washing, farming, cooking, repairs — were suspended in favour of increased patrols, including a doubling of the number of night shifts we were each required to take. In practice this meant that twice a week I was now on my feet for over thirty-six hours without sleep.

To make things worse, I was almost permanently wet. No matter how much gaffer tape I used to seal the gaps in my threadbare poncho or the eyelets in my boots, the rain always found a way through. My toes shrivelled in my soaking socks, my hair clung limply to my face, water dripping endlessly from my beard. Our stores of dry firewood had been depleted weeks earlier, so at the end of the day I would peel off my clothes and wring them out as best I could. I would lie naked, shivering under my blankets until morning, when I would attempt to repair any leaks that had appeared overnight, stretch my wet clothes back over my body. Then I'd trudge back out into the rain and do it all again.

In addition to the extended patrols, Rusty announced the installation of a complex range of defence systems and booby traps around the perimeter of the camp. Marshall himself, he assured us, had personally designed these measures, although since the morning Tyrus had died, our leader had once again retreated from view, leaving Rusty to oversee our work.

Nevertheless, the devices we were asked to construct certainly bore our Marshall's hallmarks: namely a mixture of ingenious bushcraft and extreme violence. Lengths of twine were twisted into tripwires and rigged at ankle height between trees, which Rusty explained would drive a wooden stake into the intruder's leg if triggered. Elsewhere, deep pits were dug and filled with rows of sharp spikes, before being covered over with a layer of twigs and dead leaves. Hopper was particularly excited about these "bear traps", explaining how he'd encountered something similar while serving overseas.

"They were originally used by the Vietcong over in 'Nam. Back then, they used fire-hardened bamboo for the spikes. The gooks would smear the tips in shit too, so even if you only got a flesh wound, you'd wind up with blood poisoning. Else they'd chuck a bunch of scorpions or snakes in there too — like getting a shitty spear through your leg wasn't bad enough. 'Course the modern version is a bit more sophisticated."

"Why?" I asked. "What do they use now?"

"A bloody big bomb," he answered with a grin.

"That what happened to your leg?" Butcher asked once we'd all stopped laughing. "One of those IEDs, was it?"

"Nah. As weird as it sounds, I wound up getting trench foot. All my toes went black. And the stink! Amputation was the only thing for it in the end. Snip-snip-snip."

Each of us looked down at our rain sodden boots, suddenly acutely aware of the water squelching between our toes. This time, nobody laughed.

One unexpected benefit of the relentlessly bad weather was that, almost overnight, our supplies of drinking water were replenished. Although the lack of dry firewood meant we were unable to boil it, in practice we simply drank fresh from the sky, holding out our mugs until they were full. While I was initially relieved to be rid of the cottonmouth that had bothered me throughout the long hot summer, within days my gratitude was forgotten in the wake of my all-consuming hunger. With the bad weather, our already meagre rations had been reduced to almost nothing at all. Each night I came back to an empty dinner table, with not even a rotten carrot or putrid potato to stave off the stomach cramps. Not that there was anything we could do about it. The constant rain had turned the farm into a swamp. The last time I'd visited — secretly, in the vain hope there might be something worth scavenging — I'd found nothing but a torrent of mud. There was no sign of the turnips, salads, spinach or radishes we'd planted in the run up to the feast, nor of the sprouts and leeks we'd sown in the spring in preparation for the cold winter months that lay ahead. There was only ruin and neglect. Polytunnels lay crushed and deflated, the bamboo trellises either snapped or washed away. The only thing left standing was the old chicken coop, its wire fence shimmering under the downpour, silently mocking us all.

Occasionally I would strike lucky and find something edible while out on patrol: a small bunch of ripe rose hips or hawthorn berries that had somehow clung on during the storms. Once I found a small patch of poppies under the shelter of a fallen tree. I harvested the dry heads, crushing them open and swallowing down the coarse parcel of seeds as quickly as I could, ever paranoid I would be stumbled upon by one of the others and forced to share my prize. For the most part though, I went hungry.

While I did my best to ignore the pain — guzzling water until my belly groaned, or chewing on a blade of grass to trick my body into thinking I was eating — the endless drudgery of patrols meant there was little to occupy my mind other than the thought of food. I began fantasising about meals from my old life, recalling in forensic detail a roast lamb dinner, or the glisten of grease atop a Chinese takeaway, or the steam escaping from a freshly cooked casserole. More than once I was subject to olfactory hallucinations, a phantom aroma of curry creeping through the trees, so realistic that as I returned home that night I dared to believe I might find Rusty bent over a bubbling pot. Of course, I was always left disappointed, greeted by nothing but the drenched darkness of the deserted camp.

One time in particular stands out among that slur of starving days. I was walking in the woods, moving as slowly as possible so as to conserve energy, when I stumbled across a wide circle of mushrooms, their globular white helmets bursting through the carpet of twigs and dead leaves. I leapt on them, tearing off a cap and inspecting it between my thumb and forefinger. To my ravenous eye, the tender flesh resembled a chicken breast. Almost without thinking I brought it up to my lips. Then I hesitated. I had eaten fungus in the park dozens of times. Boiled in a stew or sliced thin and scattered through a wild leaf salad, they were a familiar sight on our dinner plates. Alone though, without Rusty's culinary expertise, I was suddenly nervous. As a child, I had always been taught to stay clear of wild mushrooms, lest I accidentally pick a death cap or a destroying angel or a funeral bell, or any of the other terrifyingly named varieties that apparently haunted our innocent woodlands and parks. Indeed, as a father I had taught the lesson myself. I remembered well my panic when a just-toddling Olivia came back to us with an unclassified specimen clamped between her pudgy fingers, the prising of her jaws to check she hadn't eaten any, the bucket of hand sanitiser smeared on her palms, the endless waiting to check she'd be okay, the silent, desperate prayers.

I held the mushroom under my nose and sniffed. Nothing. No burning sensation at the back of my throat. No telltale poisoned perfume. I knew there were things to look for. A ring or skirt around the stem. A milky residue. An easily peeled cap. But what did they mean? I simply didn't know. As hungry as I was, I didn't want to die. I tossed it to the floor, then fell to my knees, beating my chest in anger and self-loathing. How could I be so useless after all these months? So incapable of providing for myself? In anguish, I began burrowing in the dirt, though what I hoped to find I still don't know. A worm? A pot of gold? I was delirious. As I dug, the deep black mud began to transform before me, looking suddenly as tempting as a rich chocolate cake. Before I knew what I was doing, I had shovelled an entire handful into my mouth. I chewed on the gritty soil, tasting nothing but clay as I swallowed it down. It was awful. Even so, I couldn't help but take another fist of dirt and force it down, the sensation of eating something better than nothing at all. It was only when I reached down for the third that I finally got hold of myself.

I stood up quickly and staggered from the spot, ashamed of my weakness. I leant against a tree, bent over and forced two fingers down my throat, prompting a cascade of black vomit to splatter my already filthy boots. When I had finished, I tipped my head to the sky, letting my mouth fill with water. It was raining so heavily that it was a long while before I realised I was crying.

CHAPTER
TWENTY

As bad as our physical suffering was, our mental health was in far worse shape. Since Tyrus' death, morale among the men had slumped to an all-time low. Wherever possible we went out of our way to avoid each other. Without the gravity of regular meals or campfires to pull us together, this was easier than it sounds. Depending on my shifts, I was able to go up to two days without seeing anyone at all. Conversations, when they did occur, were clipped and to the point. Nobody was keen to expend any more energy than was strictly necessary. Besides, we were wary of each other. Though it was never openly acknowledged, the rules had changed. It was every man for himself now. Or at least, every mouth for itself. We became paranoid and suspicious, permanently convinced that everyone else was eating more than us, that they had somehow found a secret stash of supplies and were keeping it to themselves.

Of course in retrospect — and with a clear mind — it's obvious we were all equal partners in adversity. In the months since the summer, we'd all grown visibly thinner, the meat slipping from our bones with every passing day, until our ribs protruded alarmingly through our wet shirts and we were forced to tie our trousers with ever-tightening nooses of rope.

We suffered in other ways too. Things not so easy to see. I was tired all the time, and prone to dizzy spells. I couldn't get warm and I stopped going to the toilet. My thinking was muddled. Several times I caught myself mumbling strange, broken phrases, or else repeating my own name, over and over again, a subliminal reminder to the world that I was still there, that I still existed.

"Adam, Adam, Adam, Adam . . . "

Still, I was by no means the worst off. Zebee, for instance, seemed especially ill. As the eldest in the group, he'd taken the decline in conditions the hardest. His brown skin grew eerily pale, taking on a translucent quality. He developed a persistent hacking cough that announced his arrival long before he came limping into view. After the first few weeks, Rusty excused him from patrols altogether. On night shifts I would hear his wheezes echoing through the camp. Privately I wondered how long it would be before we woke one morning to find his tent had fallen permanently silent.

Much to my pleasure, Butcher had also taken ill, having succumbed to some violent gastrointestinal disorder. In fact, his sickness was one of the few common talking points among the men, especially once a rumour — originating with Fingers — went round that Butcher had fallen sick after finding and eating a dead rat. ("Greedy bastard kept the whole thing for himself too!" Fingers was quick to point out.)

Whether or not it was true I never found out. Still, the sound of Butcher's cries as he crashed through the trees in the direction of Squit Creek never failed to raise a bitter smile.

The only other topic of conversation was Sneed. Despite the hardships we faced, the murder of Tyrus seemed to have silenced for good any reservations we had about Marshall's leadership. Instead our vitriol was reserved solely for the coward who had caused our comfortable world to disintegrate before our eyes. Not content with simply telling and retelling the stories of his many heinous crimes, we shamelessly revised history in order to accommodate his sheer wickedness. By this point, for example, I'd been entirely written out of the story of the swan. The way it was now framed, Sneed had been alone when he'd killed "our sacred bird", our eating of which had also been conveniently forgotten. It was Sneed who had built the effigy of Marshall and sneaked it onto the bonfire. Not only had he murdered our chickens and poisoned poor Tyrus — that noble and universally adored saint of a mutt — but there were now half a dozen men who would willingly swear they had witnessed him do so. It was Sneed's fault that the fruit had rotted on the branches. It was down to him that the farm had fallen into disrepair. He was held responsible for the stink of our breath and the rumble in our bellies, the ache of our backs and the blisters on our feet. Even the rain was deemed to be his doing.

Once or twice I asked around, trying to establish what had happened the previous autumn, or the one before. Were things always this desperate? Was starvation an annual event? The answers I received in return were as blunt as they were unlikely.

"We had more food than we knew what to do with."

"It was five-course dinners, three times a day."

"We had rabbit and pheasant."

"Duck and deer."

"Every year we had blazing sun until December."

"Indian summers."

"We all got along quite happily. Until he came."

Yes, the one thing everybody agreed on was that Sneed was the source of all our misery and if only we could find him, then all our trouble would be over. Food would grow. The sun would shine. Marshall would return to lead us again.

And so we kept going, day after day, swallowing down our hunger as we searched the woods and the fields for signs of life, with only our hatred keeping us upright, only our anger keeping us marching on.

One afternoon I was standing near the old boating lake. I'd half hoped I might be able to catch a fish, but after an hour or so of poking around with a stick there was no sign of any life there. Now, I stood staring out over the water.

To my surprise, I'd woken that morning to find it had finally stopped raining. Over the weeks I'd grown accustomed to the steady static crackle of rain falling on wet leaves, and its sudden absence left the world feeling out of balance, like the whine of tinnitus following a loud concert. Still, it was a pleasant novelty to dispense of my poncho for once. And, while it was by no means warm, the thin bars of blue sky that fractured the gloom gave rise to an unfamiliar optimism in me. Perhaps that Indian Summer was on its way after all. One last hurrah of sunshine that would burn away the dark clouds that had gathered around our little tribe ever since that fateful Midsummer night.

I don't know how long I stood there by the lake. Everything remained motionless. A photograph. A still-life painting. Suddenly a sound rang out, echoing across the water. Birds took to the skies in fright. A breeze blew. The park was awake.

I was slow to react at first. My head felt as waterlogged as the earth, hearing muffled, my vision blurred. The noise came again. This time I heard it more clearly. It sounded like a cry. It sounded human. I began walking towards it.

I didn't bother keeping to the bushes. They were too sparse to conceal me anyway, their leaves having long ago withered and turned to mulch. If Sneed wanted to kill me, let him try. At least it would be over, one way or another. The cry came again. I staggered onwards, dragging my spear behind me.

I was a few metres from the play park when I spotted her, standing with her back to me. The scuffed school blazer, the brown hair. It could only be one person. She tipped back her head and called out again.

"Da-ddy!"

The word rang out bright and true. It vibrated inside my head and around my gut. It diffused through my bloodstream and breached my cell walls. This was not "Dad", you understand, that throwaway, monosyllabic

213

grunt of begrudging familiarity. No, it was "Daddy". Deliberate, babyish. Even Flynn hardly used it anymore. It must have been over a decade since I'd last heard it fall from Olivia's lips. And yet here she was, standing in the park with her hands cupped to her mouth, calling for her daddy. Without another thought, I let the spear fall to the floor and ran to her.

I was fifteen feet away when she finally turned to face me. I had meant to hug her, to smother her in kisses, but something in her face stopped me in my tracks. Fear, maybe. Or pity. I dropped my arms, flinching under the scorch of her gaze.

"Ollie?"

"Oh, Dad," she said, the second syllable conspicuous by its absence, the spell broken now that she was faced by this filthy, malnourished imposter. I knew what the missing "y" meant. I was not the man she'd been calling for. I felt embarrassed for us both.

"You look . . . " She stopped, forcing herself to meet my eyes. "How have you been?" Her tone shifted as she battled to maintain her composure. The wall had gone up again. She was making conversation with a stranger now, choosing her words carefully. I was a door-to-door salesman, a pensioner at the bus stop. Despite her efforts, at distance her eyes still gave her away. They sparkled in the fading light; a kohl-blackened dam that might breach at any moment.

"You know. Not too bad," I mumbled, keen to move things along as her bottom lip gave an involuntary tremble. "How's Flynn getting on? And your mum?"

Her face flashed sourly, the polite young woman instantly replaced by a surly teenager. "You know," she said, parroting me. "Not too bad."

A spiky silence rattled between us as I struggled for something to fill the void. I'd spent so much time alone recently that the words wouldn't come, my thoughts muddled and unwieldy. I realised it would take practice if I was going to learn how to be a person again.

"Listen, Ollie . . . " I said, stalling for time.

"I brought something for you," she said blankly, holding up a small white carrier bag, the handles coiled around her skinny wrist.

I reached out, not taking my eyes from her. She had changed yet again, her timid movements transforming her back into a little girl. She seemed stuck between two places, one foot firmly planted in her childhood, the other tentatively toeing the future. I envied the options still open to her.

"Thanks," I said as I took the bag. Before I could open it, however, there was a crash from somewhere nearby. A bird maybe? Or something far, far worse?

Though Olivia didn't seem to notice, my whole body froze as I strained to listen. The fog in my brain temporarily parted, Butcher's threats rushing back to choke me.

They'll be nothing left of her by the time we've finished.

The crash came again, closer this time. There was no mistaking it. Somebody was coming.

"You shouldn't be here," I said gruffly. "You need to leave."

215

Olivia's face flushed with confusion, the dam creaking. A single tear escaped, trailing silently along the curve of her nose. "What? But I thought . . . "

The crash came again. Whoever was coming would be here in less than a minute. There was no time for my heart to break. "I said GO!"

She backed away then, doubling the distance between us. "You don't even know what day it is, do you?"

Nearby, footsteps pounded the mud. "Please, Olivia," I begged. "Please just go. Now."

Finally, she seemed to make a decision. Though still crying, her expression hardened into something like contempt. "Yeah. Well. I don't know what I expected from a loser like you," she said, her nostrils flaring in anger. "Happy birthday, Adam."

And with that she turned and stormed away.

Later on, while I lay shivering in my tent, I would replay this scene over and over again, her words, and the look that accompanied them, like a serrated blade to my gut. I would wonder why I didn't simply go with her, why I let that lone spark of warmth and generosity slip so carelessly from my grasp. Right then, however, I was too relieved to have her out of harm's way for the words to really sink in.

As I watched her go, I gradually became aware of the carrier bag she'd given me, still gripped tightly in my hand. I opened it a fraction and peaked inside to see a handmade card, a large box of chocolates and — Olivia's idea of a joke — a stick of deodorant. I closed the bag and stuffed it into the folds of my jacket. No sooner had I finished stashing it away, did I hear somebody clear their throat directly behind me.

I spun around to find not Butcher, but Ox. He didn't move, eyeing me like a starving cat might watch a caged canary. The hungry days and weeks had done little to diminish his stature. He towered above me, looking down. I wondered how long he'd been standing there.

"Hey, Ox," I said, doing my best to keep it light. "How's it going?"

Still the big man didn't answer. His eyes flickered past me. It took all of my willpower not to turn to check Olivia was safely out of view. Finally, he looked back at me and let out a long sigh. "Boss wants to see you," he said.

"Me?" I said, already a guilty sweat prickling at my neck. "Why? What have I done?"

Ox stared at me quizzically for a moment, some unknown calculations grinding behind those big empty eyes. "Not you," he said eventually. "All of us. He has an announcement. Something big."

"Oh. Right. Well, come on then," I said. I started back towards the camp, eager to put as much distance between us and Olivia as possible.

"So what does Rusty want then?" I asked as we lumbered through the trees.

"Not Rusty," he said, shaking his head. "Marshall."

"Marshall's back?"

Ox nodded, his lips parting to reveal a set of horrible yellow teeth. I realised he was smiling. "Yeah," he said. "They're saying he's caught Sneed."

CHAPTER
TWENTY-ONE

I followed Ox to the old marl pit. Despite the drizzle, the faint orange glow of a fire was visible between the branches. As we descended the bank I caught the acrid scent of petrol on the breeze. Sure enough, as we reached the bottom I saw Marshall hunched over a small campfire, a green jerry can at his feet. The others were clustered around him in an excited semicircle, waiting for the show to begin.

This was the first time I'd returned to the pit since the disaster of the Midsummer Feast. In the wet months that had passed, the ground had transformed into a bog. As we splashed our way through the darkness towards the small circle of light, nobody turned to look at us. I took my place silently between Hopper and Al Pacino, scanning the rapt faces of the men who surrounded me. To my surprise, everyone was there, even Zebee. In the weeks since I'd last seen him, he'd grown even frailer, the flickering firelight carving dark shadows in his sunken cheeks.

It wasn't just Zebee. The months of depravation had taken its toll on all of us. Fingers — who after all this time still wore shorts, having not found a replacement for the trousers we'd burned — looked like he hadn't slept in weeks, his eyes bruised black. Al Pacino, meanwhile, was as dishevelled as I'd ever seen him, his ordinarily immaculate clothes torn and filthy, his hair wild, his beard matted. Hopper appeared little better off, the gap between his trouser and boot revealing the warped plastic and rusting joints of his disintegrating prosthetic foot. Butcher, I noted with satisfaction, looked perhaps worse than anyone else, having apparently befallen some sort of accident. A nasty scratch ran from the bottom of his ear to the corner of his mouth, giving him a permanent, lopsided grin. It looked like he might have lost a couple of teeth too, though I couldn't be certain in the poor light. Even Rusty seemed to have lost weight, though it was difficult to tell beneath his mane of hair, which by now engulfed his entire upper body, as thick and tangled as Bruno's tail.

Despite their bedraggled appearances, all of the men seemed surprisingly upbeat, the firelight picking out a wall of wet lips and gleaming eyes as they turned to Marshall in anticipation. Rusty was positively beaming. I guess it wasn't hard to see why they were excited. After months of only fleeting views, our leader had become something of a ghost about the camp. He was a myth, a shadow, his earthly wishes communicated to Rusty alone. To have him physically before us once again — no matter how lean he had grown in the intervening months — represented the fulfilling of a promise, a righting of wrongs. His return could only mean one thing: justice was coming.

219

Marshall stood facing the fire, his head bowed, as if deep in prayer. I could just see the top of his sunglasses, the flames reflected in his lenses. In one hand was the gun. I wondered if he was planning to use it.

Minutes passed in silence as we waited for something to happen. We watched Marshall watching the fire. Still he didn't move. I began to grow restless, and sensed a similar twitchiness among the other men. Was it really possible that he'd captured the traitor Sneed? Perhaps Ox had got it wrong? I glanced nervously at the bushes around us, unable to see anything but darkness. After months of fruitlessly searching the park, it felt unnecessarily cruel to make us wait any longer. Glancing back over at Rusty, I saw his smile had become stretched, an impatient crease forming between the tufts of his eyebrows.

Finally, as if responding to some unseen signal, Marshall jerked into life. He straightened up and looked around, as if only noticing us for the first time. Then, without a word, he stooped slightly and swapped the gun for the jerry can, unscrewing the cap. Again I was hit by the smell of petrol as he poured out a small measure and flung it towards the dwindling fire. The response was immediate. A bloom of orange and red erupted from the hearth, basking us all in a brief blaze of heat.

"It's amazing," Marshall said, finally breaking his silence once the flames had settled down. "The difference a fire can make to a long night. It doesn't matter how cold or tired or miserable you are, the moment you see that glow, you know you're going to be alright. You know you're home."

We all nodded in agreement. I had forgotten the unique power of a campfire to bewitch an evening. Suspended in that golden bubble of light, the warmth radiating through my bones, it was easy to forget there was any world beyond this small band of men. And yet waiting in the shadows, possibly only a few feet away, was the man who had sought to destroy us all. I held my breath.

"Our earliest ancestors understood how important it was to keep the home fires burning," Marshall continued. "That which illuminates our path. That which feeds and nourishes. That which keeps the wickedness of the world at bay. They knew that without that spark, that light, that heat, they were nothing. It was what separated them from the apes. It made people out of beasts. And knowing that, they did whatever it damn well took to make sure the fire never went out. Day or night, they had somebody stand on post and watch over it. They fed it. They nurtured it. They respected the fire. And in turn, it respected them. Yet somewhere along the way we forgot to do the same. We took it for granted. We got complacent. We forgot, on those balmy summer evenings, just how easily the flames can be stomped out."

At this point he swung out a boot, scattering a meteor shower of orange ashes in our direction, which sent Bruno yelping away into the darkness. Marshall unscrewed the jerry can and flung another capful. Immediately the fire sprung back into life.

221

"There's no point in pretending, boys. We've been lost lately. Cold and hungry and stumbling around in the dark. I hardly need to remind you of the horrors we've seen along the way. Our farm destroyed. Our animals dead. We even lost dear Tyrus. Our flame became nothing but a flicker."

There was a murmur from the crowd, as they sensed Marshall finally hitting his stride. I glanced over at Rusty, who's grin was now frozen in rictus, his eyes blazing with something like hunger.

"But tonight, we're here to put all of that behind us!" With this, he hurled another capful of petrol toward the fire, so that it roared more fiercely than ever. "Tonight we build the fire afresh. And this time we'll keep it burning! Are you with me?"

We gave a wild cheer, our faces glowing in the firelight.

"Are you with me?" he asked again.

We grew louder still, beating our chests, howling at the moon.

"Good," said Marshall once we had fallen quiet. "I knew I could count on you. But first there is business to attend to. Before we can build a brighter fire tomorrow, we must first sweep away the ashes of the past . . ."

He paused and turned from us then, calling to the darkness outside the circle, speaking to the shadows and the trees. "Are you coming out then? Or do I drag you out myself?"

Nobody spoke. The silence was so complete that for a moment I fancied my heartbeat was audible through

222

my jacket. Everyone followed Marshall's gaze, though nothing seemed to stir.

And then, so slowly that at first I thought it was a trick of the light, a figure appeared. It was Sneed.

CHAPTER
TWENTY-TWO

He looked different to how I remembered him. Shorter, but fatter too. Unlike the rest of us, he actually appeared to have a put on a significant amount of weight, his face bloated, his eyes puffy. As he shuffled towards the light, I saw he was no longer dressed in army surplus, but instead sported a grey tracksuit top and jogging bottoms, the tags still dangling on the outside. With his hair cut short to his head and skin scrubbed clean, he resembled a sort of oversized toddler. I remember thinking it was funny that someone so soft and inoffensive could have haunted my dreams for so long. In fact, he would almost have been unrecognisable, if it wasn't for those enormous eyes bulging from his skull, the extra weight he'd piled on somehow rendering them bigger and more reptilian than ever. As he turned slightly, I saw that one of his eyes was underlined with a dark bruise, as if he'd been recently hit.

There was a faint but perceptible ripple of movement among the crowd as Sneed drew closer, a silent bristling of muscles. Even Bruno seemed to sense it as he slunk back to Rusty's side, a low growl catching at the back of his throat. To see the receptacle of our collective hatred in the flesh after all these months was a surreal experience. Sneed seemed to sense the animosity in the air. With each step towards us he grew visibly smaller, his hunch becoming more pronounced, as if he were attempting to climb inside his own body. Not once did he look up from his feet, which I noticed were also clad in a pair of new trainers. As he reached the far edge of the circle, he stopped, his shadow unravelling in the firelight, stretching out beneath him. With a solemn nod, Marshall turned back to us to speak.

"What is it that makes a good leader?" he began. "It's a question I've asked myself constantly over the past few weeks. A question to which there are no easy answers. Lately though, I've come to the conclusion that *one* of the most important qualities of a good leader is the wisdom to admit when you've got something wrong, and, more importantly" — and here he took a small but definite step towards Sneed — "the courage to put those things right."

We all nodded vigorously, bracing ourselves for the inevitable explosion of violence.

"Before we get into that, however, I'd like to explain how it is I came to track down this slippery young fellow. Now, as I'm sure you all know, I've spent a good deal of my time recently engaged in a series of covert operations. It's been a tough couple of months. But, after calling in a few favours with some former colleagues, I finally had a break through last week and made contact with Sneed, who I discovered has been staying in a hostel not two miles from this very spot."

225

We looked again in disgust at the flabby figure at the edge of the circle. That he had chosen walls and windows, a soft bed and a full belly, over life with us came as little surprise. As far as we were concerned, he deserved everything that was coming to him, though what form that punishment would take I couldn't imagine. One thousand laps around the park would hardly scratch the surface, especially now there was no Tyrus to nip at his heels. Neither was cutting his rations an option, seeing as there were no longer any rations to cut. No, Sneed would have to find another, more substantial way to pay for his crimes. We turned back to Marshall, eager to hear the specific details of the penance that was to be handed down.

"As you can imagine, he was more than a little surprised to see me. I admit we got off to a what you might call a bumpy start."

There was a dark gurgle of laughter as we glanced again at Sneed's bruised eye.

"But I'm a fair man. After we'd overcome our initial *teething* problems, we did manage to talk properly. Actually, we spoke for hours. And what I heard rocked me to my very core."

Marshall took another step towards Sneed. Close enough to crush his windpipe, or bury a blade in his chest.

"That's why," he continued, "in front of all of you gathered here tonight, I would like to prove my leadership once and for all, by making amends for the biggest mistake I've made since I arrived here. Perhaps the biggest mistake of my life full stop."

226

We watched as Marshall's hand snaked out, closing the distance between him and Sneed. Rather than grabbing him by the throat, however, it rested gently on his shoulder.

"On behalf of everyone here, I'd like to apologise," Marshall said. "We got it wrong. I got it wrong. I know now you've done nothing wrong and, if you're interested, you're more than welcome to take your place alongside us, here in the park."

Sneed finally lifted his head. To my surprise, I saw what looked like tears shimmering in those bulging, alien eyes.

At this point, Rusty could contain himself no longer. Breaking rank, he took one lurching footstep over the fire, so that he was stood directly between the two men. "What the bleedin' heck are you talkin' about? What about the chickens? What about Tyrus?"

Marshall smiled generously. "Ah, Rusty. I was just getting to that. You see, once Sneed and I had a chance to talk, I realised it was all just an unfortunate misunderstanding."

"Misunderstanding? He murdered my bloody birds!"

"No, he didn't. Your birds were killed. No one's disputing that. But there's not one shred of evidence to suggest that Sneed was involved. In fact, I've seen evidence to the contrary. Hostel records, dated and stamped. He wasn't here, Rust. Now, maybe those bloody foxes got in again, or . . . "

"Foxes!" Rusty interrupted. "Bleedin' foxes? Will you listen to yourself, boss? It doesn't even begin to make sense. Now I suppose you're going to try and convince me that foxes upped and poisoned Tyrus too, did they?"

Marshall's smile remained, yet his eyes were cold. "I'm not here to argue with you Rusty. I'm here to tell you we got the wrong man. Now, in the spirit of reconciliation, I'd like the two of you to shake hands so we can draw a line under this and move on. Okay?"

Rusty didn't move. From my spot on the far side of the fire I was unable to see his face, but his shoulders seemed frozen around his ears.

"RUSTY!" Marshall barked.

This time Rusty did move, his arm coming up in slow motion.

Only he didn't shake Sneed's hand.

Instead he reached up and grabbed Sneed by each of his ears. A look of realisation, then horror flashed across Sneed's face.

There was a sound like wet fabric being ripped as Rusty yanked his hands away. At the same time Sneed's eyes bulged wider than ever and he made an "o" shape with his mouth, though no sound came out. To his left, Marshall raised both his hands in the air and held them there, as if unsure whether to reach for Rusty or Sneed, and instead did neither. For a moment nobody moved or said anything, the three of them frozen together in a strange tableau. Finally, Rusty turned back to face us. Pinched between each of his thumbs and forefingers was a bloody ear, looking oddly limp and shrivelled now they were no longer connected to Sneed's head. He considered them for a moment and then, with a grim nod of satisfaction, he tossed them to Bruno, who

228

leapt up and swallowed them both in one spluttering bite.

Bruno's jaws snapping shut acted like a starting gun. At once Sneed let out a horrifying scream, clutching the side of his head as he attempted to stem the blood that was steadily streaming down the side of his neck, staining the collar of his new tracksuit. Marshall too started shouting, though he was too shocked to either form proper words or move. Instead he stood rooted to the spot, barking a stream of nonsensical threats and curses. Rusty merely shook his head though. He was a weary workman now, no more, no less. Here was a problem. Here was a solution. From somewhere in his jacket a tool was fetched. Then, with an almost bored expression on his face, he turned to the still squealing Sneed, slashed, and then did the same to Marshall. The entire operation was over in less than two seconds. When he stepped back both men's throats gaped open.

Again the tableau was fixed: Rusty holding the knife by his side, Sneed and Marshall too stunned to react. A dark fountain cascaded down their chests as their tongues attempted to escape their mouths. While Sneed clutched his neck, I saw Marshall struggling to make sense of the situation. Somewhere along the line he'd lost his sunglasses, and I watched as his face cycled rapidly through a range of emotions: disbelief, anger, self-pity and, finally, resignation. His eyes rolled white in their sockets. And then, as if by some prior agreement, the pair of them crumpled in tandem, an oddly graceful movement. They knelt for a moment, tottered, and then fell face first into the dirt, close enough to kiss. They twitch-twitch-twitched. And then they twitched no more.

We didn't move.

"He had it comin'," Rusty said eventually, though he didn't specify which of the dead men he was referring to.

Still no one moved.

After a while I caught the scent of smoke on the breeze. Singed hair, with an undertone of burnt bacon. I looked down and saw Marshall's arm had somehow landed in the fire, his sleeve now silently smouldering, the tips of his fingers already turning black in the flames. Another moment passed and the smell grew stronger, turning my stomach. It was so bad I was about to step forwards and kick the arm free, when Fingers spoke out. "Well, I suppose we should bury them then?"

Everyone turned to look at him.

"What?" he said. "We can't just leave them here, can we?"

At last Rusty turned to face us. He was still holding the knife, a military-style dagger I'd never seen before, its serrated blade engineered to inflict the maximum possible damage to its victims. "I'm not sure that is the best idea, actually," he said, licking his lips. "I mean, it seems a cryin' shame to let good meat go to waste, eh?"

I looked around at the men to try and gauge whether Rusty was joking, but they had already begun to move, shoving and jostling each other to claim their place around the bodies. Even Zebee looked re-energised, clawing his way between Ox and Butcher to get to

Rusty, who by then had knelt alongside Marshall and begun to hack at the charred arm. At the sight of more blood they fell on him, moving as a pack, snorting and grunting as they tore into the flesh.

I stayed where I was for a moment, watching the scene. Someone had hacked off the rest of Sneed's head and tossed it into the fire. He stared out at me from the flames until his eyeballs began to melt. It was time to leave.

I started to back away. The men were too busy on the floor to notice me. I kept walking, the coolness of the night a relief as I dissolved into the shadows.

And then I stopped.

Rusty had stood up and was peering in my direction, his hand cupped to his eyes, his white beard smeared red. For a moment I wasn't sure if he could see me. And then he spoke.

"And where do you think you're goin'?"

WINTER

CHAPTER
TWENTY-THREE

At first light the men blinked and looked up at each other. The carnival had lasted all night. For hours, the dancing and screaming had hardly let up. They had decorated the trees with entrails. They had painted their faces with gore. All of the petrol had been used up to keep the fire going. For the most part I had sat motionless beside Rusty, having feigned illness as an excuse for my lack of appetite. Every now and then I would glance upwards, trying to distract myself from the constant crunching of gristle, the slurping of marrow. The sky though was black and unknowable, not a single star penetrating the darkness. I felt as if a bag had been forced over my head, as if I had been kidnapped and bundled into a speeding car. I stayed still and tried to say as little as possible, weighing up whether or not I should stay put or risk making a break for it. Either way, I realised, I was probably dead.

Just after dawn, when the fire had eventually burnt itself down to a black smudge on the grass, there was a lull in the madness. The men seemed stoned from the meat and sat dazed and awkward, avoiding eye contact with each other. Whereas only an hour earlier they had howled and hollered songs with their arms around each other's necks, daybreak had shrouded everything in shame. The spell was broken, and now they seemed embarrassed by the bloody remains that surrounded them. Without speaking, a few of the men got up and began to gather up the inedible parts — the clothing, boots, a length of shinbone, Marshall's charred skull — and piled them together next to the fire.

"What're you doin'?" Rusty asked.

Ox shrugged. "Thought maybe we could burn it? Can't leave it around here, can we? What if someone came?"

"Who's gonna come round 'ere?" Rusty snapped. "Besides we're out of petrol. You won't get that lot lit. Even if you did it wouldn't be hot enough. Them crematoriums get up to about a thousand degrees. Nah. I say we dig a hole and bury him next to his dog. He'd have liked that."

Everyone agreed this was the best solution. And, taking off his poncho and using it as a makeshift sack, Ox began to clear the body parts and clothing away. As he reached Sneed's tracksuit however, Rusty stopped him again.

"Now what the bleedin' hell are you doin'?"

Ox looked up, confused. "What?"

"I said we'd bury the gaffer. I didn't say nothin' about bringing that treacherous scumbag up to the farm. I won't have his decomposin' whatsits pollutin' my land. Our vegetables grow in that soil. You want to be eatin' that muck?"

Ox hesitated, the bloodstained jacket still in his hand. For a second I thought he might point out the

236

bits of Sneed that were still stuck in Rusty's beard, but in the end he simply nodded and tossed the jacket to the floor. "So what do you want us to do with him then?"

"Who cares?" Rusty shrugged. "Leave him for the rats."

We stood around the grave, peering down. It was a grim sight. Although situated next to the mounds that contained Tyrus and the chickens, it was only about half their length, on account of there being so little left of Marshall to bury. Ox had carved out the hole with a few quick slices of the soil and then stood back as Butcher dumped the whole poncho inside. Bruno let out a couple of quick barks, earning him a sharp slap on the snout, before we all leant forward and peered down. A couple of pieces had slopped out as the poncho had hit the bottom, including a pale hand, severed just below the wrist. It looked faintly absurd lying there like that, dirt still visible under the yellowing nails, a gold signet ring glistening on the little finger. I found myself wondering who had given him the ring, and when. Was it a gift from a lover? An inheritance from a parent? I'd never thought to ask. Now I never would.

I looked down. My own fingernails were equally filthy, though my platinum wedding band still gleamed in defiance. Burying my hand in my pocket, I felt a sharp bulge in my stomach, remembering for the first time the bag containing Olivia's birthday card and gifts, tucked into the top of my trousers. I decided then and there that no matter what happened, I would not end up in the ground alongside Marshall. I would not be the fourth mound. I would see my daughter again.

When I looked up, Rusty was staring at me. For a moment I thought I'd given myself away, that he was going to challenge me. Instead he opened his arms in a wide, Marshall-like gesture and addressed us all.

"I've never liked funerals, me. Nah, miserable business, ain't they? No wonder everyone has to go and get themselves steamin' drunk right away afterwards so they can try and forget about it." He paused, allowing himself a little chuckle, before growing serious again. "But I know they're important too. You've got to say goodbye, haven't you? So you can move on. They're also a good chance to get things off your chest I find. Clear the air and whatnot. Therefore, if anyone's got anythin' they've been wantin' to say, either to me or the gaffer, I'd suggest this is the time to say it, or for ever shut their gob . . . "

I felt Rusty's gaze once again burning into me, challenging me to open my mouth. In the end, however, it was not me but Hopper who spoke.

"Do you think we did the right thing?"

There was a rustling as everyone turned round to look at him. Like the rest of the men, his beard and lips were stained red. His voice sounded weak, his eyes squinting with worry.

"What's that then?" Rusty snapped.

"I just mean with the gaffer. With the whole . . . With everything that happened."

Rusty nodded. "I see what you mean, sonny. And I want you to know somethin'. I want you *all* to know somethin'. We didn't kill the gaffer. Not on your nelly. If it was anyone who put a knife to his throat, it was that freak Sneed. Fillin' his head with all that guff about foxes and whatnot. He should have finished him off the second he got a chance instead of sittin' there listenin' to him. 'Course, I wouldn't be surprised if Sneed slipped a little somethin' in his tea to make him a little more suggestible."

"What do you mean?" asked Hopper.

"I dunno. I just read somethin' about herbal preparations that can do that to a man. Voodoo, I mean. Like them Haitian witchdoctors use. Else he could've been hypnotised . . . "

"You really think Sneed knew about that stuff?" Fingers asked.

Rusty shrugged. "All I'm sayin' is it wouldn't surprise me is all. And we all know the gaffer was a little . . . sensitive about things."

Everyone nodded at this.

"So you see," Rusty continued, "when I say you don't have to feel bad about this, I really do mean that. Sneed killed the boss and we killed Sneed. That's all there is to it."

We stood quietly for a moment, staring down at the pale, disembodied hand. It was still raining and the hole had begun to fill with water, a black puddle that lapped at Marshall's fingers.

"Right then," Rusty said at last. "I suppose we'd better fill the poor bastard in."

Without a word, Ox began shovelling again, and within a minute all that was left of Marshall was a small mountain of earth. Once Ox had stamped it down a bit, Rusty hoisted up the rifle and let off a single shot salute — "I'd do twenty-one but I've gotta think about the ammo" — before we once again fell silent.

A few minutes passed and I began to grow aware of just how cold I was. Last night's fire was now a distant memory as I felt the familiar squelch of water between my toes, the prickle of rain on my neck. After a while I realised that Rusty and a few of the others were staring at me again. It was a look I'd seen before, in casinos and bookies around the world. They were weighing me up, mentally shaking me down as they tried to decide what I was hiding, what I was worth — how dangerous I was.

In my old life I did everything I could to blend in, to hide any defining features. My suits were well cut but not flashy. I opted for muted tones; beige, navy, black. My hair was average length, average colour. I had no tattoos, piercings or visible scars. I'd once been told that the best gamblers are invisible. They do not chomp on cigars or go around with a harem of hookers. They do not wear Cuban heels or ace of spades cufflinks. They melt into the background. They are impossible to read. Here though, I felt exposed, my blood-free fingers and face marking me out as different. As an outsider. Again I thought about making a bolt for the trees, before Fingers suddenly interrupted my thoughts.

"What about the gaffer's place?" he asked.

We turned to him blankly.

"The tree house."

"What about it?" Rusty asked.

"Well, shouldn't we go and sort it out? Now that he's . . . You know. Gone."

A rippled of excitement stirred through the circle. Now there was no Marshall, there was nothing to stop us trampling over this prohibited space, the only no-go zone in the entire park. There was no reason not to go and discover for ourselves the forbidden treasures he'd undoubtedly been keeping from us all this time. The *food* he'd been keeping from us.

We all seemed to arrive at this final possibility simultaneously, for Rusty was quick to try and quell our excitement. "Well, I don't know about that. I'm sure there's nothin' up there that can't wait a few days for the dust to settle. Poor bugger's only been in the ground five minutes." He paused, scratching his beard with exaggerated indifference. "Still, now that you mention it, maybe I should go up and check everything's in order. Just in case, y'know?"

"I don't think so," Butcher answered.

Rusty's smile evaporated. "What do you mean?"

"If anyone goes up, it should be me," said Fingers.

"How'd you work that one out?" asked Al Pacino.

"Yeah," said Hopper. "How's that fair?"

"If anyone goes," said Ox, his booming voice instantly drowning the others out, "we all go."

Everyone agreed with that, and so, with an increasing sense of panic we turned our back on the grave and began to walk, then jog, then run in the direction of the camp.

As we drew nearer, the jostling intensified, the men clawing at each other as they raced to be the first to the rope ladder. For a brief moment I thought I might be able to slip away unnoticed. Before I had a chance, however, I felt a tight pinch around my upper arm. It was Rusty.

"Thought I'd lost you for a second there, sonny!" he grinned.

I laughed and showed my teeth, my stomach a hollow pit.

We surged through the camp as one, a cheer going up as the tree house came into sight. The men swarmed around it, Al Pacino getting there first, though as he attempted to haul himself up, the others began clambering over him. They tugged at his legs and tried to dislodge him. I stood back for a moment and watched the writhing human chain ascend the rope ladder, before I felt the butt of the rifle pressing into my back.

"After you, sonny."

I dutifully took hold of the ladder and pulled myself onto the first rung, ducking to avoid Hopper's false leg, which thrashed behind him as he attempted to drag himself up. Below me I could hear Bruno snarling. I kept going, putting one hand in front of another, the wind whipping my face, the rope cutting into my fingers, up, up, up.

By the time I reached the top there was hardly any room to get inside the small, nest-like structure

Marshall had constructed up in the tree. Glancing back over the side I saw Rusty was still only halfway up. It was even higher than it looked from the ground, the platform creaking unnervingly under the weight of so many people. I turned away and squeezed past Hopper, stooping to enter the dimly lit room.

It took a second for my eyes to adjust. The floor was uneven, an amateurish patchwork of random wooden planks and rickety-looking fence panels. Large gaps ran along the length of the structure, wide enough that if you were to drop something, it would likely slip through and plunge to the ground below. The walls and ceiling were even more primitive, a few flimsy supporting beams holding up a canopy of woven twigs and branches through which the morning sun streamed in. A few squares of tarpaulin had been strung up at strategic angles, while in one corner it looked like an attempt at wattle and daub had been abandoned. Architectural quirks aside, there was very little else to see. There was certainly no sign of a secret food mountain, or booze, or weapons, or anything else that might conceivably be of use to us. The men stood huddled together around a single khaki sleeping bag and pillow, which, apart from a small pile of underwear, appeared to be his only possessions. The place was empty.

Behind us, Rusty finally appeared at the door. "Well?" he asked, doubling over to catch his breath.

Butcher shook his head. "Nothing. Not even a lousy porno mag. The guy lived like a fucking monk!"

It was true. Outside the wind rattled through the bone-bare branches of the tree, while underneath us the old planks of wood creaked their discontent.

"So," said Fingers eventually. "What do we do now?"

CHAPTER
TWENTY-FOUR

Now that Sneed was gone, the days quickly lost their shape, stretching out into long, aimless weeks. Without the need to constantly patrol the park, I found I spent longer and longer curled up under a blanket, trying my best to fend off the bitter wind that swept through the camp and shook loose the final few leaves that had clung stubbornly to the hunched black trees. For hours at a time I would lie there listening to the whip and rustle of the faded canvas above my head, trying to block out the endless griping of my stomach.

The first thing I'd done when I got back to my tent after the "funeral" was to take out the card, the deodorant and the small box of Quality Street that Olivia had brought me. Without thinking I unwrapped six and swallowed them whole. I probably would have devoured the entire box if it wasn't for my body's intervention. It had been so long since I'd eaten anything at this point that the sudden introduction of so much sugar triggered an instant reaction in my gut. I was struck by a debilitating cramp, as if I'd swallowed six shards of glass. When I finally recovered enough to sit up, I emptied the remainder of the box onto my bed. There were twenty-eight chocolates left in all, the various shades of metallic foil glistening like treasure. I stashed the contraband inside my pillow, having decided to ration myself to two a day, enough for two weeks. After that I figured I had two choices: starve or escape.

The latter, however, was to prove more difficult than I could have possibly imagined. While Rusty had claimed the tree house as his own and now spent much of his time there, I quickly discovered I was still never left alone for a second. On the first night after Marshall and Sneed's murder, I lay awake once it got dark. When I was certain that no one was around, I got up and slipped on my boots, before stuffing my sleeping bag with my sheets, hoping to buy myself a couple of hours should anyone happen to glance in on me. Then, with a final deep breath, I stepped out into the night, ready to sprint as fast as I could.

"Alright there, mate?"

I looked up to find Butcher leaning against a tree opposite my tent. In his hand he held a wooden spear, his scar exaggerating the leer on his face. "Going somewhere?"

"Just . . . struggling to sleep."

He nodded, not believing me.

"What about you?" I asked quickly. "I thought the night watch had finished now?"

Butcher shrugged. "Rust said he thought we might as well keep it going. Just to make sure everyone was safe."

"Oh. Well. That makes sense I suppose."

We stood in silence for another moment, each of us despising the other. "Well, that should do it," I said as I eventually turned back to my tent. "I think I'll try and get my head down again."

"Sleep tight," Butcher sang.

The next night I tried the same thing, only to find Ox guarding me. The night after, Rusty himself was sat on a stool, Bruno at his feet. After that I gave up, resolving instead to try and break away during the day. That too though, quickly proved impossible. Everywhere I went, somebody shadowed me. By the time I was down to fourteen chocolates, I'd more or less given up on the idea of escape altogether. Instead I lay shivering in my sheets while a deluge of old memories washed over me, my life not so much flashing as crawling before my eyes.

It was strange. During those dreary, purgatorial days, I found myself remembering things I'd forgotten about, or hadn't thought about in years. I recalled conversations with my parents, school friends, colleagues, old girlfriends, rerunning seemingly inconsequential moments in my mind. Often I thought of the children. I'd remember a day out bowling with Flynn, or one of the rare Sunday mornings I woke without a hangover to find a barely toddling Olivia bouncing on the bed. There'd been a pillow fight that had collapsed into a riot of tickles. The scratch of my stubble on her bare feet, raspberries blown on her belly. I could still remember her scent, the talcum powder tinge of her hair, the hot chocolate fingers, the faint milky smell of her breath. She smelt clean, good, untarnished by the world.

Big events came back to me too, somehow more vivid than they were the first time round. I remembered the day Flynn was born in spectacular detail: the midwife's face, her shoes, even her name — Anne-Marie. I remembered there were lilies in the room, the flickering blue curtains that wouldn't quite shut, the irregular speckled pattern on the grey vinyl floor, the squeak of the hospital trolley. The promises I'd whispered to my little boy as he slithered out into the world. It all came back to me, those details I thought I'd missed in the rush of the never-ending present. Yet it turned out nothing was lost. Nothing.

More than anything, I thought about Lydia. I turned our private history over and over like a puzzle, looking for the joins, trying to spot the dead ends, the wrong turns, the places I got lost. There was our first kiss, played out in a gooey haze of rosé wine and first-date nerves. There was our first house, our wedding day. The day we brought home Olivia. More powerful than those milestones though, were the everyday moments of affection that I'd somehow allowed to pass me by. An unprompted cup of coffee left by my side the morning after a heavy night. Her understanding and concern every time I'd call last minute to cancel our plans because a client had unexpectedly arrived in town or, later, because Tamara insisted. I remember the total lack of resentment she showed every time I failed to show at a parents' evening or school play or her mother's birthday. The way she had just *accepted* everything with a sad smile and a shrug. How could she stand to put up with me? And more to the point, how could I not have recognised how good I had it? How could I have been so careless?

One morning I awoke to the clatter of pans. I sat upright, convinced for a moment that it had all been a dream, that Marshall had returned from the dead to lead us to salvation. Then I heard a familiar laugh.

"Right then, you lazy wotsits. Holidays are over!"

I dressed slowly, hardly able to bring myself to leave the tent. When I finally poked my head outside I found Ox there. He nodded, and we made our way to the clearing, arriving to find everyone apart from Zebee was already there. They stood facing Rusty, their hands plunged into their pockets, their heads hung low, their expressions despondent. I was glad I wasn't the only one sceptical that Rusty had anything of value to share with us.

"Right then," Rusty began as we took our place. "I thought we could begin with a nice spot of yoga, followed by a lovely run. What do you say?"

The men snapped their heads up in disbelief, only to find Rusty grinning back at them.

"Nah, I'm just pullin' your legs. As much I loved the gaffer, I have to say I'm glad we don't have to mess around with all that nonsense no more. Squattin' Llama? Pain in the arse more like!"

Though nobody laughed at his joke, he ploughed on undeterred. "I do miss the sense of order we used to have in the old days though. Not to mention the food. I don't know about you, but my belly ain't shut up for weeks now. 'Course, if the gaffer hadn't got so bogged down with us catchin' Sneed, we'd be tuckin' into a nice root vegetable stew round about now, but that's another story . . . "

There was a long pause.

"What's your point, Rust?" Fingers asked.

"My point," Rusty snapped, "is that we need to get back to the farm. I was up there yesterday. It's a bloody disgrace, the state it's in. Now, I reckon if we all pile in, we'll have it shipshape by the end of the week. Sooner if we roll our sleeves up."

No one said anything.

"Well?" Rusty said, his smile now faded. "What are we waitin' for?"

Still nobody moved.

"Ah, lay off it, Rusty," Hopper said eventually. "It's over. Even if we did manage to sort the farm out, what's going to grow now? It'll take months, and we're hungry. Starving. I'm telling you, we've missed the boat. Now, I say we cut our losses and head down to the soup kitchen. There's one I used to go to just down the — "

Before Hopper had a chance to finish his sentence, Rusty was on him. He moved surprisingly quickly, and in two bounding steps his hand was coiled tight around Hopper's throat while Bruno reared up around them, barking. We watched as Hopper choked, his face turning first mottled pink, then purple. Rubbery, wet snorts escaped from his lips as he tried hopelessly to draw breath. His eyes widened then rolled, his arms carving out useless circles in the air until finally his legs gave way and he began to fit. Only then did Rusty release him, stepping back as Hopper dropped to the floor and flopped around like a hooked fish, his prosthetic foot clacking noisily each time it slapped against the dirt. Ignoring him, Rusty turned back to us and grinned broadly. "Now, does anyone else think we should go and join the queue for hand-outs with all the other bums?"

We looked at our feet.

"Good!" Rusty said. "Cos we're not bums. Or tramps. Or hobos. Or any of the other names you used to get called on the streets. Or perhaps you've forgotten? Maybe you don't remember what it's like to be looked down on with pity or contempt. To be constantly moved along or spat at. To live with your hand constantly out, or else shakin' a cup, relyin' on the charity of strangers just so you can get a bit of grub down you. Hopin' some bloke in a fancy suit'll put a hand in his pocket just so you can carry on existin'. *Charity*. Now there's a blinkin' dirty word if there were one. Sticks in my throat like a bleedin' chicken bone. Bruno here learnt early on what I think of those who beg" — and here Rusty brought down his boot on the dog's paw, provoking a startled yelp — "he understands that if he acts like a dog, then I'll treat him like a dog."

On the floor, Hopper sat up and massaged his throat. Already two thick black bruises were visible below his ears.

"Ah, nice of you to join us, Private Schwarz. I was just checkin' with the fellers here that we're all readin' from the same page of the users' manual." He turned to us and winked. "Right then. Let's get a wiggle on, shall we? Them spuds ain't gonna plant themselves!"

At first it seemed impossible. We worked for hours in the frozen soil, hardly able to scratch the surface. Although only a few months had passed since we'd last worked on the farm, nature had moved quickly to reclaim the land. The bamboo stakes and trellises we'd replaced after the chicken massacre now lay snapped and strewn across the site. The beds were choked with brown trails of stinging nettles, bramble and bindweed. The place looked like a wasteland.

As ever, we split into teams, some digging, others weeding, or else gathering and bagging dead leaves to make mulch. It was backbreaking work. My fingers quickly grew numb as I sought out the thin brown roots of the invading species, while behind me the others grunted over picks and shovels. As the morning nudged towards the afternoon, however, I began to lose myself in the familiar rhythm of labour. Despite the cold, I found I began to work up a sweat, my muscles burning pleasantly after so many months of inactivity. Pausing to remove my fleece, I saw we were gradually beginning to make progress. The beds were turned and raked, making space for neat rows of onions, garlic and broad beans. A trench was dug for runner beans, while the trellises were fixed with twine. It was taking shape.

The hours rolled by, but still we didn't stop. There was something at stake now, something that went far beyond obeying Rusty's demands. I sensed the old

252

spark of competition, as silently we speeded up, seeking to out-dig and out-weed each other. It had been so long since we'd worked like this, side by side, that I'd forgotten how satisfying it could be. With each root I pulled I felt our recent troubles recede further into the distance. After a while I was almost able to ignore the fact that Rusty was standing unnecessarily close to me, the rifle in his hand. I could pretend that he wasn't watching my every move, ready to shoot me down if I so much as thought of making a run for it.

As the light began to fade, a familiar baritone rumbled through the farm as Ox began to sing. It wasn't his usual soft rock, but something I'd never heard before. It had no words, just a slow and mournful drone. After a while we began to join in, a call-and-response evolving organically as we traced Ox's lilting melody. We worked like that then, our heads bent forwards, our tools striking the earth in time to the tune, our sad, sweet music filling the cold evening air.

Eventually we were finished. We downed our shovels and trowels and stepped back. Even in the dim light, the transformation was undeniable. The ground turned and raked, the borders clearly defined, the leaves swept and bagged. We had taken back the land as our own. It had submitted to our collective will. There was still nothing to eat, but it didn't matter. In time there would be a harvest. Until then we would find a way.

I allowed myself to be led back to my tent, nodding and smiling as if I had a choice in the matter. I laughed at Rusty's terrible jokes and ignored the fact he was walking so close beside me I could practically taste his terrible breath. I wished them all goodnight, kicked off my boots and climbed under my blankets, all the time pretending that Ox or Butcher weren't standing just outside, a spear in their hand, watching me.

Lying there in the darkness, I cradled my exhausted head in my hands and dreamt of the farm in bloom: ropes of green beans snaking up poles, fat marrows exploding under bushes, rows of juicy carrots being shaken from the earth — a feast fit to feed an army.

That night the snow began to fall.

CHAPTER
TWENTY-FIVE

Before I'd even opened my eyes, I was able to sense a shift in the light, an eerie brightness that pierced the thin membrane of my eyelids. I sat up, confused for a moment before I spotted the roof above me sagging under the weight of the snow. It had been a heavy fall. I thought of the farm, my heart sinking. All of our work had been for nothing. Quickly eclipsing my disappointment however, was the realisation that I was likely to be unguarded. It was time to leave.

I pulled on my boots and fumbled for the entrance. Then I paused. The snow was even deeper than I'd thought, the world blanketed entirely white. For a second I was transfixed by the beauty of it all. The camp looked pure and new, the snow completely masking the dirt that lay underneath.

I stared around nervously, looking for signs of life. I had no idea what time it was, but there didn't seem to be anyone around yet, the great white expanse of the field unscarred by footprints. I took a tentative step forwards. The snow compacted under my boot with a satisfying crunch. I filled my lungs with crisp morning air. And then I saw it. Almost directly opposite me, stood at the base of a tree, was a snowman. He stared at me with black-pebble eyes, his dead-stick arms reaching towards the sky, though of course there was no carrot for his nose. At that moment, Al Pacino stepped out from behind the tree, a patch of yellow spreading out behind him.

"Morning, mate," he said as he shook himself off and retrieved his spear from against the tree. He looked cold, his cheeks flushed bright red, his black hair speckled with snow. I wondered whether he'd been out there all night.

"So what do you think?" he grinned, gesturing towards the snowman. "Have you said hello to my little friend?"

That morning there was talk among the men about going back to the farm. By the afternoon though, the snow was falling again, this time heavier than ever. There was nothing for it but to go back to our tents and wait it out. I lay there in the curious, too-bright light, unable to sleep, my teeth chattering, my stomach attempting to digest itself. Outside I heard my guard clearing his throat. I took a chocolate from under my pillow and held it on my tongue, being careful not to bite it, trying to make it last. I closed my eyes. Somewhere in the distance, Bruno began to howl.

As the days passed, it became clear that the weather was not going to let up anytime soon. The men had long since stopped chucking snowballs around, the novelty having quickly given way to chapped fingers and wet socks. One morning the news went round the

256

camp that Zebee had been found dead in his tent. My query as to what had killed him was met with a shrug.

"Froze to death?" Fingers suggested.

That evening, Rusty called us to dinner. A platter of raw meat sat on the table, the snow and lack of petrol presumably making cooking impossible. There were no complaints though, only the sound of chewing. Again I refused a plate, holding my belly and blaming a non-specific illness. Nobody even looked up.

After they'd eaten, we made our way to the farm and watched as Ox dug a hole in the snow. It was difficult to know exactly where the other graves were, and in the end Rusty had gestured to a random spot. Beneath the snow, the ground was so hard that even Ox struggled to make much of a dent. Still, there was little of Zebee to bury. His belongings — which consisted of a modest handful of clothing — had been redistributed among the men. Fingers in particular was delighted to finally swap his shorts for a pair of trousers. As for Zebee's body, most of it had been carved up, with some set aside in the snow for later and the bones saved for Bruno. What remained fit easily inside a small carrier bag. This, Rusty tossed indifferently into the shallow ditch. There were no words this time, no gunshot. We stood shivering as yet more snow began to drift down, like ashes blown from a distant chimney, and left the moment Ox had patted down the final shovelful of dirt.

As we trudged our way back to the camp, I sidled up alongside Hopper. "Should we tell someone?" I asked as quietly as I could.

Hopper, who had been struggling with his foot in recent days, looked up in shock. "Tell? What do you mean, tell?"

"I don't know. His family? We could try and get a message out."

Hopper relaxed slightly. "Oh. No, Zeb didn't have any family."

Now it was my turn to look shocked. "What do you mean? He was always talking about his wife and daughters. I thought he was going to move to be with them again soon?"

"Well, I guess he's done that, the poor sod. See I was already here when Zeb arrived. The gaffer found him and brought him to us. He was in a terrible state. Pissed out of his head he was. Crying too. He told us how his family had died in a house fire years ago. He was the only one who made it out. I guess he'd been on the streets ever since. Of course by the morning, he'd forgotten all about telling us. We played along, naturally. Seemed cruel to let on we knew. Anyway, give us a hand with this bloody leg will you. I swear, it's killing me . . . "

Eventually the snow did stop falling, though it refused to thaw. Instead, it packed down and froze over, the surface of the park becoming glazed and slippery, as if encased in glass. Twice I slipped, earning myself dark bruises on my arms and legs that took days to disappear. Still, I found the pain served as a useful distraction from the endless hunger that stalked my waking hours. I was down to six chocolates by then,

258

having recently made the decision to cut my rations in half. Apart from these lonely bursts of sugar at the end of each the day, all I had to eat was fistfuls of snow, which I compulsively shovelled into my mouth in a vain attempt to fill myself up. I was acutely aware that every day I stayed there the more difficult it would be to rouse the energy I'd need to escape. So far though, there hadn't been a single opportunity. At night I lay awake, listening to the heavy breathing outside my tent and fantasising about overpowering my guard, though in truth I knew I was so weak I'd have struggled to overpower Flynn.

Despite the snow and ice making chores impossible, every morning we still woke to the clatter of saucepans, though what we were being summoned for was never clear. During daylight hours, we huddled silently together in the clearing where we used to practice yoga, avoiding eye contact. I never failed to be shocked at how frail everyone looked. All of the men were pale and gaunt, the lean winter months having filed their cheekbones down to right angles. It wasn't just the weight loss though. Al Pacino's hair appeared to be falling out on one side of his head, a shiny patch of scalp visible beneath the flap of his bobble hat. Fingers had come out in a mysterious rash, his face and hands covered in angry red welts. As for Butcher, I was pleased to see his scar looked no closer to healing. Only Ox and Rusty seemed to have dodged physical affliction, though both were showing signs of exhaustion. Dark black bags underscored their eyes, while the deep creases in Rusty's face seemed to run deeper than ever. At his feet lay Bruno, a marimba of ribs beginning to show under his fur.

It was Hopper, however, who was undoubtedly suffering the most. The ice had rendered much of the campsite virtually impassable for him, and several times I'd had to help him up off his back following a fall. In addition to this, the wound around his prosthesis had stubbornly refused to heal and was now infected, a yellow crust formed around the socket. One morning I got a glimpse of it as he rolled up his trouser leg to pack snow around his stump. Ominous red streaks had spread up his shin, the skin around his calf marbled purple and black.

I didn't know if was my imagination, but during those long, cold days the other men seemed to pay Hopper an uncomfortable amount of attention. Every time he winced they'd nudge each other, exchanging silent looks loaded with meaning. Once or twice I caught them staring longingly at his ruined leg as he pressed a block of ice to it. And in their eyes I thought I saw hunger.

The final chocolate was an orange crème. I divided it into four, holding a tiny fragment on my tongue each night, the artificial sweetness the only bright spot in my otherwise grey existence. When the evening of the last quarter finally arrived I was almost too afraid to eat it. I held the sticky glob up to my face and examined it in the dim light. It was hardly as big as my little fingernail.

In my old life, I never ate chocolate. Lydia had spent a fair portion of the last decade waging a war on refined sugar and, with the begrudging exception of Flynn's breakfast cereals, our kitchen was a junk-free zone. Thinking back, it was hard to believe I'd taken so much for granted. Grapes from Senegal, strawberries from Morocco, tomatoes from Saudi Arabia, all of it flown halfway around the world just so we could get our five-a-day, regardless of the time of year. What I wouldn't give for a single bite of an Italian apple or a Costa Rican banana. Jesus, half the time we treated our fruit as ornaments, leaving it to go mouldy in the bowl and then chucking it away. It was criminal.

I considered the chocolate again. Up close I could see the tiny hairs it had attracted from where it had lain inside my tent. I closed my eyes and placed it in my mouth, all the time dreaming of home.

"What are you fucking looking at, huh?"

I turned slowly, struggling to focus on who was speaking. This was three or four days after the last chocolate had run out. Hopper had stopped leaving his tent by this point, but the rest of us still responded to Rusty's call each morning, dragging ourselves out to huddle aimlessly in the clearing. That morning I sat on a frozen tree stump, staring at nothing, thinking nothing. I wasn't sure how long I'd been sat there. Come to think of it, I wasn't even sure it was still morning.

"I said, what the *fuck* are you looking at, freak?"

This time I realised it was Al Pacino who'd spoken. He was glaring at me, his lips parted, his teeth showing. He wasn't joking. I opened my mouth to answer, to tell him I wasn't looking at anything, but the words wouldn't come. It had been days since I'd said a thing to anyone, and my throat felt cracked and raw. Instinctively I reached for a scoop of snow to ease my dryness. It was at that moment that he launched himself at me. His fist connected with my chin, sending me staggering to the floor. Before I understood what was happening, he was over me, blows landing in my belly, my ribs, my kidneys.

"You think this is funny, motherfucker?" he screamed at me. "You think my hair's a fucking joke?"

I couldn't speak. One of Al's punches found my mouth, loosening something in my gums. I tasted blood.

The beating continued, until all at once a smeared shadow blotted the sky above me.

"Come on, you clowns! That's enough!"

A pair of large hands gripped under my arms and dragged me to my feet. It was Rusty. He'd come to save me.

"That motherfucker was laughing at my hair. He fucking *disrespected* me!" Al Pacino screamed.

"Sounds like you need to learn when to be quiet, sonny," Rusty said as he propped me back on the tree stump. "You'll want to get some ice on that. Fortunately there's no shortage of that around."

I stood up uncertainly and began to pick my way back through the snow towards my tent. I could hardly see.

Without a word, Ox stood up and followed me.

The next day I woke to a bellow of anger. Hopper had gone. During the night, while Butcher had been stationed outside my tent and the others had slept, he'd somehow managed to pack up the entire contents of his tent and leave the park without anyone noticing. It seemed impossible, especially with the state his leg was in, but there was no denying it. He'd escaped.

The ice made it difficult to track him, but eventually Ox picked up his trail. It was unmistakably Hopper: one heavy indent, accompanied by a lighter mark, leading away from the camp. We followed the trail of footprints, past the farm and through the woods. Halfway across the football field, the prints abruptly stopped. We hunted around, doubling back on ourselves to see if he had branched off earlier, but there was no sign of any extra tracks. It was as if he had simply evaporated, along with everything he owned.

Rusty was beside himself with rage. He was angrier than I'd ever seen him before. He blamed Butcher for not spotting him. He blamed Bruno for not barking. He blamed the rest of us for not waking up. But most of all, he blamed Hopper for having the audacity to leave in the first place. We stood and watched while he attacked Hopper's empty tent with a stick, thrashing wildly at the canvas, all the while screaming about what he'd do if he ever got his hands on "that one-legged cocksucker!"

In the end he flattened the tent altogether.

Afterwards, when Rusty had retreated to brood in the tree house, the others crouched over the crumpled canvas, scavenging pegs and rope to make repairs to their own leaky hovels.

"Reckon he had the right idea, if you ask me," said Fingers.

The others nodded gravely.

"Probably chewing on a juicy hamburger as we speak," said Butcher.

"Or sitting somewhere warm," said Al Pacino. "With a pint of beer."

"The fucking one-legged cocksucker," said Ox.

Everyone agreed.

The fucking one-legged cocksucker.

The day after Hopper left, I woke as usual to the sound of saucepans. Fearing Rusty's dark mood, I dragged my feet getting ready. When I eventually emerged, I found Butcher was waiting outside my tent. He looked disconcertingly smug, as if he had just remembered the punchline to an elaborate dirty joke.

"Morning!" he trilled, slapping me hard between the shoulder blades. "Sleep well?"

I didn't answer.

When we joined the others, I found to my surprise that Rusty too was beaming, the frustrations of the day before seemingly forgotten. In fact, everyone seemed mysteriously buoyant, a ripple of barely suppressed excitement coursing through the small band of men. Even Ox was smiling.

Before I'd even taken a seat, Fingers began hopping up and down. "Can we tell him? Can we tell him?" he asked.

264

Rusty smiled generously. "Well, he's going to find out sooner or later, ain't he?"

Fingers turned back to me and clapped his hands together. "It's Christmas!" he yelled. "Or at least, it is tomorrow. It's Christmas Eve today. Rusty's just told us. Isn't that right Rust?"

Rusty nodded. "Jingle all the bleedin' way!"

I didn't say anything.

"Jeez, don't look so pleased!" said Fingers, visibly deflating at my lack of enthusiasm. "Don't you know what that means?"

"Feast!" Butcher answered for him.

"Feast!" said Ox.

"Feast!" said Al. "Feast, feast, feast!"

Rusty chuckled. "That's right!" he said. "But first we've got work to do."

There was wood to gather, a fire to build. I wasn't sure how Rusty planned to burn it, but the instructions were clear. As before, we were to construct it at the bottom of the marl pit. After that, the table was to be fetched, a canopy erected. Ox had chopped down a small conifer that was to be decorated as a makeshift Christmas tree.

The ice made the work difficult and painfully slow. Despite this, the men remained in high spirits, singing carols and telling jokes as they went about the preparations. As I set to work scavenging the few dry branches I could find, I found myself wondering how Rusty had come to know the date. It didn't seem long enough had passed since Midsummer's Day for it to be Christmas already, but when I tried to think back to count the weeks it was hopeless. I found it hard to remember much of anything that had taken place before winter, before the sore fingers, the chattering teeth, the endless, grinding hunger. In the end I decided that even if it wasn't Christmas, it didn't really matter. As far as I was concerned, this year couldn't end soon enough.

At last we were done. We sat around the camp in the fading light, hugging ourselves to keep warm. I was just preparing to go to bed, when a loud voice boomed out from the trees.

"Ho, ho, ho!"

We all looked up as Rusty stepped from the trees. He was dressed in the same red coat he'd been wearing on my very first night here, all those months ago. Although he'd lost a considerable amount of weight since then, he still bore a striking likeness to Saint Nick.

"Well, I guess it's time to find out who's been naughty or nice," he said.

The men laughed along good naturedly as Rusty proceeded to hand around a set of old socks — one for each of us.

"Now don't forget to hang these up in your tents tonight," he said. "Else Santa won't be bringin' you nothin' — ya hear me?"

The joke dragged on for a while, with Rusty insisting we called Bruno Rudolph and instructing us to leave out a carrot and a large glass of brandy, until it was time to turn in. We took our socks and bid each other good night.

266

"You lot better be up extra early!" he called to us as we ambled towards our tents. "I mean it! I've got a surprise planned for you in the mornin'. Ho, ho, ho!"

Despite my exhaustion, it took me a long time to fall asleep that night. For one thing, Al Pacino was stationed directly outside my tent. I'd noticed he'd developed a bad cough lately, and every few minutes he would hack violently, sending solid-sounding lumps whistling through the night air. It wasn't just that though. My head throbbed with festive nostalgia. I remembered my own childhood Christmases spent with my parents, a time when magic still existed and Santa Claus didn't carry an air rifle. Then of course there was my own family. The first Christmas I spent with Lydia, years before the money and madness ruined everything. It was an unmitigated disaster: an under-cooked turkey abandoned in favour of a frozen pizza; later my mother, drunk and abusive on the phone. Yet none of it mattered. Our love and our youth combined to make us bulletproof. Everything was ahead of us then.

And of course, there were the Christmases with the kids. The ritual dangling of stockings, the manic five a.m. shrieks as they woke to discover a sack literally splitting with presents. The tears and tantrums over missing batteries and un-assemblable toys. There were arguments about which TV channel to watch, the battle over Brussels sprouts, the living death of the endless post-dinner Christmas afternoon, with nothing to watch, nothing to open, nowhere to be. But none of that mattered. I saw that now. It was part of it. It was Christmas. It was perfect.

And where were my children tonight? Were they lying in bed, listening for sleigh bells? For footsteps on the roof, for a rustling in the chimney?

Or were they lying awake, listening for their daddy instead?

I opened my eyes. It was still dark. I rolled over, intending to go back to sleep. Then I stopped. Something was wrong. Someone was in my tent. I sat up to look around. Instantly I felt a hand press hard over my mouth. The hand smelt of fire and dirt and dog. I began to wriggle, trying to break free, but the man pulled me closer to him, squeezing me so tight I heard the faint crack of something deep inside me. After that I stopped moving.

"Surprise," said the man.

CHAPTER
TWENTY-SIX

It was all so obvious. The building of the fire. The preparation for the "feast". I saw now that I'd made a terrible miscalculation. I should have risked running earlier, perhaps the morning we'd followed Hopper's footprints through the snow. Or even earlier. Months earlier. I should have left the night they'd turned on Marshall, or right after the chickens died, or before the whole ridiculous business with the swan. Or earlier still. The moment Rusty had leapt from the bushes and flattened me. Before I'd even entered the bloody park in the first place. Before I'd lost my job, or ended up in bed with Tamara, or gambled away my house and my marriage and my children's futures. Before, before, before! My head spun as I considered the near infinite junctures I'd passed on the way to reach this point. So many missed opportunities to make the break, to cut my losses, to change course. Now all I was left with was the familiar hollow remorse of having stayed too long in the casino, of not cashing out while I was ahead.

They say a good gambler knows when to quit. Yeah, well, *they* would say that wouldn't they. Those pious, self-satisfied people, with their dreary, drama-free lives. No, like most clichés, the idea of quitting ahead originates with people who don't live by the roll of a dice, the slice of a pack. In my world, there was no quitting. Not really. Not when there was still money on the table that could be in your pocket. No, for gamblers there is only winning and losing, all or nothing. The winners stayed alive long enough to see off all other competitors. You became big and bloated and bilious enough to swallow everyone else. Or else your luck failed and you withered away. Walking was never an option.

And now, finally, my luck had run out.

I lay prostrate on the icy floor, my hands bound with a coarse length of rope. I had been dragged from my tent and beaten, though not with any real commitment. I suspected it was simply a way of sending a message. Lie still. Do not run. We will hurt you if you try to escape.

I'm not sure how long I lay there, bleeding and broken beside my tent. At some point morning had blistered over my head, a foul blue light that stung my rapidly swelling eyes. I wasn't sure what the men were waiting for. They hovered close by, muttering among themselves. Eventually I was hoisted from the ground and slung over Ox's shoulders. As they carried me through the camp and down the slope, I recalled another time, months earlier, when I'd been carried to the lake on a sea of hands. That was how it had all began. My baptism. My rebirth. It seemed strangely appropriate that it should end so similarly, with me surrendering all control, a sacrificial lamb, my life in the their hands.

When they finally dumped me on the floor of the marl pit beside the stack of firewood, I finally realised what my fate was. I was to be roasted on the Christmas bonfire I had helped build the day before. Again, there was something fitting about it. To have gathered the wood that would cook me. After all, wasn't that what I'd been doing all along? I only hoped the end would be quick.

"I expect you're wonderin' how it's come to this, eh, sonny?"

I had passed out. Or perhaps I hadn't. There was a wooziness to the world that made it difficult to keep track of time and place. I opened my eyes to find Rusty silhouetted against a background of absolute white. With the halo of the new morning behind him, he almost looked like an angel.

"Because I've got to be honest, Adam," he continued. "I'm kind of wonderin' myself. Now, you know I like you. Hell, I'm the one who invited you here in the first place and treated you as one of my own. We all did, ain't that right, boys?"

The men murmured in agreement. There was an odd theatricality to the proceedings, as if I was being put on trial. Rusty was to be the judge of this kangaroo court, while the other men acted as jury, and later, executioners.

"And sure you were always a little odd. Not as *proactive* as the others, shall we say? A little self-absorbed. You had a few funny ideas about this and that. But we let it slide. We felt sorry for you. Besides, you seemed harmless enough . . . "

I didn't move, didn't speak to offer an opinion. There was no point.

"Which was why I couldn't believe me bleedin' eyes when, during a routine tent inspection, we discovered this little treasure trove of goodies!"

Rusty brandished the evidence with a theatrical flourish.

This was what I had been waiting for. The charges against me. I squinted and saw the tatty outline of a birthday card, a stick of deodorant and an empty box of chocolates, the possession of which I presumed would sentence me to death. As Rusty held up the incriminating material for the men to see, a few of the empty wrappers fluttered down to me, the brightly coloured cellophane glistening like baubles on a tree.

"So!" Rusty roared, showering me with flecks of brown spit. "This whole time us lot were sat around starvin' to death, you had your own private supply of grub waitin' for you in your tent. No wonder you couldn't wait to get to bed each night. Makes me wonder what else you had stashed away. A nice steak dinner? A lamb hot pot maybe?"

The men's murmurs grew louder.

"Traitor!" Fingers yelled.

"Not only that, but according to this little card, it looks like he were havin' his meals hand delivered. 'Dear Dad'? Thought you'd get the family in on the act, did you? Not to mention the fact that you brought people here, to our home. What did you think this was, a bleedin' campin' trip? *The Great Interactive Homeless Experience*? Thought you'd come and rough it with us for a few months before you scurried back to your nice little life, eh? You disgust me! I thought you was one of us, Adam. Turns out you're nothin' but a bleedin' tourist!"

The men were screaming now, baying for my blood. Yet still I said nothing. They needed this, I realised. This spectacle. This catharsis. They had to justify it somehow. To reassure themselves that in killing me, they were righting some catastrophic wrong. That they were not merely monsters. They shouldn't have bothered. I had raised no objection to the proceedings. After all, was this not the way of the world? Darwin placed no stock in compassion or mercy. It was survival of the fittest, to the detriment of all else. You take the weak and devour them, so you can become strong. Those were the only rules. This was nothing personal. I was simply on the wrong side of evolution.

Rusty stepped over me. The trial was over. Now it was time for sentencing. I watched as he held up the birthday card and tore it in two, tossing the remains onto the pile of wood. Then, as if performing a magic trick, he reached into his jacket and produced a small can of lighter fluid.

"I've been savin' this for a special occasion," he said, aiming a long squirt towards the pile. Next a match was produced, struck, dropped. The fire jerked into life.

The men were silent now, solemn. They crowded closer, blocking the heat from the fire. Rusty searched his jacket again. I caught a flash of silver.

I looked beyond the men. Among the trees that fringed the clearing, a bird sat quivering on a branch. It was a robin, it's breast splashed with a shock of red, as if mortally wounded. Clutched in its beak, some small, pink thing writhed helplessly. A worm, plucked from the earth for no reason other than because it happened to be there and was too weak to protest. The robin stared at me with its beetle-black eyes, utterly indifferent to my suffering. It tipped back its head and the worm vanished.

As the circle collapsed in on me, time stretched and stalled. I reminded myself that my death would be no major loss to the universe. It was no great tragedy. I thought of Marshall, the look of disbelief as he fell to his knees. I thought of Sneed's panic, of Zebee alone in his tent. Every day, people faced the certainty of their annihilation head on. I was no different. Perhaps in the end it would even come as a relief.

Rusty knelt above me, the knife raised. I searched the men's faces for any sign of doubt, but there was none. Only hunger. I glanced past them, searching for the robin. It was gone. A strange calmness washed over me. This was it. The ice, the sky, the smoke. I closed my eyes.

And then . . .

Nothing.

I waited. Still nothing. I opened my eyes and saw that Rusty had frozen, the blade paused midway on its journey to my throat. He turned his head. He'd heard something. They all had. The sound came again, and this time I heard it too, carried on the wind. There was no mistaking it. It was a voice, faint and fragile as glass, but definitely a voice.

"*Da-ddy!*"

Someone was calling me.

Olivia was here.

CHAPTER
TWENTY-SEVEN

I was dying. Either that or I'd fainted. This was all some terrible nightmare taking place in the microseconds before the knife swooped down and severed the final threads tying me to the world. Because this couldn't be happening. Not now. The universe couldn't possibly be this cruel.

"*Da-ddy!*" Olivia called again. Something about her intonation awoke a buried childhood memory, a game of hide-and-seek that had gone on far too long, panic and doubt displacing excitement. *What if they weren't hiding? What if they'd really gone?*

"*Da-ddy!*"

There was no doubting it now. Olivia was in the park. If anything, she sounded closer. Rusty stepped back, the blade dropping limply to his side as he turned his head slowly, trying to ascertain which direction the voice was coming from.

"*Da-ddy!*"

This time he paused, chuckling lightly to himself. "This your idea of a rescue party, eh?" he asked, turning his back on me. "Looks like it really is Christmas, lads. We've got ourselves dessert too!"

Without a word, the men fanned out into the trees.

276

Rusty paced the perimeter of the clearing with Bruno at his side. Every now and then he would pause to peer up into dark bars of the trees that surrounded us, shaking his head in disgust every minute the men failed to materialise.

Olivia meanwhile continued to call out intermittently, oblivious to the danger she was in. The sound of her voice was like a tonic. Suddenly the ache of my ribs from the boot blows was negligible, as was the frozen earth digging into my knees. All of my pain had at once become remote. It seemed Olivia — or at least the adrenaline her voice injected into me — had endowed me with superpowers. I felt stronger than I had in weeks. For a moment, I felt as if I could break the ropes that bound my hands by simply flexing my wrists. Sadly though, after struggling for a few minutes, I found this wasn't the case.

On the other side of the fire, Rusty continued to prowl. Every second that passed he grew more agitated, his fingers twitching as he chuntered to himself. Olivia hadn't called out for a few minutes and fear seeped into the vacuum she left behind, sapping my strength. I needed to get to her. I needed to go now.

Rusty's back was still turned. I looked around, calculating the number of steps it would take me to reach the cover of the trees. If only I could get to my feet. I tried rocking over onto my side, but only succeeded in planting my face into the ice, bashing my teeth against my lips in the process. I tasted blood again, but managed to swallow my yelp. I glanced up, terrified. Thankfully, it seemed Rusty hadn't noticed.

"*Da-ddy!*"

Olivia's voice was like a defibrillator, jolting me back to life. She sounded closer than ever, perhaps just beyond the trees at the top of the pit. It was now or never. Risking a final glance in Rusty's direction, I rolled back over, using my momentum to hurl myself up onto the balls of my feet. The moment I was upright I lurched towards the bushes — *five steps to the trees, four steps* — not looking behind me, not stopping — *three steps, two steps* — I knew I was being too noisy, but Rusty hadn't called out yet and maybe, just maybe my luck was going to hold — *one step . . .*

Inches from the trees I froze.

A scream echoed out, high above me. A girl's scream. It only lasted for a moment, before stopping abruptly. I felt my strength drain away as dread coursed through my veins, threatening to shut off my air supply.

"Goin' somewhere, sonny?"

I span around. On the far side of the clearing, Rusty was facing me. Even at that distance I could make out the malice on his face, his mouth twisted into a mocking grin. I held his gaze for a second.

And then flung myself into the trees.

Within moments of entering the woods, I understood I'd been mistaken. I was no superhero. Despite the imminent danger I was facing, the many months of malnutrition had left me weak and sluggish. Coupled with my recent beating and the icy terrain, I found it

278

almost impossible to scramble up the steep slope of the pit. With my hands still firmly fastened behind my back, I slipped several times. Halfway up, I twisted my ankle, and for one awful moment I teetered on the brink of falling backwards. I somehow managed to stay upright and kept going, dragging my useless foot behind me while I recited my daughter's name under my breath, like a prayer.

Olivia. Olivia. Olivia.

Meanwhile, Rusty was closing in on me. So were the others. I could hear the crash of foliage, the cry of startled birds, the snapping of twigs. The grunts and curses of starving men. Any moment I expected Bruno to pounce from the bushes. I pictured his jaws clamping around my ankle, my arm, my throat.

I kept staggering onwards, onwards, until miraculously the trees parted, abruptly giving way to the frozen clearing that lay between the camp and the farm. I paused for a moment, unsure of which way to run. Now that I was out in the open, I realised I had no real idea which direction Olivia's cries had been coming from. She still hadn't called out since the muffled scream, though I didn't dare dwell too long on what that might mean. Behind me I heard a strangled bark, the snapping of sharp teeth. I closed my eyes. There had been a time not so long ago that I'd regularly gamble the sum of my worldly possessions on the roll of a dice, the spin of a wheel. Now though I floundered, feeling hopelessly indecisive. Then again, the stakes had never been this high before.

Another bark sounded nearby, and surely within seconds Bruno would be on me. *Last bets, please!* It was time to choose. I opened my eyes and began to run, aiming for neither the camp nor the farm, but towards the woods that divided our territory from the rest of the park. My plan was to head for the old playground, hoping Olivia might think to return to the place we'd first met.

I powered through the ice, my lungs burning, the ropes biting into my wrists, my ankle pounding. I ignored the pain. Behind me I heard footsteps, yells, ferocious snarls — certain death. I ignored them too. If I was a religious man, I might have called on a higher power to deliver me from evil, to spare my only daughter, to light the way. But I am not a religious man. Instead I prayed to the closest thing to a doctrine I'd ever followed. I thought back to *Seventy-Seven Steps to Sterling Success*. I didn't have a mirror in which to visualise my reward, but it didn't matter. I didn't need one. Because for the first time I understood exactly what success — true success — looked like.

And it didn't have a thing to do with money.

I was halfway across the woods when the shout went up. It was a man's voice, though this time it wasn't Rusty. The noise seemed to ricochet off the trees, again making it difficult to discern exactly where it had come from. Was it a cheer of victory? A bellow of frustration? It was impossible to tell. Against my will, I pictured Butcher's leering face as he towered over Olivia.

It was at this moment my luck ran out.

280

Momentarily distracted, my foot snagged on a concealed knot of tree roots and I went down. Even before I hit the ground, I knew it was going to be bad. With no hands to break my fall, my face took the majority of the impact. I felt my nose pop under my weight, my eyes immediately flooding with tears.

I lay there for a second or two, willing myself to get up. The image of Butcher flashed back into my mind, and somehow I managed to clamber to my knees. A steady stream of blood dripped from my nose, splattering the snow a startling red. I spat once, twice, and staggered to my feet.

And then someone spoke behind me.

"It's over," they said.

I turned around. Rusty stood twenty paces from me. He looked exhausted, leaning against a tree trunk for support, his forehead glistening with perspiration. Even so, he was smiling. He held Bruno by the scruff of his neck. A low growl rumbled in the dog's throat as he strained to escape his master's grip.

"It's over," Rusty said again. "We've got her. We've got your little girl."

There's a phenomena in poker called the "crying call". Taking place in the last round of betting, it describes the act of placing your bet to see your opponent's hand, even though you know you're holding nothing. Now, as the name implies, the crying call is rarely, if ever, a happy circumstance. It normally comes at the end of the night, when you've drunk too much and stayed too long and invested too much money in the pot, so that even though you've got next to no chance of winning, you can't bear the thought of just walking away. Again, as the name implies, I've seen real tears in the eyes of grown men at this stage in the game. In my experience, there's little in this life that sobers you as quickly as the realisation you're about to put twenty more years on your mortgage for the sake of a pair of twos.

Generally speaking, there's only one thing you're clinging onto when making this kind of call. That is the hope that the guy or girl sat opposite you is somehow even more full of shit than you are. Of course this is rare, but occasionally it does happen. You spot the bluff. You match their bets. And you call them out. Like I say, it doesn't happen that often. I've seen professionals get it wrong. But when it comes off, when you open the window and step out, only to have your fall broken by a concealed ledge? Well, it's like seeing the face of God. Other people look at you differently too. You're transformed suddenly, so that rather than being just another drunken idiot chasing a broken dream, you're crazy old David facing down Goliath. Only you did it without the slingshot. They shake your hand for it, these people, imagining you knew what you were doing the whole time. They shake your hand and they call you a hero.

I stared at Rusty. It's funny how you stop seeing people when you're around them too often. It's like you get so used to someone's face that you stop noticing their features, and instead use a sort of a crude child's drawing as a mental placeholder while you concentrate on more important things. Seeing Rusty now, I mean *really* seeing him, I was shocked at how much he'd aged. Or had he? It occurred to me I'd perhaps got some things fundamentally wrong about him. His rosy cheeks, for example. In my head I'd always taken them as an outward sign of his cheery nature, his rude, outdoorsy health. Now though, I saw that the red smudges on his cheeks were simply the burst capillaries of a former heavy drinker. Similarly, I'd associated his long white beard with a sort of jolly, British eccentricity. Looking closer however, there was something almost malevolent in its breadth and unkemptness. I saw not Santa Claus, but Harold Shipman, Charlie Manson. The guy was clearly a psychopath. But was he a liar?

There was only one way to find out.

"Prove it," I said.

Rusty blinked twice. It was fast, but I saw it. "You what?"

"You heard me. Prove you've got my daughter."

At this, Rusty laughed. He laughed so hard that he began to cough, phlegm rattling in his chest. He sounded like he was drowning. "It's not up to me to prove anything, sonny," he said once he'd got his breath back. "I don't care one way or the other if you believe me or not. I only thought you might like to know is all. 'Specially after what Butcher and the boys have got planned for her. Not that I blame 'em. It's so hard bein' cooped up with a bunch of fellers the whole time, ain't it? A man needs a good *release* now and then or he's liable to go a bit funny in the head."

I felt my jaw clench involuntarily, a surge of fury scorching my chest. I pictured myself taking a rock to Rusty's skull. Still, I didn't move. He was playing me, I was sure of it. He was pressing buttons, searching for points of weakness. Trying to unbalance me. I held his eye and stood my ground. "I don't believe you. If you've got her, then where is she? Where are the others?"

Rusty laughed again, but this time less heartily. He was struggling to disguise his irritation. "Look, Adam, we've had some fun, haven't we? But it's time to stop messin' around now. Why don't you come back with me and we'll see if we can't sort all this out? Who knows, if we talk to the lads nicely we might even be able to get them to let that little girly of yours go free."

I stared at him, this wheezing old wreck of a human. He was a pitiful sight. It wasn't just his physical state though. When you spend as much time in casinos as I have, you learn to recognise desperation when you see it. It bleeds from you, a wound that's impossible to staunch. It stains everything you say or do. It doesn't matter how expensive the cut of your suit or the name on your watch, when you're truly desperate, you're a marked man. After that, it's only ever a matter of time before the sharks begin to circle, preparing to drag you down.

"I don't think I will do that," I said, not taking my eyes from him. "In fact, I'm going to leave now. Goodbye, Rusty."

284

Rusty's face twisted in fury. "So what? You're gonna run away, are you? She said you're good at that . . . "

I shrugged, a familiar feeling of weightlessness already settling over me. Nothing he could say could hurt me now. I'd placed my bet. There was nothing left to do but wait to see what he was holding.

"Goodbye, Rusty," I repeated, already turning from him.

At that moment, there was a thunder of paws behind me. I looked back to see Bruno bounding in my direction, a savage blur of hair and drool and teeth. I tried to move out of the way, but it was hopeless. Even without the icy floor and the twisted ankle and the bound-up hands, I'd never have escaped him. He was just too quick. I braced myself for the impact, while behind him Rusty laughed.

And then something strange happened.

Bruno vanished. One moment he was charging at me, his jaws parted, his fangs bared, the next he was gone. He'd disappeared, as suddenly as a puppet plucked away from the stage by its strings.

Still too stunned to do anything else, I inched forward to investigate. Rusty had stopped laughing now. I took another step, peering down.

And then I saw him.

Bruno was lying at the bottom of a deep trench, a wooden stake protruding from his side, a trail of blood already leaking from his ear. It was one of Marshall's concealed bear pits, rendered invisible by the recent snowfall. It was a miracle I hadn't stepped on it myself.

"Ah, Jesus. No, boy. No!"

Rusty rushed forwards, dropping to his knees as he attempted to free the stricken beast. I had a feeling it was too late for that.

"OH GOD, NO!"

This time I didn't hesitate. I turned and I ran, Rusty's roars ringing in my ears. I didn't look back.

The play park was deserted when I arrived there. There was no sign of Olivia. No sign of anyone. I ran frantically from one side to the other, convinced I'd somehow missed her — that at any moment she'd pop out from behind the rusting swings, the broken slide. I circled the tiny play park three, four times. But she wasn't there. She wasn't there.

That's when the pain engulfed me. For the first time in my life I appreciated why people used the term "heartbroken". For that's where it hit me, a sudden visceral cramp directly in the centre of my chest, so sharp it stole my breath. It was like every loss I'd ever experienced in my life distilled into a single, burning drop of anguish. Every dud horse. Every busted flush. They were nothing compared to this. I'd gambled on my daughter's life and come up short. They had her. They had her. And there was nothing I could do about it. It was over.

I stumbled backwards, my limbs finally preparing to give way after carrying me so far for nothing, when I noticed a flash of movement in the distance, over by the entrance to the park. At first I assumed it was one of the men. Ox or Butcher perhaps, swaggering over to

286

gloat or finish me off. Good, I thought. I won't stop them this time.

As the figure drew closer, however, I realised it was too short to be any of them. The clothes too fitted. The hair too long.

And then I was running towards her.

"Daddy!" she squealed, terrified and delighted in equal measure as she ran to meet me. "I tried calling but you didn't come. I wanted to wish you happy Christmas. Oh, what's happened to your face?"

She stopped dead a couple of feet from me, her smile dissolving into a look of horror.

"And your hands? Who's done this to you?"

I tried to talk, tried to apologise, but no words would come. Only tears. My Olivia. I fell to my knees, my head pressed against her legs while she patted my hair awkwardly.

"Daddy? What's going on? You're scaring me."

My Olivia. I wanted to explain, but no words would come.

Instead I kissed her. I kissed her and I cried.

It was all I could do.

SPRING

We have tarmacked the forests. We have filled the sky with concrete. We have choked the ocean, fouled the air, scorched the fields. What once was green is now grey. What once was blue is black.

In the same spots where wild deer roamed and adders coiled under a sleepy midday sun, there is now nothing but a spaghetti-knot of carriageways. Where drunken bees once bumbled through meadows and orchards, hordes of pale zombies now shuffle to offices, pinching and plucking at digital screens.

We have levelled mountains and drained swamps in order to construct labyrinthine shopping centres and vast multistorey car parks, monuments to nothing but bottomless greed and consumption, to our own terrible appetites. We have torn out the trees and replaced them with satellite dishes and mobile phone masts, so that we can talk and talk and never feel alone.

We are gods now, each and every one of us. All seeing. All knowing. All speaking, hearing, buying, destroying.

But oh, what careless gods we turned out to be.

All this I think while staring out from the window of my small council flat.

This is where I live now. This is my home.

I'd intended to take Olivia back to Lydia, but instead she led me to the hospital. She's changed a lot in the time I've been away. She's more mature now. Wiser. I can see how much I've put her through. She's old beyond her years.

I'll always be sorry for that.

They kept me on the ward for weeks. I lost track of my various ailments. A fractured ankle, a broken nose, chipped teeth, cracked ribs, bronchitis, impetigo, anaemia, mild frostbite, dehydration and malnutrition. They attached me to an endless bank of machines and drips. They washed and cleaned my wounds. They evaluated my mental health. They assigned me a caseworker.

And then, finally, they let me go.

Lydia wouldn't see me. I wasn't surprised and I didn't insist. After my Lazarus-like return there were "implications" that needed to be considered. Legal. Financial. Not to mention personal. I wasn't allowed to see Flynn either. That was tougher to accept. The letter from Lydia's solicitor explained that, while he had bounced back well from my disappearance, the new situation would need to be negotiated delicately. There was talk of more counselling.

Olivia visited though. Not every day, but enough to keep me sane. I was staying in a hostel at this point, though I wouldn't let her meet me there. I would take her to a café round the corner. There she would sit and spoon the froth from sugary lattes and moan to me about school, about Lydia, about boys, while I sat and nodded, stunned that this beautiful, vivacious young woman would see fit to include me in her life. I still went to pieces every time she called me Dad.

We talked about everything on those long, caffeinated afternoons. Everything except what had happened in the park.

Eventually I was allocated my own place, a small one bedroom flat on the seedier side of town. The walls were magnolia, the carpets grey. The whole place stank of cat piss and stale marijuana.

I couldn't sleep there at first. I still couldn't get used to walls and ceilings. To radiators and curtains. To lights that came on at the flick of a switch. Most of all, I couldn't get used to being alone. After the first few exhausted nights, I hatched a plan. I carried my bedding through to the kitchen and draped a sheet over the table. Then I took my pillow and blanket and

290

climbed underneath, snuggling down into the dim safety of the den I'd built.

After that, I slept in the kitchen every night.

As the weeks and months passed, I found myself thinking more and more about the guys in the park. I wondered how they were doing. What — or who — they were eating. In spite of everything, I still felt guilty for leaving them.

Of course it crossed my mind to contact the police, but in the end I decided against it. I wouldn't know what to tell them. Besides, the park was another world. What happened there was governed by an altogether different set of rules.

At least, that's what we told ourselves. Else how could we ever hope to sleep at night?

One day I opened the newspaper and read a small article that mentioned Adenbury Community Gardens. It said the whole place was about to be redeveloped — flattened to make way for an exclusive range of apartments and penthouses. A "bespoke living sphere", the article called it. There would be a selection of restaurants, a private cinema, a fitness suite. There would be a twenty-four-hour concierge and secure underground parking. There would be a business lounge.

It sounded like hell on earth.

After that I spent many evenings walking the streets, scanning the doorways and underpasses. I always expected to see a familiar face huddled in a sleeping bag or digging through bins. My heart would leap whenever a wizened hand would reach from the shadows to nudge a tin towards me or ask for a cigarette. But then they would turn their heads and it was never them.

The men and women I saw there were a different breed to the guys at the park. They were invariably mentally ill or drunk, or else broken in some other fundamental way. They stared at the floor when I passed, or mumbled for change. They seemed ashamed.

Compared to us, they were like domestic dogs to wolves.

As for the park, I never did risk returning there. Perhaps I wasn't as interested in seeing the others as I thought I was. Or maybe it was just time to accept that that part of my life was over for good.

As the months crawled by, I began to wonder what I was going to do with the rest of my life. I still wasn't able to see Flynn, and Olivia's visits had become less frequent now that she was sure I wasn't about to drop dead or disappear again. I didn't begrudge her absence though. Far from it. I knew she had a whole story ahead of her to write, in which I would only ever be a minor character.

For a long time I admit I didn't do very much of anything. I sat in my small, dank flat and stared at the walls, brooding. In many ways, it felt as if I had lost two lives. My entire pre-park career had been built on reputation, on the illusion I was disciplined, organised, well-adjusted. Now that I'd comprehensively burned all of that to the ground, it was difficult to see how I would ever work again. Not that I was sure I even wanted to. The world I'd returned to seemed miserably sedate in comparison to my life in the park. If I was hungry, I simply had to walk to the shops and pick up a vacuum-packed steak or a breast of chicken or a tin of tuna, all of it neatly stacked and labelled, all traces of its nature scrubbed and skinned and stripped away. If I was thirsty, I needed only to turn on the tap. If I was bored, the television or the Internet was only ever a click away.

At first it was a revelation. But the novelty quickly faded. It felt like cheating, to have everything made so easy for me. Besides, what was a person supposed to do all day? With the challenge of everyday survival removed, I was left with a dangerous amount of time to think. And what I thought mostly was this: how could anyone ever be expected to truly value something if there was no effort involved in getting it?

One day, Olivia arrived at my flat with a present. It was a small pot plant.

"What's this?" I asked. "It was my birthday months ago. You already got me a card?"

She laughed. "I just thought some flowers might brighten the place up a bit. Stop it being so . . . shit."

"Thanks, Ollie. It's lovely," I said, examining the small shrub. "But this isn't a flower."

"Isn't it?" she asked distractedly. She was already bored of the conversation, her hand twitching for her mobile phone. "I just picked it up from the shop."

I smiled. "No. It's a tomato plant. Look, cherry tomatoes."

"Mmmm? I thought it might be a rose or something. Listen, Dad, I can't stay. I'm supposed to be meeting Kyle . . ."

I put the tomato plant on my windowsill.

It's been sunnier lately, the snow and ice of the winter fading to nothing but a distant memory. Everywhere I look, green shoots are beginning to appear, needling their way through the cracks in the pavement and the gaps in the brickwork. The trees too have shrugged off the cold, their boughs suddenly plump with flurries of pink-and-white blossom, like fireworks frozen mid-detonation. The city might still be predominantly grey, but nature is waging a guerilla war on us. I don't think it would take much for the balance to shift in its favour. You see, nature has a secret weapon, one that for all of our technical brilliance, we have never mastered:

Patience.

One day we will all be gone. The cars will rust, the buildings will crumble. And nature will be there, waiting, ready to fill the void, to swallow our carnage and reclaim the land, until there is no trace of us at all.

Until we are but a dream.

I have added more plants to my modest indoor garden. Chilli peppers, aubergines, a few herbs. They crowd my windowsill, so that I can no longer shut the curtains. I do my best to care for them, watering them regularly, feeding them fertiliser, turning them to make sure they get enough light. Whether they will ever fruit is anyone's guess. I'm vaguely aware that at some point in the not too distant future I'll need to repot them, to plant them outside. Beyond that though, I have no idea. At the park there was always someone to tell me what to do. Now it's just me.

One of my plants died last week. One of the chillies. I don't know what happened. I treated it the same as all the others, but it just stopped growing. The leaves went brown and it shrivelled to nothing. I threw it out in the rubbish the next day.

I'm scared that the same will happen to the rest of them. I even went to the library and took out a few books on gardening. That only made it worse. There's so much to consider, so much that can go wrong. Fungus. Disease. Pests. No matter what I do, they'll always be under threat from something. Life is so fragile. I try my best, but the truth is I'm making it up as I go along.

But I'm learning. I'm learning.

Acknowledgements

Huge thanks go to the following:

My complicated and unwieldy family.

My early readers/confidants/counsellors: Mum, Dad, Aidan, Ciara, Fiona, Lauren

Also special thanks to Michael Langan, whose comments and suggestions on the embryonic drafts of this novel almost a decade ago (!) still resonate today

Adelle Stripe & Ben Myers for their friendship, encouragement and support, Jonathan Davidson and all at Writing West Midlands, all at Room 204 (past, present and future!), Aki Schilz and all at TLC, Riz at RK Animation, Gem Sidnell at Moo Moo Art & Photography, Sam Mills & Thom Cuell at Dodo Ink, Marek at Almond Press, Roz at West Midlands Readers' Network, *LossLit Magazine*, *Bare Fiction Magazine*, Rob Burgon for his advice on self-defence, John Oakley for his comments about "hope", Freelance Mourners, Birmingham Central Library (where large portions of this book were written), the nice people at Birmingham City Council Parks Department for not having me arrested

Independent bookshops/publishers

Readers everywhere

Wind, rain, mud

Extra special thanks to Tom, Lauren, Lottie, Lucy, Rob and all at Legend Press for their hard work and continued faith in my writing

Finally, to Simone, without whom none of this would have been possible. Until our jetpacks fail.

THE SONGBIRD

Marcia Willett

When Mattie invites her old friend Tim to stay in one of her family cottages on the edge of Dartmoor, she senses there is something he is not telling her. But as he gets to know the rest of the warm jumble of family who live by the moor, Tim discovers that everyone there has their own secrets. There is Kat, a retired ballet dancer who longs for the stage again; Charlotte, a young navy wife struggling to bring up her son while her husband is at sea; William, who guards a dark past he cannot share with the others; and Mattie, who has loved Tim in silence for years. As Tim begins to open up, Mattie falls deeper in love. And as summer warms the wild Dartmoor landscape, new hope begins to bloom . . .

DEAR FANG, WITH LOVE

Rufi Thorpe

Vera is seventeen — the same age her parents were when, blindingly in love, they decided to have a baby. Now in their thirties and long since separated, "seventeen" is already a lifetime ago. So when Vera suffers a terrifying psychotic break, they scramble to try and comprehend what has happened to their wild-hearted, inimitable daughter. Vera's father Lucas takes her to Lithuania, his grandmother's homeland, for the summer. Here, in the city of Vilnius, Lucas hopes to save Vera from the sorrow of her diagnosis. Meanwhile, Vera pours her heart out in letters to her boyfriend, Fang. She is searching for answers of her own. Why did Lucas abandon her as a baby? What really happened the night of her breakdown? And who can she trust with the truth?